VISIONS IV

BOOKS FROM LILLICAT PUBLISHERS

VISIONS SERIES
VISIONS: LEAVING EARTH (2014)
VISIONS II: MOONS OF SATURN (2015)
VISIONS III: INSIDE THE KUIPER BELT (2015)
VISIONS IV: SPACE BETWEEN STARS (2016)
VISIONS V: MILKY WAY (ABOUT AUGUST 2016)

THE FUTURE IS SHORT: SCIENCE FICTION IN A FLASH (2014)

SUNSHINE & SHADOW: MEMORIES FROM A LONG LIFE (2014)

VISIONS IV

SPACE BETWEEN STARS

EDITED BY

CARROL FIX

LILLICAT PUBLISHERS
USA

VISIONS IV
SPACE BETWEEN STARS

"Veil Nebula" Credit: NASA, ESA, and the Hubble Heritage (STScI/AURA)-ESA/Hubble Collaboration. Acknowledgment: J. Hester (Arizona State University)
"V838 Monocerotis" Credit: NASA/ESA
"Tarantula Nebula" Courtesy NASA, ESA, and D. Lennon (ESA/STSci)

Special thanks to DeeAnn and Timothy Heins.

Lillicat Publishers books may be ordered through booksellers or by contacting:
Lillicat Publishers
www.lillicatpublishers.com

POD ISBN: 978-0-9966255-5-5
EPUB ISBN: 978-0-9966255-6-2
MOBI ISBN: 978-0-9966255-7-9
Printed in the United States of America

V838 Monocerotis
Credit: NASA/ESA

SPACE BETWEEN STARS

CONTENTS

STEPPING STONES TO ETERNITY

The *Visions* series tells the story of how humanity must ultimately venture outward from our tiny home and explore the Universe.

Visions: Leaving Earth, the first volume, describes our first faltering steps to rise from Earth's surface and build homes in space.

Visions II: Moons of Saturn confirms that humankind has left the Earth and is at home in the other planetary systems of our solar system.

Visions III: Inside the Kuiper Belt proclaims humankind's domination of all that dwells within the solar system—from our Sun to the outermost reaches of the Kuiper Belt.

Visions IV: Space Between Stars astounds us with the infinite possibilities of adventure and danger far from any suns or planets—in the cold, dark regions of deepest space.

Beyond these volumes, we will explore outside our solar system: exploring and colonizing the *Milky Way*, and understanding the *Universe*.

Our vision is limitless.

Introduction

The Visions Series presents imaginative stories from authors who spend most of their time speculating on the future of humanity. We have explored the possible paths of humankind's first steps off our mother planet, the colonizing of the solar system, and the establishment of homes and commercial ventures beyond the known planets of our system, and pondered the mysteries of the Kuiper Belt and Oort Cloud. Visions IV pushes outward and expands our imaginations to encompass all the area between our heliosphere and our star neighbors.

Imagine the deepest regions of space between the stars of the Milky Way. Cold, empty, silent, and vast. In the quest to achieve immortality for our species, someday, humankind will reach those realms.

Television and movies often depict spaceships spending weeks and months, sometimes years, traveling from one star to another...and even to distant galaxies. Other times, the unimaginably huge distances are traversed in what seems like the blink of an eye. Science fiction concepts do not always match what astrophysicists believe to be true. But, in some rare instances, a seemingly incredible idea turns out to be close to reality.

In early scifi adventures, the idea of a "black hole" was grounds for unrestrained scoffing and snorting from the general scientific community. Today, it is even accepted that "black holes" *could be* "wormholes" to other galaxies.

Using current technology, it would take many generations to reach even the nearest star. When science overcomes those limitations, humankind will encounter endless opportunities for strange and exciting adventures between the stars.

Possibly, cold sleep will be used. Generations ships could carry whole populations to a new home. Black holes, space warps, faster than light travel, or something never thought of before, will transport future voyagers through the dark distances.

Visions IV: Space Between Stars leads the reader into the soaring minds of fifteen authors—talented award-winners—whose delight in life is to imagine the impossible and bring it to us in exciting and believable stories.

The Editor honors differences in international writing styles by leaving most spellings and conventions as the author prefers. No matter where you are reading this, please keep in mind that typos and misspellings could be variations in regional interpretations of the English language.

Carrol Fix
Editor
Lillicat Publishers
April 22, 2016

Tarantula Nebula · 30 Doradus
HST WFC3/UVIS ACS/WFC · ESO 2.2m

When an influenza decimates everyone else aboard the colony ship, SS New Hope, Evalynn Santori discovers unexpected companions. Together they must undo the Captain's dying act and re-route the ship away from a fiery death in the clutches of a dying Red Giant.

COMPANIONS

By

S. M. Kraftchak

They weren't on any pre-flight checklists, Remote Survival classes, or mentioned in Advanced Theory: The Art of Negotiation. They weren't even on the personnel manifest, but they stole aboard and waited.

Boldest of them all, Optimism openly wandered the corridors of our colony ship. It shadowed each mission specialist as they double and triple checked technical specs, and had us children giddy with the thrill of space travel and a grand plan to create a new life on a distant planet. Optimism blinded the whole crew to the truth, while Loneliness and Fear oozed out of the quiet corners, claiming one isolated victim at a time.

Perhaps if Command and Strategic planning had not studiously herded us out of the way, or used electronic diversions to lure us into complacency, we might have demanded a stock of spray like the one used to keep monsters out from under our bunks; a different formula of course. Most of us would have gladly suffered an addition to the dozen or so inoculations we received to protect us from identifiable virulent conditions, just to keep Them at bay. However, the unsuspecting *Star Ship New Hope* began its ten-year voyage to establish a new colony on the planet of New Haven, totally unprepared to deal with a host of unwanted Companions.

Cookie, my guardian and the ship's cook, said I was the lucky one. I'm not quite sure how he figured that, other than I was a healthy teenage girl, too young to assume a regular assignment, but too old to be corralled into the nursery. I split my time between Cookie and the Captain.

With Cookie, I spent many companionable hours studying and discussing every subject from engine maintenance to the influence of color on psychology, and on to xenobiology while I made myself useful stirring sauces and rolling out biscuit dough. Even though others dismissed Cookie's wildly fantastic rocket stories as fabricated because he was, after all just a cook, I listened in rapture, knowing he held a doctorate from LIT, Lunar Institute of Technology, and had simply decided cooking was his passion.

Captain Chaplin always seemed pleased to see me when Cookie chased me from the Galley to make friends. When I entered the bridge, I'd call, "Good morning, Captain Chap," and smother my giggle like the other officers on the bridge.

"That's Chaplin," he'd say.

"Oh, I thought you were the Captain?"

"Exactly and you're late for your lessons. My office, now."

And I'd usually high-five Jessie, the Com Officer, on my way into his office, where I'd spend several hours debating philosophy from nearly every great mind in History, arguing over command strategies or listening to stories of his wild adventures on Granterra. I knew our time was up when he'd fall silent after a long laugh and then say, "One day, I'll have a daughter just like you."

Seven years, three months and fourteen days into our ten-year journey was a day like any other. Optimism and Hope continued to fill the corridors with their light after a second wedding, the birth of a seventh child, and the discovery in Astral Navigation of a stunning space anomaly that masked the endless blackness of space with its spectacular light and color. That afternoon the stench of Fear, pungent and unexpected, wafted through the ship, banishing Hope and Optimism. By evening, nine children in the nursery fell ill with a phantom illness. By the end of the week, Death stole aboard from the gloom of space and seized all nine, newborn to two-year-olds, and then loitered nearby waiting for a mutated strain of virulent influenza to sweep the other eighteen two to ten-year-olds children onboard into its clutches.

Over that week, Cookie and I held hands next to weeping parents, teenaged siblings, and crew. We watched two, and then three, tightly wrapped little bodies set adrift into the frozen void. I refused to look into the dark corners of the launch bay where fang-toothed Fear stood gloating over trampled Optimism and Hope. I felt Fear's surging warmth grow with careless, hushed words that asked, "Who's next?" The day we watched seven more of the eighteen small bundles float away, Cookie whispered, "Like tears on the face of God", and then quickly escorted me from the bay.

Fear strutted the corridors the following week, escorting Death to the quarters of my teenaged classmates. With Optimism and Hope all but gone, Captain Chap quarantined the whole ship, except for a handful of essential personnel who were required to wear environmental suits outside of their quarters. When Doc realized I was the only one under the age of seventeen not in sickbay, I was summoned and became a professional pincushion. He syphoned a vial or two of blood from me daily in a frantic attempt to isolate the antibody that kept me healthy.

As a captive of sickbay, Insomnia and I kept watch on Death. I was too afraid to succumb to Sleep's welcoming arms because each time I awoke; another friend had been enveloped by Death's dark cloak. Exhaustion took Doc each night, usually in the lonely hours of morning, and sprawled him across his chair with his mouth wide open.

One morning while he was snoring especially loudly, I shouldered Fear and Death aside and rushed to help Sean from engineering with his wife Anna, who was seven months pregnant, as she stumbled into Sickbay, weak and feverish. After rousing Doc, I helped where I could with making her comfortable, until Sean took notice of me. He grabbed my arm and pulled me away from Anna. "How are you still healthy? What special medicine does the Captain's pet get that the rest of the crew isn't good enough for?" His eyes were bloodshot and his features distorted by Fear.

"I don't know what you're talking about," I said trying to pull away, but his fingernails bit through my uniform sleeve. "Ooww, you're hurting me!"

"It's you! You're the one who's making everyone sick. You're a typhoid Mary! Get away from me! Stay away from Anna. Haven't you killed enough children?" He tossed my arm so hard I spun, lost my balance, and landed on my hands and knees. He glanced around, grabbed Doc's empty coffee mug, and raised to bludgeon me.

"Sean Patrick Martin! Put that down and leave Eva alone. She may be the only one who can save any of us. Anna needs you, now get back over here," Doc shouted.

Sean looked between Doc and me as I crabbed away on the floor. "You stay away!" he said and then returned to his wife.

Doc whispered something to Sean and then hurried to help me to my feet.

"I didn't do anything. It's not my fault." I willingly followed Doc to the far side of the open bay.

"I know. Everyone is just scared." Doc said in a calm voice as he held both biceps to scan my whole body for injury.

"Like I'm not?"

Doc nodded and escorted me to Sickbay's quarantine. "Maybe you'd better stay in here for now."

"But..."

"Please don't argue, Eva. I know you're trying to help, and you didn't purposely make everyone sick..."

"I didn't make anyone sick!" I said, yanking my arm from Doc's hand, and then watched him enter the quarantine activation code. As the blue boundary hummed to life between us, he gave me a sad smile that told me he believed I was the cause. Bewildered, I sat hugging my knees and staring at the wall until I finally succumbed to Sleep's siren call.

The next day from the safety of my bubble, I watched Theresa Leigh Martin lifted from her dying mother. A week later I stood with Cookie's arms wrapped protectively around me as Anna, the first adult to die from the influenza, followed by her infant daughter's body looked like an exclamation point warning others to avoid our dying ship. Fear bullied the crew for the next two weeks, forcing me into protective custody in Cookie's quarters. Slowly, Fear's grip weakened as Despair and Sadness draped across everyone's shoulders. After two more uneventful weeks, Captain Chap lifted the quarantine allowing Relief to escort the ship's crew slowly toward normalcy. Smiles appeared on tear-stained faces. All the children were gone, except for me, but the adults appeared healthy.

Without classmates and still fearful of the crew's reaction to me, I spent more time by myself and met Loneliness for the first time. Cookie had insisted all along that I spend time with kids my age saying, "You need to develop a rapport with those you will someday command." I had laughed at the notion I would one day command a ship but had tried to fit in with the others. I was now secretly glad I hadn't succeeded very well. Loneliness seemed preferable to the awkwardness of trying to ignore the occasional hate-filled glance from bereaved parents, until it began to smother me.

Determined to find Optimism and escort it back into the ship's corridors, I shirked off Loneliness with a new zeal and boldly began connecting with the crew. Many of them, reluctantly at first, encouraged me and eventually came to depend on me as qualified assistance. I confided in Cookie I was pleased that my youthful exuberance brought a shy Optimism back wherever I went. Each night when we had dinner together in his quarters, I'd rattle on about all the things I was learning and how I was feeling like a real member of the crew instead of a passenger. At the end of each night Cookie made a comment I didn't understand, about Hope trailing out my back pocket.

A month later, when things felt almost normal and Optimism greeted people in the corridors, Fear pounced again. Two crew members from Command, three more from Engineering, and three from Maintenance fell ill with symptoms of the flu. I panicked and ran to sickbay.

"Doc! It's happening again. I know now it *must* be me."

Doc shook his head and quietly escorted me away from the eight ill crew members. "Don't be ridiculous. With one hundred and seventy-two people on board, we're bound to have a handful sick at any one time."

"But I've been helping each one of them and their symptoms are just like the ones the children had before they..."

"They are much milder and generic to nearly a dozen different maladies." Doc lowered his head to look Eva in the eyes. "They'll be fine."

"Please, lock me in quarantine again. I don't want to make anyone else sick."

"Eva, don't be absurd. You're not sick and we don't know that you've made them sick. I've heard what a good job you've been doing, and with the crew out for a couple of days," Doc motioned over his shoulder with his thumb, "the Captain will need your help."

"But—"

"No. Now I need to tend to my patients. If you're that concerned, come by every morning and I'll give you the once over to be sure you're not passing anything along."

The next morning, sickbay was full and patients were being returned to their quarters on mobile monitor. "Are you ready to quarantine me yet?" I felt tears burning my eyes at the thought that all the pain, suffering, and death might somehow be my fault.

"Captain Chaplin agrees there's nothing to be gained by quarantining you. It didn't stop..." Doc turned his face away and cleared his throat. "Your new expertise at a variety of stations makes you more valuable than ever. You need to report to the Captain for assignment."

Like with the children, once someone became ill, it took no more than a week before they died. In a belated, futile attempt to prevent others from getting ill, Captain

Chap assigned me to assist Doc. Three days later, I had the onerous duty of forcing Doc to bed. Harder yet, was informing Captain Chap.

"Sickbay to Captain." My voice wheezed past the lump in my throat.

"Captain here. Is that you, Eva?"

I cleared my throat in an effort to sound professional. "Yes, Captain. I need to inform you that Doc has taken ill."

I repeated myself after a long silence. "Captain? Doc has it."

"Do you require more assistance running sickbay?"

"I...I...don't think so. There are two nurses who aren't sick yet."

"Good, have them assume care of the patients. You stay with Doc and help him however you can, but keep him in bed. Are any of the patients improving?"

"No, Sir." I suddenly needed air and inhaled deeply. "We lost Ensign Fray and Commander Macy an hour ago."

The Captain took a full minute to respond and then his voice sounded strained. "Do your best. Captain out."

In the wee hours of morning, I stood outside the Captain's quarters and pressed his call button. Cookie's hand rested on my shoulder.

"Come," the voice through the intercom said and a moment later the door slid into the wall.

It took several seconds before I could trust my body to step into the captain's quarters. Cookie's squeeze on the shoulder helped me forward. "Captain Chaplin, I need to speak with you."

"Eva?" The Captain turned from his panoramic window. "What is it?"

"I regret to inform...I regret to..." I cleared my throat and tried again. "I regret to inform you..."

"Doc is dead," he said and bowed his head.

All I could do was nod.

"Thank you, Eva. I know you did your best. I need you to assist me and the remaining crew in covering critical positions. Are you up to that?"

"But Captain, I don't want to make..."

Captain Chaplain slapped his desk and jumped to his feet. "I will hear none of that nonsense. You will report first thing in the morning. Cookie, I expect you to see she is properly fed and fully rested when she reports. Dismissed."

Two painfully long months later, after watching one hundred and sixty-nine crew members slip silently into the void, Cookie and I stood hand in hand next to a flag draped bundle.

"Do you want to say anything?" Cookie asked.

"Yes," I whispered. It took me a minute to find my voice. "Captain Chap was a good man. His loss..." Tears spilled from my eyes and I began to shake. "...is devastating. No one's heart was bigger. No one's patience was longer. No one's trust was more profound. God speed, Captain Chap," I said as his bundled body slipped into the void from under the flag of the Colonial Expansion Alliance for Species Existence. Staring at the limp flag I suggested they might have considered a better name for our mission. Cookie scowled at me for a moment then allowed his snowy topped head to tip backward, shaking side to side. A moment later, he tugged my hand. "Let's get some ice cream, the real frozen stuff."

In the Galley, Cookie sat across from me, tugged a thin blanket close around his neck, and began reciting the same pabulum I had heard for the past month and a half. "There's nothing to worry about. The ship's course is set. Ninety percent of the ship's systems are automated so they only need to be monitored. We'll arrive at New Haven safely and on time. There are manuals detailing each automated..." He seemed to need to recite it, so I silently confirmed my basic knowledge of each system as he rattled off the list.

I sucked ice cream off my spoon, several measured swipes for each spoonful to keep from getting brain-freeze, while trying to ignore Loneliness darting from corner to corner and peering over Cookie's shoulder at me. He seemed unaware as he slowly stirred his melting treat and continued half-hearted reassurances.

"A second Colony ship, Courage, is scheduled to arrive at New Haven two years after us. We can stay shipboard until they arrive. Since we have fewer...our supplies will last well past *New Hope's* scheduled arrival."

Once the reassurances and my ice cream were finished, I watched Cookie's melted ice cream silently drip from his spoon creating ripples his bowl. I tried to voice my deepest, most immediate concern. With a glance at Loneliness, I asked, "What if you...?" I couldn't say the words, so I shifted tactics. "Would you mind if I stayed in your quarters tonight?"

The plop of his spoon, the splash of sweet vanilla milk on both our faces, and a wide toothy smile, followed by, "I think that would be a wonderful idea," instantly banished Loneliness.

Despite a wracking cough and raging fever that often made him delirious, Cookie spent every waking moment diligently drilling me on procedural manuals and reviewing every non-automated detail I'd need to perform in order to survive, except how to deal with Loneliness. We toured the bridge where he explained each station and even let me sit in the Captain's chair, supposedly for the first time.

"How do you expect me to cram all this into my brain? It took years for the crew to learn their jobs."

"You don't have to understand it, just be aware of it. The computer will take care of it. You just need to know what to tell the computer."

"And what if the computer fails? Can I fix it?" I asked as I followed an imaginary maze around the rows of different buttons on the Command Panel.

"The Computer will fix itself. It can find a solution for everything."

"Then why hasn't it figured out a cure for this flu?" I stared into Cookie's blue eyes, trying to keep my own from spilling my fears.

Cookie crossed his arms on his chest pulling the corners of his blanket in to create a sort of straitjacket effect and scowled at me. "Doc was working on that."

"So then everything important isn't automated," I corrected him. Cookie's deeply creased brow didn't faze me.

"You know that. Sometimes...things take time and...he did have enough."

"How many more pints of my blood does the computer need? I'd give every last drop of blood to save you."

Cookie's mouth dropped open; his thin white eyebrows nearly disappearing into the creases in his forehead. After a few seconds he pressed his lips together and then said, "You know you're the most—"

He stopped, when I held his gaze, and then said, "Let's go review the Med Suite."

Eight days later, every kid's dream of having no bedtime, or nagging adult to say they should tend to their studies, or do their chores was now mine. As I watched Cookie's body drift away from the ship, Loneliness boldly stepped forward and turned my dream into a nightmare. I ignored it for a long while. The clock became my opponent and companion, as I raced the empty corridors or practiced half a dozen emergency drills by myself. I explored every corner of the ship normally off limits, except the dangerous ones of course. But far too soon, the time ceased to matter. Loneliness paced me, patient and attentive. It kept its distance when I lost myself in an e-reader, devouring books and manuals, until one day when Loneliness walked up and tapped me on the shoulder.

Loneliness sounds like such a lovely name for something so heart-wrenching and cold. At first I shrugged away from her sharp talons, determined not to give in and nestle my cheek against her frigid breast. Hours of video games, studying theory and history, and a routine of exercise and checking the ship's systems only kept her at bay until I settled into Cookie's bunk at night. Then, she'd crawl in next to me and I'd sob into my pillow until Sleep gently nudged her away, only to return when Sleep left. Loneliness thrived in space.

With no weapons to protect myself, I slowly allowed Loneliness to become my companion. She followed me as

I scoured every crew member's personal quarters and brought back all the hard-copy pictures I could find and plastered first one wall of Cookie's quarters and then filled up ten feet of corridor. Loneliness was comfortable and far friendlier than venomous Desperation that periodically seeped in the portals from the vast emptiness of space, ambushing me and plunging me into catatonia for a day or two at a time. The only demand Loneliness made was to be with me, and I let her.

The day I discovered how to view videos messages, sent and received, from the crew, Loneliness sat forlornly in the corner. Peeking into one hundred and seventy-two lives lifted my spirits, for a while. The longer I watched, the closer Loneliness inched until she finally wrapped her arms around my shoulders and squeezed until tears streamed down my face. I found the pleas of families and loved ones on the second colony ship, Courage, desperate for a response or update. Several times I began to send a response, but froze with the reality of not knowing what to say. I wondered how they'd feel at the other end if they knew the truth. Not sending any response was a practicality to keep Desperation at bay. I was here, safe, and healthy. They were there and couldn't help me, so I agreed with Cookie's axiom, "No news is good news". It wasn't until I began viewing Captain Chap's personal video log, that I finally understood Cookie's saying and how getting some news was bad news.

Loneliness fled when Anger snatched me from the Captain's chair and sent my bowl of fish-shaped cheese crackers flying. I rewound the vid to just past Captain Chap's last bloody coughing fit. Tears rolled down my cheeks as his words settled into my heart.

"Our hope of curing or at least containing this influenza died with Doc at 02:30. Seventy percent of our crew is dead and all but Eva are sick. Perhaps that's a blessing in disguise for Eva since I'm not sure how much more blood she could have given. Doc's daily analysis of her blood hasn't revealed why she alone is still healthy. There's nothing to prove or disprove she's the 'Typhoid Mary', though logic clearly points to her.

As a last desperate hope, Doc had me relay his research to the Courage. Hopefully further analysis by clearer minds will reap results. Maybe some of the crew..." he coughed a little and then continued. "...will survive, but even if they do, I can't allow this contagion to reach New Haven."

I watched the Captain pinch his lower lip as he took a long pause. He seemed to be staring into the distance off camera. Then with a giant sigh, he continued in a strained voice. "I've directed the ship light-years off course so we cannot be found. I sent word to Courage and Star Command of my intention to self-destruct *New Hope.*"

I slammed the pause button and stared wide-eyed at Captain Chap's ashen face. Fear, Panic and Despair danced around me like a Maypole, tying me in knots. It took several minutes until I was calm enough to continue listening.

"Even though I've stated my intentions, I cannot bring myself to sentence any survivors to death; they deserve a chance if they survive. *SS New Hope* will live out her days orbiting the Red Giant, G72, until she runs out of power and becomes derelict, or is destroyed when G72 goes supernova; expected in no more than five years. I've disabled our locator beacon and run up the black plague-flag. God bless us all, especially my sweet Eva."

Anger cloaked me like a second skin for days, igniting tantrums where whatever could be thrown or shattered was quickly destroyed. When Anger wore thin, Exhaustion sprawled me on the floor or against a wall, rendering me unconscious until I'd wake to my own shouts, desperately trying to rouse the corpses drifting silently across the galaxy. When they refused to answer, Anger again draped my shoulders and kindled another round of tirades.

Days and nights melded together until Anger finally released my exhausted body into the sturdy arms of Desperation. Her beguiling song entombed me. Only the call of my body to visit the head rose above her mesmerizing chorus. With little desire for food or water, the need to move at all grew less frequent and I wished

Death would lose patience, crawl out of the corner, and take me.

I'm not sure if it was delirium, some mystical intervention or simply fate that picked me up off the floor of Cookie's quarters. He would have said it was Hope trailing out of my back pocket. I chose to believe that.

A forty-five-minute shower was an extravagant waste, but I didn't care. There was plenty of water to wash away Desperation's stench. In fact, there were thousands of gallons that one hundred and seventy-two people would have used on the way to New Haven; two lifetime's worth for just me. Water, undeniably a critical concern in space, was the least of my problems. As the hottest water I could stand turned my skin bright pink, Hope and I laid out a plan for my future.

Hope sat across from me and nodded encouragement as I began to speak into the captain's ship recorder. "Survivor's Log Day 1. This is Evalynn Santori, new ship's Captain, and only survivor of the influenza that decimated the entire crew of the *Starship New Hope*. It's been three weeks since Cookie died. Other than slightly under-nourished from my recent bout with Desperation, I'm still healthy, or reasonably so. It's finally apparent I must institute a regime of normalcy to survive, which includes learning all I can about my ship. *New Hope* is on course to orbit the Red Giant, G72, because it's predicted to go supernova in no more than five years and will prevent the spread of the contagion that killed the crew. Hopefully I have time to master the necessary ship's systems to redirect *New Hope* back toward New Haven. I'm not so naïve as to believe that I will be welcomed, and have a minor concern about being turned away, but I am willing to live onboard New Hope in isolation until they find a cure. I want a long life, even if I have to live with Loneliness."

Survivor's Log Day 344: Desperation tried to seduce me today, but I traded her siren's song for a strange celebration of life. I commemorated the anniversary of

Cookie's death by taking the crew's pictures from the giant collage in our quarters and reposted them around the ship where they had lived and worked. It felt more natural to see human faces in the proper places instead of just cold structural steel or endless miles of pale blue, plastic corridor walls. I've actually started smiling at them and asking about their job and families. Jealous Desperation occasionally flings a picture or two on the floor, but Hope and I quickly replace them and have sent Desperation packing.

Some would say Insanity had seeped in alongside Desperation and was impossible to evict, but I don't consider my conversations out of the ordinary. It seems natural to call on Cookie's ethereal guidance, real or imagined, when I struggle with engineering manuals. I'm certain once or twice he even led me to the answer, but never the easy way. I still hear his words, "If I give you all the answers, you'll never learn anything."

Survivor's Log Day 515: Loneliness and Patience are constant companions while studying manual after manual, showing every subroutine and circuitry diagram on both the automated and non-automated systems. Patience introduced me to Logic when I discovered the O2 scrubbers in the aft part of the ship were working at only fifty percent capacity. Instead of allowing me to panic, Logic insisted this wasn't a major issue, yet, since I could turn them off and seal off the back third of the ship. Spare parts might actually last longer in a low O2 atmosphere.

Survivor's Log Day 517: Hope is soaring now that I've finished the systems review and maintenance tasks, because I can focus on learning navigation. Cookie said my knack for numbers would serve me well in navigation. I decided the twenty-minute walk between Cookie's and Captain Chap's quarters was a waste of precious time, so Hope followed me when I assumed my rightful place, awkward though it might be, in the Captain's quarters. Here I have access to his navigation records, personal logs, and private manuals. With only 220 more days until we achieve orbit around the dying Red Giant, I need every minute. Each day I wake in one piece instead of blown to bits by G72 is a gift, one I don't plan to waste."

"Survivor's Log Day 749: Hope keeps wandering away and leaving me with Despair. Navigation is decidedly more difficult than Cookie had said it would be. Red Giant G72 has filled the forward view screen for over two weeks now. Mariah, at the Science Station, says there are increasing signs of instability. Ralph, in Engineering, has raised his concern about several peculiarities in the ship's Systems. Everywhere I turn, someone is demanding more input. I refuse to take time from my navigational studies, but will in another day or so."

"Survivor's Log Day 827: Hope abandoned me at 03:00 yesterday when I determined how to lay in a proper course, got it laid in, and then found the Captain's change of course was locked in. A twelve, two-digit sequence security code was required to unlock the course. Anger trashed the Captain's quarters as I watched helplessly and then flung me sobbing back into Desperation's arms. After a restless night on the floor of the Bridge, Hope tapped me on the shoulder, suggesting I search the Captain's personnel record, and the code might reveal itself. "I'll never find it in time," I sighed, "but I have to try."

Flopping backward onto the bed, I called the vid-screen on the far wall to life, scanned the hundred or so folders, and growled when I still couldn't find what I was looking for. "Computer, record Survivor's Log Day 1095." <Recording.> "Loneliness and I are now best friends. Hope occasionally whispers from the corners. Desperation and Anger abandoned me to the stingy care of Futility. After three years alone, I've learned that caring hasn't changed anything. *SS New Hope* will need no help from G72, since her systems are going offline one by one. I've searched manual after manual and found nothing to explain the methodical deactivation of the ship's systems. Nothing I try stops the progressive shut-down. Water, heat, and atmosphere are about all that is running, and only in the Bridge, Captain's quarters, the Galley and a few corridors in-between. The ship's degrading orbit appears to be accelerating and will most likely put *New Hope* in the permanent clutches of G72 within two weeks.

On the bright side, I've discovered the first three and the last three pairs in the twelve, two-pair security sequence. Since remembering numbers was easiest when I related them to important things or people, I assumed Captain Chap did the same. The day we left Granterra, 01-10-57, was the first set of numbers. The day *New Hope* was supposed to arrive at New Haven, 02-07-67, locked in the last three places. I presume the other six numbers correlate to two more dates of importance to the captain, but have found nothing that seems to work. I've tried the birth and death dates of every notable person in History that he might have admired. I even thought about just plugging in numbers one at a time until they lock, but the numbers seem to be in sets of three and only lock as a set. I started to have the computer run the permutations, but stopped it because it estimates a solution would take another three years. I've reviewed every log entry from the captain since the day we left until the day he died, and run out of ideas. I'm running out of time."

Staring at Captain Chap's files on the vid-screen, I scrolled down and opened VIDEOS to distract me from Desperation's proximity. Bored with the many choices I'd scanned dozens of times before, I scrolled to the end and almost closed the file but stopped when I spotted one named Honey. I didn't remember seeing it before.

"Computer, open file named Honey."

The screen was black with tiny pieces of light dancing across the screen like an ancient celluloid film and then suddenly there was a blissful young woman with light brown hair framing her face. She smiled down at the pink bundle in her arms as she tipped slowly forward and back in a wooden rocking chair. Captain Chap's distinctive gravelly voice began talking as the camera zoomed in.

"And here are the two most beautiful women in the world..." the camera zoomed in on the woman who looked up. "...Honey," the camera panned over to the tiny infant face peeking from the pink bundle, "and Olivia, who is our brand new light in a world where such small joys are far too rare." I thought the file was corrupt when the picture froze with Honey giving a sideways glance to the camera for nearly a full minute.

"Computer..." When I started to close the file, the screen went black and a screen shot of a news article appeared. I froze, mouth agape. I had been off planet when it happened, so only knew of the headline, but felt my chest tighten as my own disaster, small by comparison, brought the reality home.

"CATACLYSMIC EARTHQUAKE ON THE NORTHERN CONTINENT: 1,000,000 DEAD; Millions more Injured. Scientists say aftershocks and additional seismic events in other parts of the world are highly likely."

The bold headline remained as an after image when the screenshot disappeared, and lingered like a ghost when a single picture of side-by-side memorial stones appeared. Honey Leigh Chaplin, Born: 07-26-31, Married: 08-17-55, Died: 06-12-56. Olivia Hope Chaplin, Born: 05-23-56, Died: 06-12-56.

<Awaiting command.>

"Delay command," I said barely loud enough for the computer to respond as Desperation, Loneliness, and I stared at the screen, not horrified, but amazed. Captain Chap used to have a family. I'd always assumed he was unmarried, since Colony Ship Captains weren't permitted families until they reached New Haven. Colonial Command believed it ensured their "Mission objectivity". Tears filled my eyes as the scab of loss peeled open. I thought back on his stoic demeanor when he presided over each child's body committed to the void, and then each adult. I'd wondered why he hadn't cried as he sent friends and their families into the void. At the time, I figured it was his duty to be a paragon of strength, but now it made sense. No other pain could cut as deeply as the loss he'd already experienced. I rolled over and sobbed for his loss until Sleep finally cradled me in her comforting arms.

I startled awake, glancing around my quarters, trying to figure out what had roused me. The soft glow of the vid-screen was the only light. My mind tumbled through millions of details that had been crammed into it over the past three years. What had woken me? Had Hope tapped me on the shoulder again? How long had I been asleep? I looked at the time stamp on the vid-screen. 01:30:45 Thursday, 02-07-67. "That's it!"

I leaped to my desk and tapped the command panel. The "Navigation Locked" screen came up as it had every day for the past three years. The first and last three-pair sequences, a cheery green, waited patiently for the second and third sequences. I typed in 07-26-31 then groaned when the numbers turned red and disappeared. I tried 08-17-55 and held my breath. When the numbers turned green, I didn't celebrate; I plugged in 05-23-56 and waited. A squeak of dismay drowned out the snicker of Desperation when the numbers turned red. Having surmised that marrying his wife was important to Captain Chap, I was sure the birth of his daughter was equally momentous.

My fingers paused above the touchscreen keypad. I had one set of numbers left to try. What if it didn't work? I watched my hand shake. I knew all my companions: Desperation, Anger, Optimism, Fear, Futility, and especially Hope would abandon me and my silent crew into the arms of Loneliness, who would cradle me until Death stepped forward to plunge me into G72. "It will work," Hope whispered at my shoulder and then gently pressed my fingers to the touch screen. One number at a time I tapped in the death date of Captain Chap's wife and daughter, 06-12-56. It would be a true irony if the worst date in his life became the best in mine. I closed my eyes, held my breath and let my finger fall onto the final 6.

<Code authenticated, please enter a new course.>

Before I could even open my eyes, or inhale to cheer, <A message drone has been detected. It is broadcasting at the outer limits of our sensor range.>

I gasped as Fear's fangs drove into my back. Desperation shouted in my mind, "All this for nothing?" Hope encircled my shoulders and said, "Listen."

"Computer, play the message." I wasn't sure I would be able to hear it above the pounding of my heart.

<...(static filled intermittent signal) Captain Larkin... *SS Courage*... message ...*New Hope* ...self-destruct(unintelligible garble) prevent your strain of influenza ...not a cure...>

Fear began to strangle me with disbelief. I'd struggled for three years, alone, and they're telling me to self-destruct? Hope demanded to hear the whole message. "Computer, boost gain and clear up signal."

<The drone is moving away from our current position. Communications are set to automatic. A clearer signal requires closer proximity to the drone and manual adjustment.>

"Set course to get closer."

<Course set.>

"Engage."

<Unable to comply. Propulsion systems are set on automatic, which allows only impulse speed.>

"Then engage impulse speed."

<We are unable to escape the gravitational pull of G72 at impulse speed.>

I stood and screamed at the ceiling. "What do I have to do to get this ship moving?"

<The propulsion system must be rebooted.>

"Don't tell me I have to figure out another code?" Desperation was prying Hope from my side.

<Propulsion systems are not locked, but must be rebooted from the main control panel in Engineering.>

"Will rebooting the propulsion system affect our orbit?"

<There is an 89.63% chance that our orbit will degrade further during the reboot.>

"Will we still be able to achieve escape velocity?"

<Based on a 7.49-minute reboot cycle, our orbit will degrade 12.3 kilometers and require a minimum of 2G acceleration to achieve escape velocity which, once the propulsion system is rebooted, will be easily achievable.>

"Good. Anything else I should know?"

<There is a 3.276 percent chance the engine reboot will fail; an environmental suit is required on the

Engineering level due to the low atmosphere; the turbo lifts are inoperative; and there is a 69.6 percent chance we will be unable to reacquire the drone's signal, which increases by one percent for every ten minutes we are delayed in following it.>

"Great, Futility is back with vengeance. Please restore atmosphere and reactivate the lifts."

<Not possible until propulsion and full energy is restored.>

"Wonderful! Hope always has the most imaginative ways to help forget about Loneliness."

Survivor's Log Day 1002: We escaped G72 with no trouble, once the ship's systems were reset. The cascading shutdown of systems was an obscure result of the long-term automation designed to preserve resources and maximize survivability wherever there were signs of life on the ship. It's taken me a week of 12-hour days to reset and complete a maintenance check on the ship's systems. I've reset our course for New Haven. It will take me a little over two years to arrive. Loneliness, Hope, and Optimism are now my constant companions, although Fear occasionally prowls my dreams, Desperation has been bundled into the void. Hope assures me the message from the drone was a good sign that the *SS Courage* is looking for us, but Fear plays the fragments of the message over and over trying to convince me New Haven or Courage will blow me up on sight. I refuse—

<Captain, contact has been made with the drone. Do you wish to hear the message?>

"Is the message complete?"

<According to my sensors, and extrapolation of the syntax of the message, it is complete.>

I stared out the window at the stars streaking past and contemplated listening to the full message. Hope whispered in one ear, while Fear traced its cold clammy fingers up and down my spine. I had decided three years ago that if I got the chance, I'd go to New Haven whether they chose to destroy the ship with me on it or permit me to live alone onboard until a cure could be found.

Listening to the message wouldn't change that. "Computer, save message without playing."

<Message saved.>

Survivor's Log Day 1701: It's been nearly two years since New Hope escaped the clutches of G72, just in time. The remnants of the explosion still make for exquisite viewing. Optimism and Hope have introduced me to Anxiousness. If the computer's estimates are correct, New Haven should be only thirty—

<Captain, we are being hailed by the *SS Courage*.>

Fear pounced and crushed me. I stumbled to a nearby wall for support. "What do they want? How can that be? We're still thirty days from New Haven."

<They are hailing again. Do you wish to respond?>

I focused on the cool air traveling my nasal passages and filling my lungs with my eyes closed, then pushed Fear away, and summoned Hope. "Computer, play the message from the *SS Courage* drone saved two years ago." My trembling knees forced me into the nearest chair.

<Message on audio.> "This is Captain Larkin of the *SS Courage* trying to contact the *SS New Hope*. Do not self-destruct. I repeat, do not self-destruct. Doctor Jonathan Rock, the premier Virologist in Star Command has achieved promising results on a serum to combat your strain of influenza. It's not a cure, yet. You are instructed to maintain quarantine and rendezvous with the *SS Courage* for resupply."

As the message ended, I pressed my trembling hands against my eyes to stop the burning tears. After five years of Loneliness, Fear, Anger, and Desperation, Optimism and Hope had brought me home. Logic quickly dismissed Fear and Desperation. Loneliness may still be a passing acquaintance, but no longer a constant companion.

<Captain, *SS Courage* is still hailing us.>

"Open a channel."

<Open.>

"*SS Courage* this is Captain Evalynn Santori of the *Starship New Hope*. It's so good to be home."

S. M. Kraftchak notes: Writing is my passion. Visiting with dragons, elves and the occasional alien in worlds of my own imagination helps me enjoy sunrises, sunsets, puppies, and the uniqueness of snowflakes. When not immersed in faraway worlds, I teach camping to Girl Scout leaders, speak at writing workshops, sew Renaissance clothing, and portray Elizabeth Tudor. My husband and three daughters are all fervent supporters of my writing. You can read more of my short fiction in these anthologies published by Lillicat Publishers. Visions III: Inside the Kuiper Belt; Visions II: Moons of Saturn; Visions I: Leaving Earth; *and* The Future Is Short: Science Fiction in a Flash. *To find more of my writing, visit my website http://www.smkraftchak.com.*

My name is Liz but they call me Lady Inked, because my body is covered with sensing, breathing tattoos. A murderer is stalking Pirate's Cove, our paradise at the outer edge of the heliosphere. Some believe my ink gives me special senses that will find the killer. Some think I'm the killer. Haunted by voices of those I've lost, I don't know who is right.

SARI SARI

By

Mary P. Madigan

You should have been here an hour ago, when all of MamaSan's friends in Pirate's Cove were there for her funeral. We were cleaned up, for once, in proper black. Palm trees were swaying over her freshly-dug grave. The suns were shining. I'd done a new tattoo for the occasion, drawn from a photo of her hammering the shelf over the bar. She was in her overalls, her short-cropped hair sticking out at all angles, cigar clenched between her teeth. I put the tattoo on my left shoulder, the last patch of my skin that was bare. It had sensors that could feel the mood in the air. I didn't need it to tell me, the mood was sad.

I was at the podium, giving a eulogy for her when the thin, leathery Police Chief Ponseca, aka Loco Pete, the former Vice President of Charon, stormed in with his battered robocops. He got behind the podium, cuffed me and declared that I, Elizabeth Aguilar, aka Lady Inked, was a suspect in the murder of my guardian, Nicole Santos, aka MamaSan, proprietor of the High Dive Bar. I was also a "person of interest" in the murders of twenty people who had been crushed to death by a serial killer, appropriately known as The Crusher.

"Who is accusing me?" I cried as he twisted my arms behind my back.

"I am," Ami Watanabe, our head waitress, shouted. She peeked out from behind the robocops, black hair streaming in the wind, her slender frame hidden behind their rusty, dented bodies.

"You jerk!" I said. "I saved your life." I don't know why Ami was out to get me. Maybe it was the bad tattoo I gave her. Or the pink shirt I borrowed and never returned.

Our Mayor, Murph, (not aka anything, just Murph) stepped forward. He said his power superseded the Police Chief's, and everyone else's for that matter. Ponseca demurred. Murph loosened his tie, flexed his substantial augmented muscles and punched Ponseca in the nose. That started a free-for-all. As fists flew, newsdroids, cop and camera drones spun wildly, weaving in and out of the mangroves, not knowing where to focus next.

When Father Thomas got knocked into the ditch dug for MamaSan's grave, I knew I had to end it. I twisted back and forth, lowered my shoulder, nudged the sleeve of my black sarong and let it drop to the floor, baring all. Newsdroids are programmed to seek out a scoop, and a young woman's bare breasts override everything.

Most men are programmed the same way. As I stood there, kinky hair flying, bare, rose-decorated breasts punctuated by the cold, they all quieted down. Father Thomas crawled out of the ditch and wiped off his stole. Murph clapped a heavy hand on Ponseca's shoulder. Pete plugged his bloody nose and took off my cuffs.

YouNews is calling it a scandal of epic proportions. MamaSan would have loved it.

Now I'm standing on the shore, watching the suns spinning in the solar wind. The warm azure waters tickle my feet. You might wonder, why don't I make a run for it?

Because I didn't kill her. At least I think I didn't. Ever since I killed my best friend Kara, my brain has gotten a little wonky.

You can decide on my guilt or innocence when you hear my story. But I have to warn you, I'm an unreliable narrator.

I was born on Asteroid UW-540, a platinum mining operation that traversed the Oort cloud. Grandma had a variety store, a place with a little bit of everything. She called it "Sari-Sari". Her side-business was cyber-tattooing, an ancient art developed in the 21st century, when humans were all-meat and nanosensors were external. She taught me how to tattoo before I could write. With my ink pen strapped tightly to my hands, I drew flowers on my knees, butterflies on my belly. I learned how to grind my own paints, and make radio sensors from ferrous dust. I made my first 3D claw from UW-540's platinum clay. I melted it, put it into the pen and formed it into a removable plastic skin. I loved making my body more than nature and science could give me, watching silicon and sweat merging into the folds of a petal.

"It's a sensual experience to make your fingertips hear, your ears breathe," Grandma said.

"Sensual?"

"Something that makes you feel happy. Like ice cream on a hot day."

She drew a picture of Mom and Dad on the back of my right hand, so I'd always see and remember them. She didn't talk about where they'd gone or how they'd died, but I knew it had something to do with the Titan Wars. Grandma never said which side they were on. She didn't care.

When the wars came to our little asteroid Grandma said, "I'm not losing you too," as she stuffed me and her paints into the escape pod. She shut the pod door behind me. I cried, pounding my fists on the door, wanting her to come in, but she couldn't. It was a tiny, cheap pod, all she could afford. There was only room for one person.

She pressed the button and launched me away. From above I saw her waving "Aloha"; hello, goodbye. Then the mercenaries came, their faces covered with scarves that made them look like grinning skulls. I screamed as they surrounded our Sari-Sari, aimed their guns and blasted Grandma into char.

I'll never forget her wave. It was a perfect arc. I saw the same arc in twists of the Oort cloud as my pod was drawn into the rescue ship. It was in the stars as we passed Charon. It was in the furrows of MamaSan's forehead when the rescuers dropped me off at Pirates Cove, when she realized she was going to have to keep her promise to her cousin and take care of a ragged, miserable, eight-year-old orphan.

Alone in my room, I drew Grandma's portrait into my arm, in grey ash, with a sensor mix that would detect the dark matter that made up poltergeists. I drew that perfect arc around it and said, "Hello?" No answer.

The next morning, I tried to hide from the world, but what child can ignore dancing suns? The beauty of the Cove hypnotized me. A domed paradise built at the cold, outer edge of the Heliosphere, glowing in friction-warmed dust grains caught in the whorls of the Bow Wave. The water was just a few feet from the bar. Mangroves, flowers, and salt-tinged mushrooms were right outside my door. Grandma's portrait, grey the night before, sparkled like a prism.

MamaSan didn't feel like talking to me in those early days. She thought if she ignored me, I'd go away. But I discovered the one subject that would get her talking for hours–infrastructure.

"How was Pirate's Cove built?" I asked her.

"Long story, kiddo. Sure you wanna hear?" she said.

I nodded, figuring if I could get her to talk, she'd like me better.

"At first, the Cove was like Earth's Big Pacific Garbage Patch, a bunch of junk that got caught in solar-wind whirlpools."

"What made the whirlpools?"

"They were made of interstellar medium pushed by edges of the great, solar-winds Bow Wave. Like waves formed by the prow of a ship. Pirates, refugees from the wars, travelers in generation ships–they all got sucked into the Cove."

"Did everyone get along?"

"They were pirates and crooks, of course they didn't get along. They had the best fights, though. Sword fights."

"Why swords?"

"Because guns and lasers in an oxygenated atmosphere make big booms."

"When did they build the dome?"

"About a hundred years ago, when a terraforming package from Acme Worldbuilding fell off the back of a cargo ship. Not too sure how that could have happened, but those who found it never said. They covered the junk pile of ships with dirt and put the dome around it. The suns gave us heat. That made weather, clouds and rain. We got lakes, put fish in them. Underneath the lakes, the ships' Jeffries tubes became caves. Some people like to go diving down there. Those are the crazy people who come to our bar."

Kara's mother, who was kind of a Hippie, told me the other side of the story. "When IonFire ships made interstellar travel cheap for the masses," she said, "this paradise turned into a tourist trap. Multi-story hotels grew like crabgrass. They bumped and scraped against the domes that held precious oxygen in. The Cove's "sky" is scarred, the water is dirty, and there's a mold in the air that paints the concrete with rot. That's what happens, when nobody pays taxes. All they care about is profit, and the environment goes to hell."

I cared about the environment, but I was too busy trying to survive to do much about it. Even if the Cove was dirty, it was still pretty. Beauty always lifted my spirits. And there was Kara.

I met Kara on the rescue ship. She asked me to make her a rose tattoo like the ones on my knees. She was everything I wanted to be; tall and willowy with silky brown hair. She was loved. She had a family.

At first, I thought she was clueless. When she found out that I couldn't afford to go to school, she said, "I wish I didn't have to go. It's so boring." She thought I went spearfishing because it was an adventure. I explained that I did it to eat. She said, "Awesome! I wish I could eat fresh fish every day." But soon I realized–other girls my age avoided me because I was poor. And weird. Kara wasn't afraid of weird. She wasn't afraid that my poverty-cooties would get on her. She wasn't afraid of anything.

When we were little, she would sneak away from school, I'd take a break from work, and we'd scuba dive, going down past the warm surface, the mangrove roots, the piles of seaweed, shells, and sand. We'd sit at the edge of the caves, cross-legged, fish swimming around our heads as we played patty cake, humming, "This old man, he played one, He played knick-knack on my thumb" through our sub-vocals.

Soon, MamaSan made me manager, and I could make my own breaks. Kara was old enough to get tattooed without her parents' permission, and she wanted gills just like mine. I told her they wouldn't be the same, they would be better. My tattoos were inspired by a person's DNA, their nano-data and, most of all, the boldness of their heart. My line was spare, practical, but occasionally twisted. Kara's line was fine calligraphy, twirling into light, baroque whorls.

She sat still, trying not to gasp as my needle twisted into her skin, bravely biting her lip. Her skin had the whiff of fresh grass. My pen and my hands moved by instinct, generating waves of gills. Then I drew a rose of nano-sensors under her ears that would let her 'see' by following the echoes of the waves.

The first time we dove into the caves, I was staggering like a drunk. Kara had to take my hand to keep me from disappearing into the darkness.

"That's a diver's high," she said. "It feels like you're floating in space."

We dove further, into the caves, where one scratch of PCP-coated stalactite could mean death. I drew a filter tattoo of purple roses over our hearts to keep the poisons away. After our last dive, I searched the neuronet and found that her "diver's high" was really the first symptom of Rubyshakes, the brain shutting down because of the extremes of pressure in a space station/diving atmosphere. I wish I'd known that before. If I had, Kara might still be alive.

A few days ago, Ami and I were hanging out at the High Dive with nothing to do. There was no crowd of first-timers celebrating the fact that they'd gone into the caves and survived, no Yakuza in the back room getting grimly smashed on Shochu. There was only the sound of rain on the roof and the tank filter bubbling. Tourists tend to stay away when a serial killer is on the loose.

Ami said to me "I want you to give me a dragon tattoo like Kara's."

I tried to think of an excuse not to do it, but I couldn't, so I ignored her, watching as the girls in the tank did their mermaid routine. Their gills fluttered, their water-soft hair slid over rose-tattooed breasts; feet rippled in wavy, blue light as they kicked their way to the depths, then gracefully rose, glancing at the clock as they reached the surface.

"Liz!" Ami shouted. "Are you going to do it or not?"

Her tattoo could never look as nice as Kara's. Her line would be like her personality, simple, and kind of unrealistic. Like a Manga cartoon.

"Your dragon will be different," I said. "Because..."

"Great! You'll do it!"

"Sure." I grumbled. I got the paints, stirred the nano-bits until they fizzed, and loaded my pen. As I drew a line over Ami's shoulder, I thought of the dreams I'd had every night since Kara died. They started out nice; Kara and I were kids again, deep in the caves, singing "This Old Man." But as we'd play, Kara's hands would get pale and cold. When the song was over her eyes would roll back until they were white.

"Can you keep a secret?" she'd say. I'd be crying so hard I couldn't answer.

"You know I can," she'd say. "Because I never told anyone that you let me die." Then her mouth opened into a wide black maw of rot. I could feel her hunger, her desire to eat me alive. I'd wake up screaming, wracked with guilt.

On our last dive, she wanted me to follow her into a cave she'd found, at the lower depths. "It's so beautiful, covered with ice. You've got to see it!"

I couldn't gather the nerve. Everyone who had gone that deep had died.

"But you must," she said. "We are doomed, but that makes everything more beautiful."

She almost convinced me with those beautiful words. I looked it up later, and found out she was quoting some guy named Homer. Still, I was afraid.

"Then stay here, scaredy-cat." I remembered the look on her face as she said that, tugging on her weight belt as she turned. It was heavier than usual. Then she fell away from me, sinking fast. That could only have happened if she was over-weighted. Dizzy with "diver's high," I'd been the last one to check her weights.

"Do you think the killer will come here?" Ami asked, squirming, as I started her dragon tattoo.

"I don't know." I tried to find something reassuring to say about the serial killer, but I was distracted by Kara's voice in my head, demanding I do the outline in blue instead of black. I tried to disagree, but Kara said "Do it! You know what happens when you don't listen to me."

I knew "Kara" was really the voice of my own guilty conscience, my way of punishing myself, but it seemed a little less crazy to pretend she was a ghost.

Holding the ink pen tight, I changed inks and lined the edges of the scales in blue. The last thing I needed was to hear about more death, but Ami kept talking.

"The Crusher killed Dal when he was sitting on the couch, drinking a beer." she said, tapping her foot nervously. "Oh my god, it was so gross, there was a trail of blood and guts right through his living room. Zavi Teng disappeared when she was doing the dishes. The Crusher ground her in the trash compactor. He got Mosley when he was sitting on the loo!"

"Shut up," I mumbled.

"What?"

"I said hold still."

"The newsdroids say the Crusher's kill rate is increasing exponentially. With the tourists gone, there's only a few thousand people in the Cove. We're all going to die!"

"Newsdroids are programmed to exaggerate," I said. "The Crusher's kill rate is more like a Fibonacci sequence. Three weeks ago five people got killed. The next week it was eight, the next week, it'll be thirteen."

Her contacts glowed as she calculated. "In eleven weeks we'll all be dead!"

She was right but I preferred to ignore that. I put the finishing touches on her dragon.

Ami walked to the bar, past the fake sparkling waterfall, the hanging lights and the reconstituted flowers. Empty Xenomorph shells sang an eerie tune as the margarita fountain splashed over them. She lifted a hatch covered with tangerine seaweed, revealing a picture of Kara. "In Memorium." Ami looked in the mirror and compared.

"It's not like Kara's. It looks like a cartoon."

"I told you…"

"Make it like hers!"

"I can't!"

"You can too!"

She sat back down and stuck her shoulder blade in my face. I sighed and fired up my pen.

"Oooh! Is this supposed to hurt?"

"It'll hurt less if you stop wiggling," I said, adjusting the tattoo gun. "Let me strap this back on."

Murph opened the door, shook the rain from his short-cropped dark hair and smiled. "Mmm. Is this a private party or can I join in?"

"Huh?" Ami said.

I coughed "Horndog," and finished adjusting the strap. "He heard us and thought we were…you know."

"Oh!" Ami gasped, giggling.

"Color me disappointed," Murph said, but he was clearly not upset by Ami's flush of desire. She was what the ex-mercs wanted, a skinny doll to hang on their beefy arms.

"No one wants a brainy girl shaped like a kamote," Kara hissed. More proof that Kara's voice was my own guilty conscience–she knew the Filipino word for sweet potato.

Trying to impress Ami, Murph took off his camo jacket, black shirt tight against his chest. I stared at his sharply-edged abs. They looked like they were cut from marble.

"You are so hot for him," Kara hissed.

Bullshit, I thought as I put the inks back in the box.

"You blushed just as much as Ami did. Look at your face."

I turned away from the mirror.

"Put the red one in last, and I promise, he'll ask you out."

Defiantly, I put the black in last.

"Now you've done it," she said. "Bad luck."

I switched the black to red. "No, that's not good enough. Take them all out and put them back, in the exact order I tell you. Or else."

Or else wasn't an idle threat. I once used the wood cleaner to polish the titanium edges of the holodeck. Kara didn't like that. An hour later, we heard about Dal.

Another time, I walked up the stairs starting with my right foot. Kara wanted me to start with my left. Zavi Teng disappeared that evening, Mosley the next day. It was more than coincidence. I took the inks out of the box and rearranged them, glancing at the tattoo of Grandma on my arm; my poltergeist detector. It didn't register any of Kara's appearances, in my dreams or when I was awake. Which meant something in my subconscious knew when these murders were about to happen.

Ami scratched her ear, reddening her new tattoo. "How does this thing work?"

"The nano bits and liquid sensors connect with the nano-cells in your ear," I said. "Then they set up a neuronet connection. You can listen to your playlist, too."

"Ooh, fun!" She wiggled her ears and frowned. "I'm not online."

"You need to go in the water. Your skin, the water and my ink are their own elements. They only work when they sing together."

"Sounds pretty whifty," Murph said. "Thought someone like you would have a bulleted list of instructions, twenty pages, single spaced."

"Someone like me?"

"You know," he leaned towards Ami and stage-whispered. "Kinda OCD."

"She hasn't always been this way," Ami said "Just since Kara died."

"She? Stop talking about me like I'm not here!" I slammed the box of inks shut.

"Okay, okay," Murph said, as he followed me into the bar. "I was supposed to meet MamaSan at noon. Where is she?"

"Somewhere else." I said.

"Why is she blowing me off? I'm mayor of this cowtown now. That should count for something."

"You won the Cove in a card game. What should that count for?" I said.

He snorted and walked to the window. The rain had stopped, but the rainbows that followed were hidden by the monstrosity next door, the Nine Luck Hotel. Built on a foundation of sand and bribes, the wobbling tower of rotten cement was squarely in the middle of our view.

"If you want some respect, do something about that kraplik hotel." I said.

"Wish I could." he said.

"Any news about the Crusher?" Ami asked.

"Yeah!" Murph said. "You gotta see this! There was a witness." He blinked a few times to download the vid onto the holoscreen. The newsdroid warned that children under 21 shouldn't watch it. "You girls are both legal. Aren't you?" Murph asked. I rolled my eyes. Ami nodded and giggled.

The vid began with a shot of a man's face, blackened eye sockets brimming with blood. The camera pulled back to show the sewer behind the face, blood dripping through the dirty grates. There was no neck or skull attached to it.

Just a face. "This was all that was left of Davy Paul after he met with the Crusher."

I gasped.

Ami said "Gug..." and ran for the loo.

The newsdroid asked the witness "Mr....um what's your name?"

"Call me D."

"Mr. D., what did you see?"

"That guy, on the street, running scared. I guess I shoulda tried to help him, but he had that look about him. Martian, Burger Boys. Didn't want to get mixed up in any gangster shit."

The newsdroid nodded in an approximation of sympathy.

"He ran in an alley. Then he started screaming. And this...thing, this slimy, tentacle thing, came through the sewer. It wrapped around his body and started squeezing. I could hear his bones cracking. It was horrible."

"Mr. D., do we have your permission to replay your internal video online?"

"Take it. I'm deleting the damned thing. Never want to see it again."

"Thank you, Mr. D." The newsdroid faced the camera and said, "People on the street are asking, 'What is the mayor going to do about this?'"

D. stuck his face back in the camera and shouted. "Yeah, Murph! Get off your ass and do something!"

Murph blinked and shut the vid off. "The rest is just everyone crapping on me. You don't want to see that."

"Yes, I do."

Sitting at the empty bar in the lotus position, I tried to concentrate on my meditation. Murph and MamaSan weren't making it easy.

MamaSan leaned back in her chair, unlit cigar between her gold teeth. "The Crusher isn't gonna come through our pipes," she said. "I got filters."

"I don't know where it is. It could be in the water supply, or it could be in the caves. I'll have to go down there and find it."

She chewed on the cigar. "That's no job for an old man."

"I can still fight the good fight." He flexed. "See?"

MamaSan caught me looking and frowned. I squeezed my eyes shut and went back to my ohms.

"Seriously? You gonna hunt this guy?"

"It's not a guy, it's a cephalopod. My best guess, a Jovian banshee. Must've come here on somebody's ship."

"Banshees are tough, but they got lizard brains. Crusher is a hunter, smart. I think it's a crazy diver, with Rubyshakes."

"But, the tentacle...?"

"A tattoo artist can 3D a tentacle."

I could feel everyone in the room turning to look at me. Sweat began to drip down my neck.

"Rubyshakes," Kara hissed. "That's you."

"Ohm," I said

"Yeah, everybody's got a theory," Murph said. "The businesspeople in Northside want me to fight it. The hippies in Southside want me to negotiate, find out how we offended it. What offends Jovian Banshees?"

"Weren't no Banshee! They chop, they don't puree."

"Anyway, I need a guide. Your best."

"Won't be cheap," MamaSan said, putting her cigar into the ashtray. "Thirty-thousand credits."

He sunk back into the chair. "Crap! Ever since I got this job, I've done nothing but spend my own money."

"Welcome to Pirate's Cove."

"Sometimes I think Old Bud threw that game on purpose."

"Took you this long to figure that out?" MamaSan cackled. She waved her hand towards the mermaid tank. "Take one, any one you want."

"I said your best." he said.

Please don't say me. Please, please...

"Liz."

Dammit!

"She don't go in the water no more," MamaSan said. "Ear problems."

Thank you, MamaSan! This ohm is for you.

Ami breezed past me, newly-painted dragon ink glistening in the sunslight. "I'm gonna try this tattoo out." she said.

"Uh huh." I said, but a moment later I realized she was headed in the wrong direction. She wasn't going in the tank; she was going outside.

Then I heard the scream, online and through the window. From my toes to my ears, her pain cut through me. I stumbled out of lotus, ran out the door, didn't think, just dove in.

My fault. All my fault. I swam down, sensors activating, gills, breathing, radar searching. Ami was struggling in the water. Alone.

As I got her in a rescue hold she said "The water... so cold! My leg cramped."

Murph was waiting at the shore, smiling at me. "Looks like your ears got better."

On the walk home, I stopped to gather the Mixtec Slugs. They came out in the evenings to feed on mushrooms that grew in the grassy sand. When boiled, they made a beautiful purple dye. I got on my knees and gathered them up, watching the sunslight swirl.

"I put poison down to kill these things." MamaSan said, kicking at the mushrooms. "But they won't die. This is what we get for using that Acme crap."

"The terraform?"

She pulled a puffy button up and tore the strands out from under the cap. "They use a mycelium base, a mushroom, to make a net under the dirt. Mycelium sticks together, grows miles wide. That's why my fruit trees don't grow—mushrooms suck food from the soil."

I got up. "Did you come out here to complain about mushrooms?"

Her drone whirred towards me, wobbling, weighted down with a plate of spam and eggs. "You need to eat, build up your strength."

"I'm too fat already." I said.

"You're a normal, healthy girl! If you were skinny like Ami, you'd freeze to death in the deep."

I pushed the spam away. "I'm not diving with Murph."

"Yes, you are."

"I can't. Every time I go near the water, I see Kara's face."

"Don't think that way. If I got wound up about every shitty thing that happened, I'd never get out of bed. "

I wiped slug slime from my hands "You think Murph can kill it?"

"No, but he's good for the money. Thirty large is enough to keep the bar in the black for a while."

"I can't do it."

"Lizzy girl, we got no customers. Everybody's scared to go out. We gotta get the money somewhere."

"No."

"Ok, there's plan B. Give the guys what they really want. You do more than just swim." She lit her cigar, the smoke merged in the light with her grey hair. "You don't have to go in the water any more. Earn money on your back."

"Are you serious?"

She blew the smoke into my face. "Of course not! You think I'm giving you all this training to make you a whore?" She smacked my shoulder. "Get some confidence, girl. You're smart, a hard worker. You got potential."

"Enough potential for a raise?"

I turned to her for an answer, but she wasn't there. Her cigar lay on the ground, smoking into the suddenly quiet air. The slugs disappeared and the frogs stopped singing. Slowly, I turned towards the water. Something splashed. It was MamaSan, kicking her feet, trying to free her throat from the thing that had slithered around it.

I tilted the drone, dumped the spam, smashed the plate and used the biggest shard to cut the tentacle that was tight around her neck. More tentacles rose from the water, burning my arms like a swarm of jellyfish. I kept cutting, despite the pain, wishing I'd built myself an armor of throwing stars.

"Let her die!" Kara screamed in my head. "She was always so mean to you."

"Shut up!" I cried as I cut through the tentacles and pulled MamaSan out of the water. She lay on the beach, gasping. I caught my own breath, held a trembling hand to help her up.

The ground shook. I struggled to keep my balance as hundreds of thin, purple tendrils snaked from the loamy ground. "No!" I cried as they wound themselves around MamaSan. I tried to tear them away but they wrapped around my wrists, holding me fast, burning through my skin. MamaSan was dragged into the water, thick tentacles winding around her, squeezing her swollen body, pulling it into the deep. I twisted myself free and tried to follow, but blood clouded the water. I turned my radar sensors on and saw something solid floating towards me. MamaSan's face, eyes gone, the skin around them burned black and red. Clutching it, I fell into the upturned dirt, tears rolling down my jelly-stung face. Kara laughed as blood washed up on shore, turning the sand a foamy pink.

The funeral was a few days later. That was where my story began. Here's how it ends.

I told the police what I saw, I showed them my internal vid, but the reception was choppy. They know vids can be faked. When they heard MamaSan left me the bar in her will, they got even more suspicious. And Ami didn't help. Now, only Murph seemed to believe me.

He said we should still do the dive. I was still afraid, but now I had no choice. I had to do it, for MamaSan. I was waiting for him, at the spot where she was killed. He was an hour late.

"Had to get my kitbag," he said, dropping a massive, camouflaged lump that clanked at my feet.

"What's that?"

"This is how the Fifteenth won the Titan Wars," he said.

"The Fifteenth what?"

"Legion!" He said, proudly displaying the pigmented Army/QR symbol on his wrist.

It was just a few centimeters above the spears embedded in his palm. Mercs like Murph were bred to fight in watery subsurface outposts like Titan. He didn't have to tattoo his gills, armor, or weaponry, they were already there. But that didn't stop him from packing a massive amount of extra heat. His kitbag had railguns, titanium spears, katana swords, and bags of quivering red blobs.

I gingerly pulled the bags out. "What are these?"

"Adhesive explosives. Stick one gram on your target and run. Merges with the target's DNA and blows it to shit."

"Ugh," I said, shuddering. "There's enough here to blow up the whole Cove!"

"If we don't kill this thing, the Cove will be just as dead."

"We should kill the Cove to save it."

"I didn't say that."

"It's what you mercenaries do."

He repacked his kitbag. "I know you hate mercs. After what happened to your grandmother, I don't blame you. We all regret the battle of five four zero. If we had only gotten there before they did..."

"It doesn't matter who got there first! 540 was a tiny asteroid, you mercs had enough weapons to blow us all to shit a hundred times over! Grandma was doomed no matter what."

"That's not true. They have weapons of massive destruction. We have weapons of massive precision. If we'd gotten there first, we could have taken them all out, without harming one hair on your granny's head."

"I don't believe that."

"I can't go into the thick of it with someone who doesn't trust me." He pulled a revolver from his kitbag, put six bullets in the cylinder and spun it.

"What are you doing?"

He pulled a leaf from the tree behind him and ran it through the pistol's sensor. "If you point this gun at my head, do you think it'll kill me?"

"Yes..."

"It won't. But it'll knock every leaf off that tree, because that's how I programmed it. You could pull the trigger once, twice, a hundred times, an inch from my face and I'll still be standing."

"But...how?"

"Massive precision. The Fifteenth never misses."

I took the gun, felt the weight of it. "Why do you believe me when I say I didn't kill MamaSan?"

"Because I trust you."

"What if I told you that I hear voices in my head. That they told me to let MamaSan die."

"I know real killers, and you're not one of them."

"You can't know for sure."

"I know my own kind." His blue eyes gazed into mine, straight and cold, sending a chill down my spine. "Now shoot me."

I put the gun to his forehead. He took a deep breath, clenched his square jaw. I thought I wanted to shoot, my rage about Grandma's death was still strong. But he was so close, so vulnerable.

I gave him the gun. "I can't."

He pushed me away and picked up his kitbag. "Stay here. I'm going in alone."

"No, wait!" I opened up my paintbox. "I have my own test—I'll give you a tattoo. Your line, it's a window to your soul. If it's strong and true, then I can trust you."

"That's ridiculous," he said.

I slid a finger along his bare chest. "Look at this pattern of scars. I could make a wolf. Or maybe a wolf morphing into a dragon."

"I...uh...No." he said. But he didn't push my hand away. I fired up my pen. "Stop!"

"Why?"

"I don't...I...uh..." he sighed. "I'm afraid of needles."

I couldn't help but smile.

"It took a lot of balls to admit that! Give me some credit."

I was about to pull my hand away, but he held it tightly. I stopped laughing. My sensors felt what he felt; fear that I would reject him. Warmth. Love. My heart felt like it was sweetly melting. Like ice cream on a warm day. "Everything is more beautiful..." I whispered, "because we're doomed."

"You will never be lovelier than you are now. We will never be here again."

"You've read Homer?"

He tapped his head. "The whole Library of Congress was downloaded into my noggin when I was ten." he smiled. "Do I pass?"

I picked up his kitbag and walked to the shore. "Let's go."

We descended past the shallows, through white lines of sunlight cutting through the cyan haze. At the entrance to the caves, I searched for the fish.

"My god," I said through the sub-vocals. "Angels, groupers, barracuda...they're all gone."

"Something's hungry."

As we descended, the water turned from blue to black. My tattoo-armor was strong, but the cold still cut through.

"This was where Kara disappeared." I switched my positioning system on and chose the map of my last deep dive, recorded on my internal vid the day she died. I'd never been able to gather the courage to watch it, but since it was linked to the positioning system, it was unavoidable. There was Kara, laughing, the way she used to, with no rage in her voice. She pulled her weight belt, turned to me, then fell. That look, shock, pain. Grief boiled in my heart as her pale face dropped into the dark, as the purple tendrils swirled around her feet.

Wait, what?

I replayed it. In real life I hadn't been able to see through the grit, but my vid recorded it clearly. She wasn't over-weighted. She was pulled down by the same thing that had killed MamaSan.

Murph bumped into me. "Why are you stopping?" he asked, but I was watching the replay so intently I barely heard him. The last time we'd been down here, the caves were crowded with stalactites. Those were gone too. There was only ice, covering the walls. Was this the ice Kara saw in the depths?

I touched it. A jolt stung my hand. I shone my flashlight on it. Purple, squirming ice, patterning itself into baroque curves.

"Stop!" I said, grabbing Murph by the flipper, "We have to go back."

"Don't chicken out on me now, honey, you've come this far."

"I know what the Crusher is. We are not ready for it."

"You said it's a jelly."

"Yes. It's a jelly. And an octopus, and a plant...and—Kara."

"You're not making sense."

"Yes, I am. What's the largest organism in the Cove?"

"The bouncer at St. Jack's."

"Be serious."

"I dunno."

"A mushroom."

"Get out."

"This whole place is built on the foundation of mycelium, one gigantic mushroom."

"Mushrooms don't have tentacles."

"We're pouring all kinds of garbage into the water. Pollution, chemicals, nanocells. Tourists bring their germs and their animals. I think this created a new kind of monster, a thing that ate Kara and somehow...incorporated her."

Murph pulled the largest railgun from his pack. "I'm not running away from a mushroom."

I shone the flashlight onto the purple-white threads that covered the walls. "This isn't ice, it's mycelium. We're in the Crusher's stomach."

A tendril grazed his ankle. The jolt cut through his suit. He screamed with pain as his flashlight flickered and went dark. "Let's get out of here." he said.

I accessed the positioning system, retraced our steps, but there was a wall where the entranceway had been. I didn't need to look at the radar to know what it was—mycelium. I unhooked my flashlight and shone it onto the squirming wall. There was a lump at the center. It opened its mouth and groaned in pain. I screamed, dropped the flashlight and fell back into my own bubbles.

Murph took the flashlight. "Mosley," he said. The walls were lined with the faces of the Crusher's victims, slithering strands winding through their hollowed eyes, curling through mouths twisted in agony.

"They're still alive. The Crusher is feeding from them."

Murph shuddered with disgust. He grabbed his drone and twisted the fuel tank cover. "This drone is fueled by nitrites. Pure poison to shrooms."

"Will it work?" I asked, but he didn't answer, he was jerked back as a mass of tendrils wrapped thick around him, ignoring his roar of rage, pulling him to the wall. With a shaking hand I reached for a sword.

"Stop!" Kara said. Her voice was harsh, but she softened it, trying not to sound like a monster. "Liz...I've missed you so much!"

"You," I gulped, my throat suddenly dry "...you have a funny way of showing it."

"I won't hurt him if you come talk to me."

"Talk? For months you've been screwing with my head. I've had enough of your talk."

"But you kept your sensors open to talk to me. We were besties."

"You're not Kara!"

"Yes, I am." The monster twisted its tendrils into classical swirls, slithering over Murph as he struggled. "See what I can draw?"

I clutched the sword tightly. Tendrils from both sides of the wall shot out from the wall and yanked the blade from my hand. "Play nice or I'll flay him alive." The sword fell into the hungry wall, like Murph, instantly mummified. "Come to me," the Crusher said.

A spark flashed at the end of the tunnel. The light illuminated what was left of Kara's body. Mycelium pierced her skin, wove through the black maw that had been her mouth. Unlike the rest of the victims, she had one eye, round and lidless. I cried for her, for the pain she must be feeling. That eye stared right through me.

"Wh...what are you? How can you do this to people?"

49

"I am to you as you are to your slugs," Crusher/Kara said as tentacles licked my legs. "Do you cry for them?"

"The Hippies were right—you're doing this because you're angry about what we've done to the environment."

The Crusher/Kara laughed. "I'm doing this because you taste good."

I hid my hand as I slowly reached for the knife in my belt. "Naughty, naughty," the Crusher/Kara said as its mycelium twisted around my wrist, burning my skin. The knife fell. More tendrils wrapped around my waist, dragged me towards the wall. The poison was cutting through my shields, all the way to my bones. I couldn't hold back the screams. Dizzy with pain, I saw Kara's hand, only a few inches from mine. "I know you're in there..." I gasped.

She laughed, her blackened mouth twisted into Crusher's rictus grin.

Murph screamed. A thin stream of blood floated past my face.

"You said you wouldn't hurt him!"

"I trap humans and slowly eat them alive. You're surprised that I lie?"

Murph screamed again, but this one was different. Victorious. An explosion rocked the cave. Bits of withered tendrils fell around us. Through pain and tears, I could see Kara's face and the Crusher's crazy grin, shifting from one to another, flickering like a character in a cheap hologame. Tentacles began flying, twisting in fits of rage, knotting into each other. I couldn't tell if Murph was free, but, somehow, he was pissing off the Crusher. When it was distracted, Kara seemed to come back.

"This old man..." I said, touching Kara's hand, "he played one..."

She stared, then said, "He...played knick-knack on my thumb." Something like a smile quivered at the edge of her blackened mouth. "This old man...he played five. He played knick-knack on my eye."

With the mind-meld that best friends had, I knew just what she meant. "Are you saying... your eye?"

"Do it." A bloody tear flowed onto her cheek. "Please."

I tried to hold her hand, but the Crusher's poison was seeping through my veins, paralyzing me. I could feel the mycelium under my eyelids, licking them hungrily. "The eyes are the first to go," the Crusher hissed. I wept, struggling to open my eyes before they were gone. As I struggled, I felt Murph, cutting me free. He got me in a safety hold.

"I can't kill this thing." He gasped. "The bombs don't work; it changes its DNA pattern in microseconds."

"Kara's eye...its...weak spot."

"Roger that." He grabbed the wobbling drone, balanced the load of red bomb on it and aimed it at the eye. Then he turned, kicked and swam us out of there. I watched as mycelium twisted around the drone. Clouds of poison roiled and burned. The Crusher screamed, but Kara was laughing, the way she used to. Then an explosion, a wave of fire, slammed me through blazing shards. I awoke in a mass of starry dust, gasping for breath.

Did we destroy the Cove? Was I floating in space?

A hand touched mine, bloodied but intact. Murph. We were floating over a thick mat of stringy grit, all that was left of the Crusher. We coughed grit out of our gills, then swam in silence until we reached warmer waters. Through the wavering debris floating overhead, we saw the rot-stained concrete of the Nine Luck Hotel, still standing.

"We didn't destroy the Cove." I tried to be happy about that, but my lips quivered.

"I'm sorry about your friend," he said, swimming close.

"Me too," I said.

We stumbled on to the shore and closed our gills. My sore and tired body, suddenly weighty after coming out of the water, felt off-balance. I leaned against Murph for support. He put his warm arms around me.

One of my sensors tickled. Grandma's portrait was glowing with a prismatic light. The poltergeist detector had switched on. Behind me, the waves and the grass circled in baroque curves. I could have sworn I heard Kara, laughing.

Murph didn't see or hear any of it. "Point me to the bar." he said. "To the margarita fountain."

"You want a couple of drinks?" I said, distracted.

"I wanna swim in it."

He threw the bar door open and shouted. "We got it!" to the crowd of newsdroids and registered voters. They cheered. Murph filled a Xenomorph skull and poured a margarita over my head, shouting "Fifteenth!" I wiped the lime goop from my eyes, drank some of it and warily looked outside. Did we really get it?

The patterns were gone. My Grandma, her soft smile and kind eyes, was grey once more. Guess my sensors got wonky again.

Mary Madigan is a writer, artist, and photographer. She and her family live in New Jersey, a place whose undercurrent of weirdness inspires her sci-fi stories. She's written and published some short stories and she's currently working on a novel about an American family's lives before and after the Singularity. She's also a dot com. http://www.marypmadigan.com

Vampires in outer space. Sounds like a sci-fi parody, yet the possibilities are strangely limitless. What could happen to the polymorphous vampiric body away from the confines of sunlight and gravity? In "Whisper," a traditional, planet-bound vampire confronts his deep space brethren and discovers the answer.

WHISPER

By

Jonathan Shipley

Plummeting through the lightless vacuum of deep space, the bridge of the one-man yacht was a cacophony of in-coming beeps. In the middle of the bridge, Anton answered first one message then another, as quickly as he could, trying not to spend more than thirty seconds on any one request. Then a priority beep from Capella. He answered that immediately.

"Anton." The voice on the com was harsh with extreme range amplification. "There's been more killing in the nests in the Artra system—same pattern as all the others. Should we try to evacuate, or what?"

Anton stepped closer to the console. "Don't bother with evacuation. Kill all the Youngers. It's the only way to stop this cancer." And he rattled off a series of contain-and-destroy commands that were virtually the same as the last three incidents. *You should be able to handle this yourself based on previous experience*, he thought uncharitably. And this was his deputy back on Capella IV where the Night Nation was headquartered. His hand-picked deputy who was freezing up in this emergency, though generally competent with day-to-day affairs. The other vampires—not hand-picked, but the rank-and-file— were completely hopeless. Give them a problem, and all

55

they saw was their next meal, as though ripping out a throat was some sort of universal solution.

"But Anton, what if the..."

The harshly amplified voice faded abruptly, taking all the unanswered beeps with it. As the bridge settled into uncharacteristic silence, Anton gave a sigh of relief and pulled a bag of cooled blood plasma from the storage cabinet. Done was done. He was out of com range of Capella and the other Night Nation planets. Hopefully, he'd clarified enough details on the half dozen pending projects that his staff wouldn't be tempted to improvise. He knew his people could make decisions in his absence. He just doubted their ability to make good decisions. He would never say it, but thought it often—vampires were stupid. Despite the annoying responsibilities that came with the job, Anton fancied himself a born leader. A dumb bloodsucker he wasn't.

Given the frenetic pace of his undertakings, silence was a luxury he seldom enjoyed. He sat back in the command chair and let himself relax—truly relax—with his plasma. This far out, he had passed some invisible demarcation where not only com signals failed, but even the texture of space felt different. Free from the gravitational fields inside planetary systems, it was a sensation of nothingness, and good nothingness. No hint of the "little death," that deadly combination of light and weight, that dragged him back to his coffin at every sunrise. It wasn't the same as being alive again, but neither was it the cold misery of a corpse's sleep. He imagined he might live comfortably out here, beyond the reach of sunlight and gravity. And death.

But that was sheer indulgence, an extravagance he could ill afford. He had problems far beyond indecisive minions back at headquarters, problems that brought him to this deep space trade route. Vampire had turned against vampire. He had seen it coming a decade ago, but had failed to address it. Now the reality left a bitter taste in his mouth. So much for the bonds of undead brotherhood. It wasn't anything as sophisticated as a political uprising or an attempted coup. That, at least, he could have coped with. No, this was quite different in the chaotic way it was spreading. But it needed to be stopped regardless.

And he had a plan. Out here in the nothingness of deep space, he needed to insert loyal operatives as his eyes and ears into the nests. Sitting back, savoring the silence, he began to understand why they had adopted the name Whisperers. Some silences didn't need to be broken.

A proximity sensor beeped, bringing him back to attentiveness as the perimeter monitors auto-activated. The coordinates were wrong for the MercyMed supply ship he was rendezvousing with, so something else was out here in the nothingness. And there, three o'clock by eight o'clock from his current location, a freighter floated aimlessly just within sensor range. Derelict, he decided, as he altered course and checked energy residuals to determine how long it had been abandoned. Less than a week.

It was an easy assumption that the freighter was the victim of raiders. The hull was damaged in several locations. But the pattern was precise and familiar, the exact pattern for disabling a ship that he had taught to his operatives before sending them out to deep-space. Their whole mission was raiding cargo and transferring it to designated ports of call for resale. The Night Nation turned a nice profit on the on-going operation. But this was opportune. It gave him the chance to inspect their work before he met with them, and their work would tell him much. They had responded positively enough when he requested this meeting, but truly, who were these Whisperers of his? They had been out here a long time with minimal contact.

The yacht closed on the freighter, scanning with full spectrum sensors. No life signs, but that was expected. He sidled the yacht to a docking port that was still operational. The loading door was designed to open only from the inside, but a few bursts of pressurized nitrogen to its hinges loosened both the seals and the lock. He forced it open enough to slip through.

Inside, the absence of atmosphere or life support didn't faze him as he hadn't needed to breathe in centuries. The light panels of the freighter's corridors retained a little residual light, but everything was cast in shades of dim to dark. As he walked the length of the freighter to the crew quarters, he noted that nothing had been ransacked. He passed several cargo bays that stood open and emptied as expected, but it all looked very orderly. It was only of peripheral interest, however. What he was seeking was the crew, or at least their remains. Only those had useful information.

Reaching the quarters, he came across the first body floating near the ceiling of a lounge area. He hauled it down for inspection and only then saw it was missing a head. A quick glance around the lounge showed no sign of the head. Not much was left of the throat where it had been sliced through, but he tore at the tissue until he encountered blood vessels. The blood was frozen, not surprising for the environment, but intact.

Anton released the body to float where it would and pushed on to the commissary. Three more corpses floated above the long table, stab wounds all. He checked the state of all three and found the same condition, blood intact and frozen in the veins. The salient point was that none of the crewmen had been drained in a situation where exsanguination was usually the rule. Were the freighter's attackers blood drinkers or not?

He found an audio log in the captain's quarters along with a dead captain. "We're all going to die," the voice wailed. "What are these things? If anyone finds this log..." The voice stopped abruptly.

Curious, Anton thought as he wiped the log. This was a Terran crew with a grasp of Terran cultural lore. Why wouldn't they recognize a vampire once the fangs came out? Or had the fangs not come out, since no blood-drinking had taken place? In which case, the log's question should have been "Who are these people," not "What are these things?"

Still mulling this over, Anton returned to his yacht and undocked. The freighter had nothing more to offer him. Even the frozen blood, red ice in the veins of corpses, held no allure. But presumably, the blood had been hot and vibrant at the moment the crew died, yet still it had not enticed anyone to partake. Again, curious. It meant his Whisperers were content with the bagged plasma from MercyMed. They had turned down fresh blood for the artificially preserved medical version. Or perhaps it was more deliberate than that. To all appearances, the freighter had been attacked by living raiders who killed the crew in an expected way and confiscated the cargo. That actually was a clever way for vampires to operate. It aroused no pitchforks from the villagers.

Pulling away from the freighter, he resumed his original course. He waited until the MercyMed transport was in visual range before activating a general broadcast channel to any other ships in the void with him. "How far out are you?" he asked in a soft whisper. The com board lit with return messages, all of it in whispers that a human ear would barely detect. "Not far." "Less than an hour." "Very close."

The effect was surreal, eerie, even though he knew what to expect. For years now, all communication with his raiders in this sector had been in the softest tones. It had to do with the overly acute hearing they had developed over their length of time in the silences of deep space. "Docking now. I'll be waiting in the lower cargo hold." Anton closed the channel and took the yacht out of autopilot.

The unlovely, bulbous ship lay directly ahead. The MercyMed supply ship was the utilitarian answer to the sweep of Terran colonization getting ahead of itself. The frontier had need for tissue and organs and, of course, that fountain of all life—blood. MercyMed made it all available through regular deep space circuit runs. For Anton and his kind, these ships with cargo holds of frozen plasma were traveling supermarkets. He had purchased the cooperation of the last five pilots of this run to facilitate the feeding of his people. Money was never to be underestimated with mortals.

The sleek yacht glided into one of the many airlocks and secured itself to the bulbous transport. Twirling a flowing cloak into place on his shoulders, Anton left the yacht's bridge and followed the docking tube to the other vessel. Yes, a vampire prince in a cloak was pure stereotype, but the theatrics helped intimidate lesser vampires. Currently, he needed all the help he could get with the Night Nation.

An inner door scanned, then slid open to admit him to the MercyMed bridge. The pilot, lase-pistol in hand, jumped up to face him. Then he recognized the newcomer and relaxed.

Idiot, Anton thought in irritation. No one with half a brain would consider firing an energy weapon in an atmosphere-sealed environment. Edged weapons were far smarter. But you got what you paid for. Any mercenary pilot willing to run blood for vampires was much more mercenary than pilot.

"Thank the gods it's you," the pilot muttered, holstering his weapon. "For a moment, I thought those damned Whisperers had gotten past the door security. Those bloodsuckers give me the creeps."

Anton allowed himself a cool smile. There was a distinct advantage in being able to pass as Living. Half a dozen encounters and this pilot had yet to figure out that the stranger with the deep pockets was also a vampire. "They'll be here shortly," he said. "We'll be meeting in the lower cargo hold, so you know where not to be."

The pilot gave a shudder. "Hope you know what you're doing."

Anton flashed him a daggered look. "I *always* know what I'm doing. Something you'd be wise to remember."

"Okay, okay. Just expressing a little concern for your health, that's all." The pilot gave him a narrow look. "What about payment before the meeting, not after?"

So the concern was money, not health. No great surprise. "You deal with the Whisperers all the time," Anton commented as he initiated the credit transfer from his com ring. "I'm surprised you're suddenly so edgy."

"I deal with them one at a time," the man clarified. "And that's about my limit. A whole cargo hold full of monsters is more than I care to handle."

"Monster is such a subjective term." There would be many who would call Anton a monster for his long history of death-dealing, mostly for culinary reasons but also for political ends. The cumulative count over the centuries was extraordinarily high. Politics was a special passion of his, and he was good at it. That was why it rankled all the more that these nests raged out of control.

"I know one when I see one," the pilot shot back.

Again, that brought an amused smile to Anton's lips. *What fools these mortals be.* Perhaps this particular mortal was at the end of his usefulness. Mercenaries were easily replaced. "I'll wait in the cargo hold. Secure the door as you see fit. I won't be returning to the bridge."

He reached the lower cargo hold and waited, using the time to review his strategy. An infusion of fresh vampires, untainted by recent events, into the nests should not only change the political complexion, but also provide a wealth of information at the base level. This violence was too persistent to be random, which implied a mind behind it. But who? This wasn't some medieval melodrama with rabid peasants out to stake evil, undead creatures. The run of humanity wasn't even aware that vampiredom had followed colonization out into the reaches of space.

A clang reverberated through the hull. Then another. The Whisperers were docking their ships. Anton counted eighteen "monsters," as the fool upstairs called them. But, as Anton turned toward the door, he felt the slightest apprehension. These were his people, his children of the blood that he had sent out to raid the trade lanes, with excellent results. But there were rumors. The whispering communication had fostered tales of space ghosts in the sector, along with any number of monster stories. He hadn't actually met with them in a long while. Regular com updates, yes, but no face-to-face contact with any of them in a number of years. He frowned as he revised that estimate upward. Had it truly been decades?

He assumed a cordial smile as the door slid open, then his smile froze. "Welcome," he managed to whisper, but his eyes were wide.

The Whisperers slipped soundlessly inside, stooping to maneuver tall, spindly bodies through the human-sized doorway. Bulbous eyes. Long, dangling fingers. Bat-like ears resembling small wings. Lips parted in rictus grins to expose long canines. What were these creatures? Surely not his vampires. But the smell said otherwise. They reeked of stale blood, as all vampires did. It was oddly reassuring.

They clustered around him, great gangly shapes that made him feel small and vulnerable. Suddenly, he felt the fool. The whole plan to infiltrate the rogue nests with loyal vampires was ludicrous. None of these could ever pass as a vampire, even though they were. "You've changed," he murmured, not sure what else to say. There was no longer a point to this meeting.

"Evolved," one of the Whisperers replied. "We've evolved."

It was true that the vampiric body adapted quickly, healing itself when damaged, becoming more or less corporeal as the situation dictated. Was this then the end result of decades of living free from the constraints of gravity and sunlight? Apparently so.

"And you are pleased to evolve?" Anton asked tentatively. The answer seemed to be yes, but he had best be sure.

"We are free," another whispered. "You have given us a life free from the 'little death' each sunrise. We have no need for coffins. And you provide plasma to drink when we are thirsty. We are very pleased. What did you want to discuss with us?"

Anton thought furiously without coming up with a believable substitution. "No discussion," he finally said. "I wanted to see you all face to face and be sure your lives in deep space pleased you. Just that."

"And that pleases us." Several nodded agreements. "Have you come to join us in freedom?"

Anton shook his head. "I have an undead empire to manage. But freedom from the 'little death' is enticing."

"Is it your undead empire that troubles you so? It is obviously something. We hear it in your voice."

Perceptive, Anton realized with growing interest. On top of the carefully executed raid on the freighter, it suggested that perhaps his Whisperers truly had evolved. They certainly seemed less stupid than their planet-bound brethren. Their perspective might be valuable. "There is in-fighting in the nests," he said. "Many Youngers are going rogue for no understandable reason. It must be a contagion of some form, but I have not been able to contain it with all the constant traffic between Night Nation worlds."

There followed a soft, whispered conversation among the group that was mostly below the threshold of Anton's hearing, even though they were standing right in front of him. One finally raised the level of his voice to ask, "Are you considering killing the infected Youngers?"

Anton gave a snort. "In a heartbeat. I would kill all the infected ones, if I could isolate them. But, instead, it means killing all the Youngers in a nest to root out just the infected ones, before they can upship and spread their infection. A much greater casualty toll, but perhaps necessary."

Another whispered conference, then, "We could hover near the infected planets and kill the rogue Youngers when they leave orbit. This would suffice to contain the plague, yes?"

Unfortunately, a simplistic suggestion. "It would not suffice," Anton whispered back, "for there is no way to differentiate rogues from un-rogues in the Night Nation traffic."

"But there is," the Whisperer insisted in surprise. "Within a loud voice are the clues to both emotions and mental state. We hear this on our raids. Will you not trust that we can tell rogue from un-rogue from their com chatter?"

Anton blinked, completely blindsided. A new skill, and a clever application of it. He was fast becoming a believer in the "evolved" Whisperers. "I will indeed trust you," he nodded. "I shall transmit to you the coordinates of known infected planets, and update the list as new cases arise." He smiled. "And I am exceedingly pleased with my Whisperers."

They smiled back with great, toothy grins that looked more terrifying than joyous, but he understood. They were pleased that he was pleased.

Evolution came to mind again, when they had parted ways and Anton was again on the bridge of his yacht. Had he not gloried in the thought of freedom just a few hours earlier?

But now he saw the balance. Living weightless without the pull of gravity did things to the Undead body that was already prone to adaptation. Never sleeping, eating only frozen plasma, these also contributed in some unknowable way. Evolved his Whisperers might be, in unexpected and even enviable ways, but also evolved in ways unsuitable to planetary living. He himself wasn't ready for that. At least not yet.

The vacuum of space, devoid of light and mass. A place where the impossible can happen. From the bridge of his one-man yacht, Anton set aside thoughts of freedom from sunlight and gravity and concentrated on the details of this new strategy to cleanse the nests.

Jonathan Shipley is a Fort Worth, Texas, writer who creates in the genres of fantasy, science fiction, and horror. Over the last year, he has published ten more speculative fiction short stories to push his short fiction total over the half century mark. He was a contributing author to the **After Death** *anthology that won the 2014 Bram Stoker Award, as well as a finalist for the 2014 Washington Science Fiction Association's Small Press Award. He looks forward to pursuing more tales in the vampire/sci-fi crossover that defines "Whisper," possibly even expanding the concept into a novel. Jonathan maintains a web presence at www.shipleyscifi.com where you can find a full list of his published short stories.*

A trainee astronaut on an interstellar mission doubts she has the "right stuff" when she fails an important test. In an environment where one mistake can kill, she must solve her problem by learning the truth about a tragic event in her past.

PARADISE SAVED

By

John Moralee

FAIL FAIL FAIL flashed up on Mazina Valentov's eyewear when the simulated mission ended. Uncle Sergei cursed in Russian. His image was floating in the air in front of her, while he worked in another part of the ship. He had been monitoring her performance during her virtual spacewalk. After exhausting his native vulgarities, he switched to English with no trace of a Russian accent. "Nobody expects you to be perfect, but you can't make mistakes *like that* when you're out on the shell. We'll run the sim again and again until you get it right. Try one more time."

"Yes, Uncle," Mazina said, feeling like a little girl, not a grown-up woman aged nineteen. "I'll get it right this time. I swear it. Just give me a minute, Uncle."

"Nyet. There are no breaks outside. Start *now*."

Mazina rubbed her weary eyes and jacked back into the sim for the fourth time that morning. In the real world she was inside a zero-gee gym in the central hub of *Paradise Saved*, but she suddenly felt like she was outside the spinning arkship surrounded by deep space, clinging onto the dark-grey hull with gecko pads on her gloves and knees. The sensation made her giddy as she looked at the spiralling curve of the ship against the background of stars.

MISSION STARTS flashed up on her display.

The simulation involved repairing the outer hull after the ship sustained damage—a mission she took seriously even though it was not real. The ship's computer always altered the mission to keep her vigilant—so she didn't even know where the damage was until she switched on her coms and spoke to Milton, the ship's central AI.

"What's the problem, Milton?"

"I have a major leak, Miss Valentov. I need you to seal it for me, as my bots are unable to operate close to the tokomak fusion drives, due to a radiation spike."

"Where's the leak?" she said.

"A small rock hit the G82 lifepod. It's leaking atmosphere."

The *Paradise Saved* was shaped like a giant conch. Each part had its own solar generators and matter scoops that provided power as the ship travelled to a star system 420 light-years down the spiral arm of the Milky Way. Mazina crawled over the surface until she was on the side of module G82. A jagged fissure had appeared through the hull plating, exposing the internal atmosphere to venting. Around the edge, slashed cables sparked and spat like electric eels. Last time, she had tried to fix the problem without turning off the power to the loose cables, resulting in an oxygen explosion. This time, she addressed that problem first, cutting the power with a thermal lance aimed at a junction, then turned her attention to the fissure. There were temporary hull plates in her supply pack that she fastened to the sides with a strong resin.

"The pressure is still decreasing," Milton reported. "And there's a temperature increase in the hull layer."

"What? Where?"

"I have no data, Miss Valentov."

No data? Only in a sim would that be true. Milton had access to every sensor on the ship—but for the purpose of training her, the AI was playing stupid. *Okay—how can I figure this out?* She looked around, determined to pass this test. If a rock had really hit the ship at near light-speed, it would have punctured one side of the ship and gone through to the other side. The other side! She had not checked there. Feeling foolish, she scampered around the module until she was staring at a second small hole. Tell-tales in her suit recorded a temperature increase on the surface of 900 degrees. A fire. Inside the hull layer. She needed to cool it down with a spray of liquid nitrogen from her supply pack. She opened her pack and located the nitrogen canister—but lost her grip on the hull with her gecko pads. No longer secured to the ship by her hands, she found herself flipping backwards, disorientated, her suit's alarms wailing, Milton ordering her to use her thrusters to correct her orientation, but panic filled her. She thrashed and screamed, losing control over her suit and body. She spun away from the ship, desperately trying to right herself, but her thrusters were not working and she was slipping further and further away, just like her mother and father…

"AAAAAAaaahhh!"

"Milton, end sim!" her uncle said.

Snap. The sim ended abruptly. Mazina was back in the gym, floating harmlessly. She blinked tears, looking at her uncle's image. "I'm sorry. I messed up. I panicked again."

"That's enough for today," her uncle said, the disappointment in his voice palpable and wounding. "We will do your next lesson tomorrow. I'll see you later."

Her uncle's image disappeared as his neural link disconnected.

With effortless grace, she exited the gym, wishing she had the same balletic zero-gee skills inside the simulation. As she moved away from the central hub, the centripetal force of the spinning ship slowly increased until she was in a white-walled one-gee tunnel walking to her room in Section Q. She slumped on her bed and stared at a picture of her parents, tears stinging her eyes.

"Why can't I do it better? What's wrong with me?"

Ten minutes later, someone knocked on her door.

"What?" she yelled.

"It's me."

"Oh ... Kai." She wiped her eyes. "Come in."

A young man with blue eyes and spiky white hair entered her quarters, wearing red overalls stained with sweat and grease. Her boyfriend started eagerly removing his overalls near the door, dropping them in the laundry box for auto-processing. When he started to strip off his T-shirt, she shook her head.

"Kai, I'm sorry. I'm not in the mood."

"But we ... oh, okay." Kai stopped undressing, fidgeting like he didn't know what to do or say. "Soooo…how'd the sim training go with your uncle?"

"It was bad," she said. "I panicked again, just before completing the task. I'm never going to be accepted on Riko's squad, if I can't even get through the basic sims. Next week they do the tests for selecting the new recruits —but I don't feel ready."

Kai sat on the edge of her bed. Taking one of her feet in his hands, he massaged it gently. "What happened exactly?"

"Forget it. I don't want to talk about it."

"Don't look so miserable, Maz. I'm sure you'll do better tomorrow."

"Yeah—right. That's what I thought yesterday."

"You could always be a grease monkey like me, you know. You don't have to join the shell squad. I'd love to work with you in Engineering."

Mazina appreciated Kai's support—but she needed to prove herself worthy of joining Riko's squad. "My parents would have wanted me to do it, Kai."

"I know you feel that—but wouldn't they have been happy even if you did something else?"

"I don't know because I can't ask them." She sighed. "When my dad was alive, he used to talk about his work all of the time. He loved his job. My mom did too. It was dangerous, but it was important. Milton can't repair everything. The ship still needs humans to do some things to keep itself running. I want to do my part to get us all to Paradise System, just like my parents. On their last mission, they died saving the lives of over a million passengers. Being on the shell squad is what I've dreamt of since the day they died. I just wish I could get over my fear."

"Fear is logical considering the situation. Maybe what you need to do is face it head-on? Have you ever talked to Doctor Collins?"

"No. What good could she do?"

"Counselling helped me deal with some things after my parents divorced. I was pretty angry and self-destructive. That's not a good thing on a spaceship. Milton probably would have sent me into cryo-storage if I hadn't had therapy. Isn't that right, Milton?"

The AI was always listening in and observing everything—but it didn't intrude unless it was asked a direct question. "Therapy was my recommended course of action. I would have not allowed you to harm the other crew or passengers. Treatment was necessary."

Mazina was curious. "Milton, should I have therapy?"

"Based on my observations, I would recommend it," the computer said. "Shall I book you an appointment with Doctor Collins?"

"I'll try it," Mazina said, reluctantly.

"You can see Doctor Collins at four this afternoon, if that is convenient."

"Great," she said without enthusiasm. "I'll look forward to it."

"Cheer up," Kai said. "She'll help you."

"I hope so. I just don't like the idea of someone trawling through my memories, trying to fix me like I'm an app with a software glitch."

"It's not like that," Kai said, continuing to rub her feet, making her sigh with pleasure. "Doctor Collins won't do anything you're not comfortable with. You will be in control of the treatment. Relax now. Just enjoy this foot rub."

"We've got hours before I go," she said, with a raised eyebrow. "Want to join me for a shower?"

Kai grinned. "It's like you read my mind."

Nervous and self-conscious, Mazina entered a large circular room with white walls and a scattering of comfy furniture. A dark-haired woman was waiting. They shook hands. The doctor was wearing a light grey suit. For some reason, she reminded Mazina of her mother. They had the same colour of eyes. Mazina wondered if the doctor had chosen that eye colour just for her counselling or if it was a coincidence.

"Cookies?" Doctor Collins said, offering a selection of delicious-smelling, freshly baked oatmeal and chocolate chip cookies.

"Thanks," Mazina said. "Hmm! These are amazing." She was not lying. They were the best cookies she had ever tasted. "Worth showing up just for these. So, do you want me to lie on a couch, Doctor?"

"You can, but any chair will do. Pick what makes you comfortable. And there's no need to be formal, Mazina. You can call me Phoebe."

Mazina picked a soft chair with plump cushions. A silver drone brought her a cup of coffee that complemented her chosen cookies. The walls changed from boring white to a beautiful background of the Great Lakes on Earth, recorded many centuries ago. It felt like she was sitting on the shore. A cool breeze touched her face, brushing lightly through her hair. It was very relaxing.

Doctor Collins sat opposite her, sipping tea. "I'm glad you're here, Mazina. I believe I can help you. I've reviewed your personal history and psych profile. You lost your parents Olga and Vladimir when you were seven."

It wasn't a question, but the psychologist's pause made Mazina want to say something. "Yes…that's correct. They died in an accident on the shell. My mom was the squad leader. My dad was her second-in-command."

"It was a horrible tragedy. Your aunt and uncle became your guardians after the accident. You lived with them until this year, when you moved out to live by yourself."

Again, it was not a question. But the silence needed to be filled. "I love my aunt and uncle, but I needed some independence."

Doctor Collins nodded but said nothing.

"Um. Things got a little awkward. I have a boyfriend and their home is pretty small. They could hear things if I had my boyfriend…you know. Um. They've also recently had another baby, so they needed the extra room. I still see them every day, though. We get on well. My uncle is training me for the gecko squad. He was a gecko, until he switched jobs. Aunt Lena insisted on that after what happened to my parents. She doesn't approve of me volunteering for space duties. She thinks it is too risky—but it's what I want. I've always wanted to join the gecko squad, like my mom and dad. But I keep having these panic attacks when I'm practising. I start thinking about my parents dying and completely freak out. The attacks seem to be getting worse." She stopped for a breath. "Listen to me talk! Am I saying what you already know?"

"Yes, but I don't mind listening."

"Can you stop me panicking?"

"I can do various treatments."

"Like what?"

"I can give you a drug to inhibit your fight-or-flight response, though it might affect your reactions."

"I don't want a drug. What else is there?"

"I could suppress your memories of your parents dying in space, but I don't advise that."

"Why not?"

"It would change your personality. Without those memories, you would be a different person. It's an extreme treatment. I'd prefer to observe you under the stressful conditions of a sim mission. With your permission, Milton could monitor your mind and give me access to those memories. Then I might be able to figure out exactly what is triggering your panic. We could do the test tomorrow morning, if you are available."

"I'd like that."

That evening Mazina and Kai met her Uncle Sergei's family for dinner in the Garden Dome café. Mazina liked listening to their chatter turn into laughter as everyone enjoyed themselves. That night she was happy to listen to everyone else, until she had enjoyed a couple of glasses of wine and built up the courage to tell her uncle about the therapy.

"I have something to announce," she said during the main course. "Doctor Collins is going to treat me for my panic attacks. She'll observe me doing a sim so she can figure out what's wrong with me and recommend therapy."

"Therapy?" Uncle Sergei said. "Why would you need therapy? There's nothing wrong with you."

"I agree," Aunt Lena said. "There is nothing wrong with you. Except that you want to get yourself killed in space."

Uncle Sergei squeezed his wife's hand. "She's not going to die in space. I'm training her so that will never happen."

"The therapy will help me. It helped Kai."

Kai had been sitting quietly at the table, until all eyes turned upon him. "Doctor Collins is very good, Mr Valentov. Maz is in good hands. Believe me. She can help."

Her uncle gave Kai a stare colder than the hard vacuum outside the ship. "You don't need therapy, Mazina. You just need to try harder. That's the solution to everything. Therapy is for wimps." That comment was directed at Kai.

Kai bristled. "Are you calling me a wimp?"

"I say what I think," her uncle said.

The table fell silent. Kai and Uncle Sergei glared across it. Kai spoke first. "Therapy isn't for wimps, Mr Valentov."

"Really? I didn't hear about you *volunteering* for the gecko squad. Is that because you are afraid, kid?"

"Uncle! Kai is not a wimp. Apologise for saying that."

Her uncle folded his arms. "Nyet. I will not apologise for telling the truth."

Kai pushed his plate away. "Excuse me. I've lost my appetite." He stormed out of the café.

Mazina glared at her uncle. "Why did you have to insult my boyfriend?"

"Insult? I didn't insult him. I just spoke the truth."

Aunt Lena sighed. "Oh, be quiet Sergei. You've had too many beers. You always say the wrong thing when you're drunk."

"I am not drunk," he said. "I've only had three drinks."

"Then you are an idiot," Aunt Lena said. "And you will apologise to the boy the next time you see him."

"Nyet. I won't."

Mazina stood up. "I've lost my appetite too. I will see you in the morning, Uncle. My therapist will be accompanying me."

She caught up with Kai outside the café. "Kai, forget what my uncle said."

"Why does your uncle hate me?"

"He doesn't hate you. He's just overprotective."

"He thinks I'm not good enough for you. Is he right?"

"No!"

"I'm just an engineer. I don't risk my life out on the shell."

"The ship needs you as much as anyone. Don't let my uncle make you feel bad."

"I wanted to punch him."

"I wanted to punch him, too."

The next day Dr. Collins monitored Mazina during her sim session, which started with a simple mission to build her confidence. In her gecko suit, Mazina made her way across the ship's shell to deal with a stress fracture repair. Everything seemed fine for the first ten minutes of the mission—but then Mazina had to perform a long jump from one module to another, crossing a 120-metre gap that left her floating in space for over a minute. It was a task that caused Mazina to think of her parents spinning away into deep space. Her blood pressure spiked and her heart pounded out of control. She felt like her head was going to explode. Even though she knew the mission wasn't real, she could not stop herself hyperventilating.

FAIL FAIL FAIL flashed up as the sim ended with her bursting into tears.

"I don't understand it! That was an easy mission! I'm getting worse!"

Dr. Collins was outside the gym, looking through a window. "Okay, Mazina. That's enough for today. I've collected your memories for review. Take the rest of the day off."

"What?" her uncle said. "Doesn't she need more practice?"

"Not for today," Dr. Collins said. "That's on doctor's orders."

Dr. Collins contacted her a few hours later. They met in her office. "Mazina, I've analysed your panic reaction in the sim mission. I have to tell you that I can't see any reason for it."

"I don't understand. Are you saying you can't help me?"

"No, but I can't find a root cause in your memory. What made you think of your parents during the mission?"

"I don't know. They just popped into my head. I was doing okay until I imagined them dying."

"Okay—I have one idea that might help. Milton has neural recordings of your parents' final mission from their view points. You never saw the recordings as a child because it could have done you psychological harm, but I think it might help you now to know exactly what happened to them. It may be upsetting to watch, but it could give you closure. I can't guarantee it will help, though. It's entirely your decision. Should Milton give you access to those recordings?"

Mazina didn't want to watch her parents die—but she could see no other option. "Okay. I'll watch the recordings."

"I think you may want to lie down on the couch for this. Milton can send you the file when you are ready. I'll be here monitoring."

Mazina made herself comfortable. She closed her eyes and sent a command to Milton, giving her access to the neural recordings of her parents. Both recordings ended at the same time, 45.2 minutes into the mission.

She played her mother's recording first. Immediately, Mazina was no longer on Dr. Collins' couch. She was in an airlock, viewing through her mother's eyes. Her mother was sealing her helmet and checking her system vitals. Other members of her mother's squad were present, also making final preparations for going outside. Mazina saw her father, Vladimir, and Uncle Sergei. The current leader of the gecko squad, Riko, had been a rookie back then. Riko was taking instructions from Olga. Once the airlock's door opened, Olga looked out at the blackness of the space between the stars.

"Let's go!" she ordered, then climbed out onto the shell, fixing her boots firmly onto the ground. The whole squad set off behind her, heading for an impact crater created by a piece of deep space debris that had done serious damage to a tokamak engine. Encountering anything big enough to harm the ship was an extremely rare event—but luck had failed that day. The tokamak fusion drive was streaming super-heated plasma out of a thruster, normally used to make minor course corrections, spreading damage beyond the initial impact zone. Milton was reporting multiple breaches through the shell into the ship, where the crew and drones were fighting fires.

Olga's squad started work sealing the breaches and cutting the power to the tokamak engine—but the engine was not responding. Instead, it was increasing its output exponentially—sending arcs of plasma over the ship's surface, burning through the hull plates, frying electronics. The drive had to be deactivated at the source, if a catastrophic explosion was to be avoided.

"Riko and Banks, seal the leaks in section alpha. Sergei, cool the shell with liquid nitrogen. Vladimir, come with me. We need to get close to the fusion port. We'll need to do an emergency shutdown."

That order was the last one her mother had given. Mazina watched her mother and father charge through a gale of whipping plasma until they reached the port, where they carried out a manual redirection of the plasma flow. They managed the shutdown successfully—but it caused a sudden and rapid change in the plasma stream's direction. The final throes of the plasma jet struck them both and vaporised them in an instant. They died too quickly to have known what happened.

Mazina came out of the sim breathless. Dr. Collins offered her a glass of water. She drank it with shaking hands. "I never knew they were killed by a plasma blast. I always thought they floated off into space. I thought they died slowly—out in deep space."

"What made you think that?"

Mazina frowned. "I don't know. I think someone must have said that, but I can't remember who. My uncle was there. He saw it. Why didn't he tell me how they died?"

"I'm afraid you'll have to ask him."

Her uncle was at his home looking after his new baby when Mazina visited him. "Doctor Collins showed me what happened to my parents. They died in a plasma blast. Why didn't you tell me?"

"It was a horrible way to die," he said. "Why would I want you to know?"

"Because it makes a difference. They didn't suffer. It was all over too fast for that. You should have told me."

"Maybe," he said. "I had to make a decision. I thought it was best you didn't know. You were a child and I could not tell you they were burned to death. Olga and Vlad died right in front of me. I never wanted you to follow them into the gecko squad—endangering your life out on the shell. But I knew you'd not listen to me if I discouraged you. You are too headstrong for that. You are like your mother— always heading straight into danger. I wanted to put you off joining the gecko squad so you'd be safe. Altering the sim to make you fail each time seemed the only way. My plan might have worked, if you had not listened to your boyfriend. I don't want you to risk your life. I love you too much to lose another member of my family."

"Uncle, it's my life to lead. My life to risk. If my mom and dad had not risked their lives, the whole ship would have been destroyed. I want to do it, Uncle, and you can't stop me."

"I know," he said. "I'm sorry for interfering. You'll be a great member of the squad. I am a fool for trying to stop you."

"I am so mad with you. You'd better apologise to Kai…and mean it."

"He's a good boy," her uncle admitted. "He's got guts standing up to me. I admire that. He will be more than welcome at dinner any day."

A week later, Mazina joined the class of new recruits in an airlock, putting on her first gecko suit. She thought of her parents, but she was not afraid. Riko pressed a button to depressurise the chamber before the doors slid open and revealed the hard vacuum and the distant stars. Mazina took a deep breath. Far away, another world awaited the arrival of *Paradise Saved,* and it was her duty to make sure they all got there safely.

She grinned at the other recruits, thinking one thing:
Here we go.

John Moralee is the author of the novels **Acting Dead, Journal of the Living** *and* **The House on Willow Lane**. *He lives in the UK, where his short fiction has appeared in magazines and anthologies including* **The Mammoth Book of Jack the Ripper Stories, Crimewave,** *and the British Fantasy Society's magazine* **Peeping Tom.**

Many collections of his short stories are available as e-books and trade paperbacks. They include **The Bone Yard and Other Stories, Bloodways, Edge of Crime, Blue Ice, The Good Soldier,** *and a science fiction collection called* **The Tomorrow Tower.**

Four hundred thirty generations have come and gone since Hanno the Navigator was sent on its way. As the latest generation celebrates entering the target system, they are about to discover that the list of possibilities in interstellar space is long indeed.

CLOUD

By

J. Richard Jacobs

Deep space, they call it. That unimaginably large area between seething spheres of fusing hydrogen. It is often thought to be empty, a void, but it is not. Far from it. Debris of all kinds travel there. There are homeless planets, chunks of rock, ice, and metal. Clouds of gas, hot and cold. There are high energy particles whizzing in all directions. Dead stars and live stars flying this way and that with no place to rest, unless they happen to encounter a gravity well sufficiently large. All sorts of matter occupy the space between the stars.

Amid all this celestial refuse something foreign moved. Something that would not have been there if it were not for the arrogance of an insignificant band of savages on a minuscule rock in a distant place in the Milky Way. But there it was, a monument to the ingenuity and pretentiousness of a primitive primate. It has been out there for a long while and communication with its point of origin is no longer feasible. The major reasons are time and the fading strength of the signals. Communication as such is no longer meaningful. Even the standard pulses have disappeared. Maybe because the builders who sent it have met their end. No one knows, but it doesn't matter. There is no going back. *Hanno the Navigator* moves in deep space and is now approaching her destination, where she will become a permanent fixture in a new sky.

The occupants of *Hanno the Navigator* have based their entire future on ancient observations made from light years away.

A young boy raced through the passage to catch a tall figure moving along the garden path. When he reached his quarry's side, he blurted out between gulps of air, "Master Mim, may I...ask you some...questions?"

"You just asked me a question, young man, so I suppose we have already begun. Come, let us rest on this bench while you catch your breath."

The two sat for a moment, and when it was apparent that the boy had regained his composure, Mim said, "And who might you be?"

"Ander of the Clan Belden, sir."

"Well, young Ander of the Clan Belden, what is it you would like to know?"

"I was looking at some Erthfots in Archive One. It looked so nice, and awfully big. Lots of room to move. And there was a...a real sky. Not like here. Why did we leave such a place?"

"My, my, my, such a complex question from one so young. Ander, it is a long story, but put simply, we left because it is our way. Oh, yes, there were other things that people called reasons, but the truth is that we have always wandered in search of something. It was that way when we were trapped on Erth. Always going somewhere. Anywhere. Even if only in the mind. We are a wondering and wandering species, you see."

"But we've been inside *Hanno* for a long time, and there's no place to go in here. Just the gardens, and the Archives, and Core where we used to be able to float and play nogee games. It seems so tiny compared to where we came from. How can we stay in here so long if what we do is...is wander?"

"A long time indeed, young Ander. This is now eyar thirty-one thousand and ten. Imagine that. We have been many, many generations here in old *Hanno the Navigator*.

It is a blessing to us that we live but a short three hundred eyars or so. It saves us much frustration, you see. But even here in *Hanno*, we are wandering still. We are travelers; the people of *Hanno the Navigator*. When we reach Newerth, we will find more reasons—new reasons to wander. It is the human thing to do, you see."

"Master Mim, will I live to see Newerth?"

"Ah, I think you are in for a real treat, young man. How many eyars do you have? Nine? Ten?"

"Eleven in Nover, sir," Ander said as he puffed out his chest.

"Well now, you're almost grown, Ander. You said you used to be able to float in Core, so, is it safe for me to assume you noticed how everything always drifts to green side now and it has been that way for two eyars?"

"Yes, sir."

"There's a reason for that, young Ander. See, three eyars ago, *Hanno* made the maneuver to begin braking. Slowing down. You can't feel it because it is still quite gentle, but that's why you drift to green side in Core and why, when you put anything round on the ground, it rolls to forward side. When you are just seventy-one, old *Hanno* here will be going into what are called insertion maneuvers—changing direction and speed—to orbit Newerth's star. Lots of things will start happening then. Complicated things. You asked, so I told, but don't go talking about it quite yet. Our secret for now, yes? Clan Control will be introducing it to all in a couple of weeks and they wouldn't like it if they knew how loose old Mim is with their information."

"I won't say anything. I promise. Master Mim, why do I feel all funny inside now?"

"Maybe because you're excited, Ander. Something new has entered your life just now. To tell you the truth, I feel that way too, and I've known about it all along. So, to answer your last question, yes, you will see Newerth—and while you're still young. Me...well I'll be nearing my end, but I may see it too."

"Oh, I bet you will, Master Mim. I bet you will."

"Ander, I think I like you, and you show…promise. Would you be interested in our talking together from time to time?"

"Yes. I think I would like that, but I don't want to be a bother."

"Bother? Not at all, young Ander. Not at all. Young thoughts and questions are good for all those who have reached the age where we are called Elders. Who knows, I may learn something, you see."

Hanno the Navigator powered into her insertion trajectory following instructions from the AI, while the Control crew celebrated the arrival of a new era in the history of humankind. In a short thirty eyars they would be falling into the place where they were destined to go. They had survived a thirty-one thousand eyar trek across interstellar space without major incident. There had been problems, of course, but nothing that prevented them from arriving at this glorious moment. Their storehouse of embryos and ova remained viable and five thousand healthy people were anxious to start the process of populating their new home. A home that the sensors had already detected. The target planet remained no more than a tiny blue dot in the great telescope, but it was there to see. It was real, not a legend. Science confirmed an atmosphere of breathable constituents as predicted in the ancient record, the presence of liquid water, and life. The latter was of some concern until it was determined there were no signs of advanced technology in the atmosphere. No one was able to say what they would have done had that not been the case. Those were things only the AI knew, and it was not revealing such information. They would know soon. Forty eyars; no more, and the first of the landers would touch down on Newerth.

"A toast," Lead Control Officer Alex Vasquez said, as she stood from her place at the head of the long table in Control Section. "Here's to some fine science accomplished and an incredible journey without incident—so far." The '…so far,' alerted all to the fact that they still had a long way and a long time to go. Even though it was but a tiny fraction of their time in deep space, anything could happen during their forty year fall to Newerth rendezvous. Nearing any planetary system presented greater dangers than deep space. "*Hanno* has seen countless generations pass in our journey, but we...we are the last. We will see Newerth. To Newerth!"

Cheers and shouts rose from the gathering. "To Newerth and a new age," Vasquez reaffirmed. Glasses were tilted. It was a good day indeed.

A little over an eyar into the fall, the general alarm sounded. No one in space wants to hear that grinding notice that something is about to go wrong or has already gone wrong. No one. The com in Alex Vasquez's quarters chimed and the image of an unfamiliar face appeared on the screen.

"What is it? Why the alarm, and who are you?"

"I am Ander Belden, the new Navigation Officer, my Lead. I was running routine scans when, in an aft scan, I found something strange. According to the record, it wasn't there ten months ago."

"Well, what is it?"

"It's an...an energetic, metallic cloud. When I found it, I sounded the alarm."

"What? A metallic cloud? Be more specific."

"I can't, yet. The scans are still being processed. I took it upon myself to launch a probe to intercept and sample. The scans indicate the cloud is producing a lot of EMF in the UHF area of the spectrum. It appears to be made up of every element. Mainly metals and minerals, but there are complex organic compounds present as well. For being out here, it's incredibly warm. The readings show about two hundred seventy-five degrees Kelvin."

"How far away is it, and is it closing?"

"It's current track matches ours and it is closing. Range is six million six hundred seventy thousand kilometers. Rate of closure, two thousand two hundred forty meters per second. Estimated time to contact is a little over one thousand two hundred hours."

"Is it possible to maneuver out of its way?"

"No. It's too large. It's a good five thousand kilometers in diameter. If we change course enough to miss it, we may not have enough reserve to make our orbit good. If we accelerate, we will overshoot and it will take several eyars to trap enough H2 to recover."

"What's the density?"

"According to what I have now, it's close to five elements per cubic centimeter. It's much too far away to be certain."

"That's not too bad. There have been encounters with dust in the past that were worse. We will simply turn *Hanno* around to align our particle shield with it. That should do it."

"Yes, my Lead, but these things aren't just atoms and ions, or particles of dust. Because of the EMF it's radiating, we could be in for some serious problems with electronics. I suggest that along with what you mentioned, we should power down all the automated critical systems and the AI during its passing. The problem with that is, if this thing is spherical like the scan indicates, we'll be in it for at least forty minutes. It could be longer if the cloud is stretched out along its path. I can't determine that. Because the LiSS will be off line, we'll need to isolate ourselves in Hull Core compartments. We'll also need to suit up until it has passed. Heat won't be a problem unless it is greatly elongated."

"Okay, let's start making preparations for that. We have five thousand people to move. Gather all Control Officers in Mission Control for a briefing in one hour. How long before the probe makes contact?"

"Fifty-one hours."

"Okay. Contact Akio and Gregorio. Have them analyze what data you have and everything we get from the probe as it comes in."

"There's a fair probability its passing will affect our trajectory, my Lead."

"We'll work that one after it happens. Get the meeting set up. Oh, and you did well, Ander Belden. Thank you."

Alex cut the connection, then settled back on her berth. Space is big, she thought. So big that the odds of encountering anything larger or more massive than hydrogen atoms and the rare chunk of complex matter were small enough to be considered nil. *Hanno's* particle shield and H2 collector were eroded and cratered, but that was after thousands of eyars in space. Now this. Why hadn't this cloud of metal particles coalesced into a solid? Why was it so energetic? It didn't make any sense. She rose from the berth, took a nervous glance at the countdown display, then set off for the briefing.

Akio Fujikawa and Gregorio Katsaros were bent over a monitor, old Mim sat quietly in a corner, and Ander was pacing nervously when Alex entered the navigation station. All were so intent on what they were doing that they hadn't noticed her approach.

Alex tapped lightly on the bulkhead. The two men at the monitor jerked as if an explosion had gone off in the compartment. Ander stopped pacing. Mim remained silent.

"Ander," she began, "this compartment is restricted to Control personnel. What is this man doing here?" She nodded toward the stoic Mim.

"Elder Mim has been my counsel and mentor for many eyars. I...I wanted him here with me. Have I done wrong?"

"No. I suppose not, Ander. Greetings, Elder."

Mim gave a quick nod of recognition.

"Alex," Akio began excitedly, "we must relay all the data we have and as it comes in directly to Central Ops from now on. We've worked up a model based on what we know and it doesn't look good. This cloud will hit Newerth and two of its moons if it continues on its current path. Not a direct hit, but the outer edge will certainly contact them. Central Ops needs to begin a continual monitoring of conditions there as soon as the cloud passes us."

"Anything else?"

"No. There is nothing else we can do. Fortunately, its path is hyperbolic like our current path, but we assume it has no way of braking for insertion, so it won't return to this system."

"Well, that's a relief," Ander said.

Alex looked up at the countdown clock indicating time to contact for the probe. A little over nine hours to go. Forty-two hours had passed and they still had no idea what the cloud was or what it might do to the *Hanno* and her people.

"What about the radiation this thing is emitting?"

"Radiation, Alex? You mean, signals," Gregorio said. His voice was hollow. Quavering. He was again staring at the monitor.

"What he means, Alex, is that we found patterns. It took a lot to isolate them—so much noise, you know, but we found...patterns."

"Well? What does that mean?"

"Mmm. We found repetition. Groupings and orders that repeat, but not regularly. We wouldn't have thought much of it, if they had been regular or if there had been just a few repeats. That could be considered to be a natural function of the entity. A resonance, so to speak. But...but we found hundreds of different data sets that repeat irregularly. Like signals. A particular pattern is transmitted from one place in the cloud, then a response pattern comes from somewhere else."

Gregorio's head turned suddenly to face them. His eyes narrowed to menacing slits.

"The goddamn things are talking to each other," he growled. "They're not just bits of debris—random particles. They're talking to each other."

"What Greg is saying is that it seems to be some sort of communication, Alex."

"That's...that's ridiculous. Communication? That's a cloud of stuff out there. A...."

"Not ridiculous, Alex," Gregorio said. "We are convinced. They are transmitting and responding to intelligence. There are no contradictory data. We were at a loss as to how they produced the energy to do this, but now we know. They are organized into smaller spheres, or packets of several millions of individuals. At the center of each packet is a—for lack of a better term—a dynamo. That's where the heat is coming from. The big sphere, the cloud, is made up of trillions of smaller spheres operating autonomously, but in communication. Like a beehive."

"You're trying to tell me it's alive?"

Gregorio turned back to the monitor before speaking. "Alive? Do you mean alive like you and I? Not hardly. Alive more like our AI, Alex. That cloud out there is made up of machines. Trillions and trillions of machines. Nanomachines. Microscopic robots—and they're talking to each other."

"Wait a minute here," Ander said. "You didn't mention this before. Nanotech hasn't progressed that far."

"You mean *we* haven't been that successful with it yet," Gregorio said, his impatience dripping from each word. "Obviously someone else, somewhere else has."

"You're saying, this thing is an alien construct?" Alex said.

"If it's out here and we didn't do it, then that's what it means." Gregorio lifted his gaze from the screen and glowered at them. "Our first contact with extraterrestrial intelligence and it turns out to be a cloud of goddamned machines."

"How? How could...why would it be so large? This is a monstrous thing we're looking at."

"They reproduce themselves, Alex," Akio said. "We have no way of knowing how long this...cloud has been in existence or what the original purpose was. For all we know, it could have been an accident; an experiment gone wrong. It could be millions...billions of years old, and it has been reproducing all that time. Its growth would have been exponential, even though available materials are rare."

Alex glanced up at the clock again. Eight hours and twenty-five minutes.

"This is all speculation based on what has been detected so far, Alex," Akio said. "We will know a lot more when the probe makes contact, but I must tell you that I don't think we are wrong."

Mim said nothing. His gaze was fixed on the clock.
08:18:31

02:14:07

Mim, his age showing in his step, shuffled into Archive Seven and settled into an Infobooth.

"Subject?" the panel said.

"Nanotechnology, general. Self-replicating robot, specific."

00:15:49

"This is strange," Akio said. He looked up from the monitor and noted the time on the countdown clock.

"It's all strange," Gregorio replied sardonically. "What's happening now?"

"The number of signals have increased dramatically and the density of the cloud is increasing in the region directly in line with the probe."

"Like bees, they're swarming to protect the goddamn hive."

"Probe data is coming in now. We should alert Alex."

"She wouldn't miss the show. She'll be here."

00:03:08

Alex, Ander, and Mim entered the compartment. Mim hobbled over to his seat in the corner.

"The probe?" Alex said.

"It has been transmitting data and images for the past twelve minutes," Akio said. "We are having a hard time making any sense out of what we are getting, though, and the computer is of no help."

"Why?"

"If we knew that, we'd be able to make some sense out of it, right?" Gregorio said. "The data is deteriorating rapidly and the resolution of our imaging is degrading. Goddamn bees are swarming all over it. I told you, didn't I?"

"How can that be?" she said quietly.

Mim turned his head nervously from side to side, then stood slowly. Even in his advanced age, he was an imposing figure. He raked his fingers through long white hair.

When he spoke, his voice was soft, but commanding. "They travel through space. They replicate themselves whenever suitable matter is made available. They are eating it."

J. Richard Jacobs is an award winning author of science fiction novels and short stories. He has also published a number of anthologies and round robins. Some of his recent short stories and science articles have been published in **Perihelion Science Fiction,** *which he considers the best online hard science fiction magazine around.*

Should past knowledge always be preserved? Even if that knowledge is dangerous to what remains of the human race? The last leader of the Noah's Ark starship must decide.

IF TRUTH BE TOLD

By

Margaret Karmazin

The doomsayers had warned it would happen, but Medical nanotechnology had held such promise. As one hopeful blurb earlier in the century put it, "The technology of this coming age will let us construct a broad range of complex molecular machines and computers smaller than a human cell. Medicine will intervene in a sophisticated and controlled way at the cellular and molecular level."

So optimistic were they, naive as children, but ones that, now, will never grow up.

The voice crackled, breaking up every other word.

"See if you can do anything," said Veldt. "I've tried."

He stood, slightly hunched over, rubbing his painful back. Arthritis was something only those in World Capsules experienced. Since the milestones in nanotechnology on Earth, few there suffered the ailment.

"I don't understand it," said Wiona, his mate. "Bryan wasn't able to fix it either."

She referred to fifteen-year-old Bryan Drumm, who had lived his first three years on Earth. The majority of the other children had been born on the ship and knew little of their home world.

Wiona's expression was tight. "I have a feeling this is something we'll wish we'd never heard."

He ignored her comment, focusing on the immediate problem. "Have you considered the shields? Usually, they don't affect communication, but you never know."

"Didn't think of it," she said. "Neither did Bryan."

The kid stood against a wall, eyes fixed on the floor, one hand flapping. They were used to Bryan's idiosyncrasies. He had Asperger's, something his parents had learned only after joining the crew. Once onboard, they had no way of changing his DNA. All of the World-Capsulers accepted a total absence of nano-med technology when they signed on. At the time of launch, everyone concerned had felt it better to forego experimental medicine on the ships. Just in case.

"Unlikely for Bryan to miss anything," Wiona muttered. She walked into the next room, which held the shield controls and, in a moment, all shields were down. Immediately, they heard rubble hit the ship. "Better hurry this up," she said.

Veldt opened communications wide as possible. The voice came in now with only an occasional break. "World Capsules! You cannot return, you may never return! Step up your mission; you are all that is left of the human race. Neither you nor your descendants are ever, I repeat EVER, to return to this section of space. I'm speaking from Mars Station 8 and I only have a few minutes remaining of personal coherence. The med nanos have gone mad, separating the human or animal body into autonomous living parts. My hand or arm could fall off at any moment, and become an independent creature that breaks down into smaller autonomous beings, losing more sentience as each separates into more." A sob and a scream ended the voice. It did not continue.

Veldt felt immeasurable grief as he watched the horror on Wiona's face. Bryan's, however, registered nothing. He seemed to be counting.

"It was the one hundred and ninth transmission," said Veldt. "To think," he said, "that this was repeating after the poor man was..."

Wiona had fainted. Holding her in his arms, he gently patted her face until she was conscious, although still incoherent. With difficulty, he made out her words. "My sister, my cousin...my sweet niece, those students we knew from Nigeria...everyone. Oh God. Oh God." She burst into sobbing, shaking her head as if to negate everything she'd heard. "No!" she screamed.

Bryan flapped both hands to some intense internal rhythm.

Veldt pulled his mate to her feet, then propelled her to a chair. She fell into it, a dead weight.

After resetting the shields, he fiddled at the center computer. "We'll do what the poor man said. We're twenty-four percent of the way to Mareed, a definite Goldilocks Zone and, as far as we know, a receptive and uninhabited moon in the Dectine System. We'll set the ship to Hyperdrive 3 and put ourselves into hybersleep. Barring unforeseen circumstances, we should arrive in four years, two months, thirteen days."

Wiona stared at him, two large tears sliding down her ashen face. "If only all the middle adults hadn't died of the virus. How will we set up a colony without them? How will we do it, Veldt? It's hard enough just to control the children."

Bryan pushed away from the wall and spoke up, voice flat. "There are one hundred seventy-nine children on board, other than myself. Of those, sixty-three are five to seven years old, eighty-one are seven to ten, and the remainder between eleven and fifteen. By our projected arrival at Mareed, the oldest, including myself, will be nineteen with the others nine and up. Some will be physically ready to begin a new world..."

Veldt interrupted. "We'll concentrate in our last months before hybersleep on instruction in practical survival."

"There's little you have to teach me," Bryan said. "I've learned the salient points of the entire known history of the human race, including the hazy information on the species that seeded us. I'll be in perfect condition to instruct the builders of our new world."

There was a silence while the two adults digested this information. Wiona's expression was unreadable. "Bryan, go see to the others, will you? I can only imagine what they're up to."

"Will do," the kid said agreeably. "Form One is napping, Form Two working on language, and Form Three geometry.

"Just go see," said Veldt, and Bryan left.

Wiona fell to sobbing again. "It's such a lonely feeling," she said. "And we've lost contact with four of the other World Capsules. I can't bear it."

Veldt wrapped his arms around her. "We've only got *Ark VI* left to speak with and they'll soon phase out of range. If we put ourselves into hybersleep, we won't be talking anyway."

"I'm terrified," she said.

"Me too," said Veldt.

As soon as Wiona could pull herself together, Veldt led her through the corridors to Form Three, where the older children spent their days when not helping with lower forms. The door slid open to reveal a large group hard at work on various projects. The only disorder was at one end where two boys were mock wrestling.

"Hey," said Veldt. "This isn't the time."

The boys stopped.

"Something has happened," he said from the doorway. "Something so unbelievably terrible that it will change our lives drastically." He stepped further into the room. Everyone looked up. Wiona began to cry again.

"We received a message from Mars. A medical technology there has gone out of control. The results are, and I will spare you the details at this time, horrific. Neither we nor your descendants can ever return to our home solar system. It has become infected with something that kills all life forms larger than one celled creatures."

No one in the room spoke. Veldt could not help being grateful that Bryan was in one of the other form rooms. Right now, he did not want the boy's robotic but accurate input.

"We must, therefore, speed up locating our new home. We're headed to Mareed, an uninhabited moon in the

Dectine System, which we have previously discussed. We now need to employ Hyperdrive 3."

A girl in the back of the room stood up. She was blond and tall for her age, and immediately reminded Veldt of her mother, Deena, a gifted and much needed medic, now dead these past four years. "Yes, Tricia?" he said.

"Hyperdrive 3 means we go into hybersleep, right?" She looked frightened. "Why can't we just go on as we are?"

"Because," said Wiona, "that would take us twenty or more years. We and the other five World Capsules are all that remain of humanity. It's up to us to start new worlds."

Another fifteen-year-old spoke up. He looked more like eighteen, dark and sardonic. "How do we know we're all that's left? How do we know there aren't other humans on other worlds out there?"

"We don't, Nagan," said Wiona. "But we have no contact with them if they do exist. We have to believe that we're alone and that it's our destiny to continue our kind."

"So, it'll definitely be hybersleep then," said the boy.

"Yes," said Wiona.

There was a groan from Tricia and others turned, wide-eyed, to look at her. "You're scaring the others," Nagan said to her. "Stop it."

Children muttered among themselves. Some were visibly upset, while others remained seemingly unruffled.

"What's hybersleep like?" two girls asked in unison, thirteen-year-old twins who often spoke simultaneously. Their voices trembled.

Veldt stepped into the center of the room. "For two days before, everyone eats a liquid diet and takes something to help him or her eliminate as much as possibly from the digestive track. You will clean yourselves well and wear light, unbinding clothing. The older kids will help with the younger ones first. You will climb into the prepped body capsule, make yourself comfortable, and pull down the lid. It will automatically shut and begin the process of inserting concentrations of various drugs into the air inside, along with a gradual lowering of temperature. In a matter of seconds, you'll be deep asleep.

When the time we set for awakening comes, the capsule will fill with a different mixture of air, different drugs will be piped in and you will awaken. The lid will pop open. You must take your time getting up as you'll feel disoriented. Whoever awakens first, can help others up and out. You will be hungry. Wiona and I will set our capsules to waken first, then the oldest among you on down."

"How long will we be asleep?" asked a small boy close to Veldt. "And what will it feel like?"

"Getting to Mareed should take us a little bit over four years. We will awaken a couple of months before arrival. The scientific literature says that it will feel like normal sleep."

"So," said Nagan, "we'll be four years older? I, for instance, will be nineteen? All that time in between is erased?"

"I hadn't thought of it like that," murmured Wiona.

There was rumbling from all sides. "Why do we have to go anywhere?" a girl muttered.

"Look," said Veldt. "Most of the children on this vessel have never known any home but this. The oldest among you spent your first one to three years on Earth, but don't remember much about it. This ship has been your world. But while it is theoretically possible to spend your entire lives on here, it's not a good idea. You saw what happened when the Kiri virus was released into the ship's atmosphere. While you and Wiona and I survived and are now immune, your parents and older siblings were dead within months. Why?"

Hands shot up. "Clotilde?" Veldt nodded at a brunette, 14-year-old girl.

"Because the people in the middle had circulating sex hormones."

"And what did that cause?"

"Out of control cancer," replied Clotilde.

Veldt was sorry he'd pushed her to answer. "That is correct," he said quietly.

A girl to Veldt's right began to cry.

"Yes," said Veldt, looking directly at her, "the death of your parents was a catastrophe so horrendous that we have not recovered. Two of those people were our sons. Now our hope for the future lies in Liam and Bernalyn." His grandchildren were in two of the other forms.

"Not only our personal hope, but for the future of our species. Have we made ourselves clear on that and on why it will be necessary to hybersleep?"

The two adults, after grueling consideration, had never told the children that the Kiri virus had been planted inside the clothing stores by an ultra-conservative religious group that had campaigned against sending out World Capsules. "Starting new worlds is against God's plan," they had shouted on Earth news reports, after infecting two of the ships.

"You never answered my question," said Nagan, his voice assertive. "We will lose four years of our lives?"

A door swished behind them and Bryan walked into the room.

"Here's the source of all knowledge," muttered someone.

"We will not actually age four years," said Bryan, his tone dry and instructive. "Since metabolism is greatly slowed down and with vitals monitors in effect, anything gone off will be instantly treated to set it right. Electric muscle stimulation will be applied at regular intervals. I would estimate that we will age approximately 2.37 Earth Years during that time. Our hair and nails will grow and be a slight problem when we awaken."

"Thank you, Bryan," said Nagan before the adults had a chance to respond. "When are we going to do this?" he asked the older couple.

Veldt looked at his mate. "We'll need several meetings to discuss preparations. I estimate that hybersleep will begin in four months. That should give us enough time to prepare."

A short, studious-looking boy raised his hand. "How will we know how to do things once we land?" he asked.

"An excellent question," said Veldt. "Fortunately, the crystal files contain what we named 'MEs' after the ancient

Sumerian writings. It was never clear what the original MEs were, but each one held teachings from their 'gods' on how to do different things. For instance, there might be an ME on how to farm or make clothing. We have our own MEs on how to do all the things you will need."

"What else is in the MEs?" asked the boy.

Veldt was going to say the history of the human race, but an expression on Wiona's face stopped him. He stuttered in his confusion. "Uh, all kinds of things about Earth. We can go over that later," he finished lamely.

Wiona stepped in firmly. "Now, who would like to accompany us as we explain this to the younger ones?"

The next months passed in a blur of activity. The ship was five hundred meters long with twenty-nine decks, seven devoted to forestry and farming. These, the domestic animals and pets, had to be dealt with. The animals, if too old, were slaughtered and processed, then frozen. Younger pets would group-hybersleep (a less meticulous arrangement as that of the humans and with the possibility that some would perish), while robots would tend, to the best of their ability, the rest of the livestock.

For two adults, the hundred and eighty parentless children were not always easy to control. Veldt and Wiona had created ways of coping. They used the usual point/reward systems with favors consisting of entertainment, special food or time with friends, giving older children responsibility for younger ones, and staggered meal, class, recreation, and bedtime hours. For more serious control, they used sound. This has been Bryan's idea.

"Sound can cause discomfort," he'd told Veldt after a particularly difficult day with the second form. "I suggest you create discomfort in their area when they misbehave and when they calm down, turn it off. You don't have to tell them why they feel bad, just that when they behave, the bad feeling will stop."

"Why can't it be the other way around?" Wiona had asked. "Sound that calms, so that they choose to behave in order to hear it?"

"Kids have too much expendable energy to be controlled by that," said Bryan. "If you insist on reward sound, you'd need the double whammy of punishment for bad, reward for good. People are animals, after all."

"Perhaps they are," Wiona had retorted, "but I'd prefer to use rewards or at least the combination."

"I'll work on it," said the boy.

"I am not sure I like Bryan," she'd told her mate, afterwards.

"What do you mean?" Veldt had asked. "He has a disorder."

"I know he can't help being the way he is, but sometimes he's so...so unfeeling."

Veldt shook his head, not saying what he was thinking, that Wiona herself often lacked empathy. He'd always harbored a special fondness for the boy, born as he was with his particular disability. And the kid had come in handy more times than Veldt could count, producing brilliant solutions for various problems.

This time, Bryan rigged up a subtle but effective sound system that pumped into any room a faint cacophony at 18,000 Hz when children misbehaved and a soothing medley as a reward when the children grew still. It didn't work every time, but enough to put a good dent into discipline issues. Rarely, the older couple had had to resort to piping in a mild sedative mist. But the death of the children's parents had subdued everyone. Since then, it was as if they had all grown beyond their years.

Nagan volunteered, alongside Bryan, to lead the preparation team dealing with the agriculture levels of the ship.

Veldt instructed them. "While the robots tend most of the chores in this area, Wiona and I have had to intervene in several situations, such as when certain plant populations went slightly out of control. There were three incidents involving the bees and birds. We will be turning up robot vigilance level to one hundred percent and simply pray that when we awaken, we'll still have a food supply."

"What if we don't?" asked Nagan.

"That will present a problem," replied Bryan, "but not an insurmountable one. We haven't touched the freeze-dried and other condensed foods. There is enough to keep us for five years if necessary while our seed store can grow."

"In the meantime," said Wiona, "we will also plant them on the new planet."

"Assuming," said Nagan, "that they can grow in that soil. Assuming that there'll be soil."

"We have to believe there will," said Veldt firmly. "We have no choice. Though it may be possible to live in the ship for decades, it's just not conceivable for long term survival of our species."

At this Bryan snickered. "When we get there, we'd better get busy reproducing. Not me though, not me though." He seemed upset at what he himself had suggested and flapped his hands frantically.

"No one will make you do anything," said Nagan kindly.

Veldt chalked up another point in Nagan's favor as a likely future leader of the young group. Did the boy, he wondered, have a potential mate in mind?

Bryan nervously rocked on his heels. "Come on, Bry," Nagan said. He knew better than to put his arm around him. "Let's go get something to eat. My favorite cafeteria robo is working this shift."

"I'll be back as soon as Bryan feels better," Nagan told the adults.

Bryan allowed himself to be lead away.

"There is something we should discuss," said Wiona later, in the privacy of their quarters.

Veldt recognized uneasiness in her tone. Her expression was tight.

"There are so many things to teach them," she began.

Veldt sat down on their bed. Wiona remained standing.

"I don't want this new world to know certain things about the old one," she blurted.

"What do you mean?" said Veldt.

"Like war and all the other brutalities of the past. Violence builds on violence and if the children know about wars, it might give them license to eventually start their own."

To Veldt, this seemed a silly idea. "But surely, you remember that old novel, Lord of the Flies? The children in that story did not need anyone to tell them human history to be cruel and violent."

"But they already knew the history, didn't they?"

"Well, yeah, to some degree. But so does our group here, no?"

She hesitated before answering. "The young ones know nothing. I have left it out of the classes. I stopped the others from studying history after the Middles all died."

"Well, Bryan certainly knows his war history," protested Veldt. "He and I have had a few interesting talks." He paused. "And that was a strange thing to do, Wiona. To forbid them their own past."

She looked away. "Bryan does know a lot, doesn't he? He's a regular fountain of knowledge."

Veldt was silent while he considered what Wiona's point was. He had been with her for thirty years and knew her every tone of voice and facial expression. He had a bad feeling.

"Veldt," she said, turning to gaze at him with deceptively innocent looking eyes. "I want this new world to be different. Yes, it's possibly human nature to end up violent, to want what someone else has and take it from them; to decide that the survival of your tribe means to steal the land and resources of another. But we're setting out as one tribe, and why can't we make an effort to remain a peaceful one?"

Veldt stared at her. "Your point?"

"Let us, I beg you, my love, begin this new world by never leaving Eden."

"I'm not quite sure what you mean, Wiona."

"I want to keep these new Adams and Eves innocent. I have already destroyed the MEs that are records of Earth history relating to war."

"You WHAT? You had no right to do that! My God, who do you think you are?"

She was calm, her voice steady. "I am, one could say, currently 'queen' of this undertaking. In a short time, I shall be obsolete and one of the young will be in command. Of course, they will make their democracies, but there is still usually a ruler of some kind and that ruler has to make decisions for the preservation of all."

He was coldly furious. "And what am I, your assistant? How dare you make decisions of that scope without consulting me!"

Her eyes were now steely. "I love you more than anything in the universe, but we have a world to start. The safety of that comes before our personal love."

He stormed out of the room and headed to the main computers where he found that what she had said was true. Any ME related to war was gone.

He sat there with his head in his hands. Surely, he'd only imagined that he knew her.

Three days later, she returned to the subject as they climbed into bed. They had barely communicated since her revelation, but now she spoke up sharply.

"There remains the matter of Bryan," she said.

"What about Bryan?"

"We simply cannot let him join us on Mareed. He knows too much and he can't keep a secret. He'll see no reason to keep from telling the others."

Veldt felt icy fingers move over his shoulders and back. "Tell the others what?"

"About war. He'll tell them about war."

"My God, Wiona, what are you suggesting? That we murder him?"

She shrugged. "Well, not that we sneak up and stab him in the back, no. But we can set his hybersleep capsule to allow him to not waken. It would be simple. He would never suffer."

Veldt felt himself gasping for air. "My God, Wiona, how can you? How can you even think of such a thing? Do I even know you? Has something gone wrong with your brain?"

Now Wiona grew heated. "Stop it," she snapped. "STOP IT. Cut the holier-than-thou crap. Our entire existence is now at risk. There's no room for being soft. We have the inconceivably grave task of beginning a new world. Anything there, or here, could wipe us all out. It's likely that ten Earth years from now, no humans will be left in the universe. The very last thing we need is to let our children harbor the idea that they have the luxury of war. Every person must be of one mind with the others— survival is all that matters. That boy could, by his innocent knowledge, plant a seed of poison in their minds. I will fabricate a history of Earth for them, one of peace. I do not want a child, like Bryan, who cannot lie, overhearing and correcting me. He cannot be on that planet with us."

"So," said Veldt, "you want to solve the problem of violence by committing murder. You don't see the absurdity and hypocrisy in that?"

"I see it perfectly well," she said. "And I am willing to do what's necessary."

"I can't do it," he said. "I won't let you do it."

They did not speak much after that, passing each day in bone wearying preparations, before falling into bed exhausted. They did not make love, which he regretted. Knowing the possibility loomed that with hybersleep they might not reawaken, it was sad that they could not at least enjoy these potentially last times together. Veldt felt she had betrayed him, or the idea of her that he'd held in his heart.

Whenever he interacted with Bryan, he suffered fierce emotions. The boy rattled on as usual, spewing his endless dry information.

"I can be of important service to you and Wiona," he said once, "because I know so much. You can, in fact, make me head of the school, if you like."

"A kind offer, Bryan," Veldt said, his voice on the edge of trembling.

How did he know that she would not kill the boy some other way? Would she dare? He felt a need to protect him from the person he most loved, and what kind of situation was that for the two of them?

Everyone, including the smallest of children, labored hard. They were growing exhausted and some even looking forward to hybersleep.

"It's very disturbing to see children so listless," remarked Wiona one evening at dinner.

Veldt, lonely for her in spite of his anger, spoke back. "It bothers me too, but there is little choice. We have no other adults to help us. The food has to be harvested and processed, and so many things shut down. But we're coming to the end. I would say one more week and we'll be ready."

"Should we have a couple days of play before we..."

He nodded. "A fine idea. We all need it and it's an uplifting way to end things here."

"Not an end, a beginning," she corrected.

The last day of work, Veldt overheard two boys talking in the grain processing lab. "My uncle was in the Mars-Patter conflict and got his arm cut off. His new robo arm was so cool, you wouldn't believe it! If he wanted to, he could stick it right in fire!"

"You remember him? I don't remember anybody 'cept my parents." The speaker abruptly shut up and Veldt surmised that he did so to hold back tears.

"I'd like a robo arm," continued the first boy, "but nobody here knows how to make one."

"But you gotta have your arm blown off first," said the second.

"It's worth it!"

Veldt felt a shiver run down his back. Was this how it started? This romanticizing of war? He remembered episodes of his own boyhood and the war games he had played with his brother. Then later how that same brother had returned from the Mars-Patter conflict a broken man, one who sat and stared into space in spite of the treatments they gave him. Little boys didn't socialize with real men who returned from wars and if they did, those men did not tell them the truth.

That night he was tender with Wiona and they made love. She did not bring up the Bryan issue, and Veldt understood without her saying so that she had given up on the idea. Perhaps she was ashamed. She ought to be.

"I'm terrified," was all she said. "Afraid we might not arrive, afraid if we do."

He encircled her in his arms and rocked her to sleep.

During the next two days, each child bathed, trimmed his nails and had his head shaved by the grooming robots. Bryan and Nagan were indispensable in helping to keep everyone organized.

"The hybersleep capsules will do their best to keep us clean, but I must warn you," Veldt told everyone, "that there will be lapses. When you awaken, use the utensils provided in the capsule to cut your nails, which may resemble those of an ancient Chinese emperor, and snip off what you can of your hair. You'll get proper trims once we get things moving. If you find that your capsule didn't entirely eliminate soiling, toweling is provided, so clean up the best you can. Luxury is over, kids, and world building begins. We are pioneers."

Veldt and Wiona supervised as everyone climbed into their capsules, the younger children first. Nagan climbed into his and lowered the lid. He set his controls, gave a thumbs up and in a matter of minutes faded off to sleep.

Bryan climbed into his. "Hasta la vista!" he said as he lowered his lid.

Wiona wore an expression that Veldt could not identify. Her eyes filled with tears. "I've loved you so long, Veldt," she said. "In case we don't awaken, know it."

"I love you also and in the same way," he told her. He helped her climb into her capsule, leaned down to kiss her, closed her lid and waited until her eyes closed.

He studied her in there for a long time before he moved to a porthole where he stared for some time into cold space. "Forgive me, Creator, for what I am about to do."

He stood over Bryan's capsule. The child resembled a fairy prince, a blond angel. Somehow he seemed more delicate then he appeared when awake.

Veldt stared at the child for a long time, then paced back to the porthole, as if he might find an answer among the stars. For that potential Eden, should he do it or not? Would it do any good if he did? The two boys discussing the robo arm already knew about war; it was already in the one child's blood. It was in all of their blood, including his own.

To do what Wiona had suggested was the same mad ideology that promoted all wars. He understood her motives, mistaken though she be. He forgave her.

There was no cure for what humans were, or at least none that Veldt knew of. With a deep sigh, he took a last look at Bryan, gave a sigh of relief that he had not succumbed, and climbed into his own hybersleep capsule. Would there be life or death after, he knew not, but at least he went on with soul clear.

Margaret Karmazin's credits include stories published in literary and national magazines, including Rosebud, Chrysalis Reader, North Atlantic Review, Mobius, Confrontation, Pennsylvania Review, *and* Another Realm. *Her stories in* The MacGuffin, Eureka Literary Magazine, Licking River Review, *and* Mobius *were nominated for Pushcart awards. Her story, "The Manly Thing," was nominated for the* 2010 Million Writers Award. *She has stories included in* Still Going Strong, Ten Twisted Tales, Pieces of Eight *(Autism Acceptance),* Zero Gravity, Daughters of Icarus, *and other anthologies and has published a YA novel,* Replacing Fiona, *a children's book,* Flick-Flick & Dreamer, *and a collection of short stories,* Risk.

What happens when a society tries to curate the future, as if to place it in a museum? Past and potential futures clash, in this satirical story about politics.

THE CURATOR OF PROVIDENCE

By

Jeremy Lichtman

Katrin stood at the picture window and looked out into space, through the gossamer shroud of her own reflection. The ship rotated slowly, to a constantly changing panorama. At this moment, she had an excellent view of one of the barred spiral arms of the Milky Way. It would undoubtedly pass from sight in time, unless the ship's movement changed, but there was almost certainly something equally impressive to observe, regardless of the direction.

"They call it El Camino de Santiago," somebody said, uncomfortably close to her ear.

She turned, irritated. "The observation deck is almost empty," she said. "Do you mind?" She made an expanding gesture with her arms.

"Sorry," said the man who had interrupted her reverie. He took a small step back. "Cultural differences," he said, possibly by way of apology.

Katrin nodded, a conditional acceptance. She had seen the man before, at mealtimes, but did not know who he was. She turned back to the window.

"Dhanen," he said. "Morriña." He had a slight accent that Katrin couldn't place.

Katrin glanced at him and frowned. "The politician?" She looked towards the entryway to the room, expecting to see guards. For some reason, there were none.

"Former," he said. "Or I evidently wouldn't be here. Please call me Dan."

"I didn't vote for you," Katrin said, eager to return to her quiet study of stars.

Dan chuckled. "That's something to be thankful for," he said. "I'm often nervous of people who did. I believe that you're the méllonologist?"

Katrin frowned again. "I prefer reliquus," she said. "It seems more intentional, more involved with the physical artifacts themselves."

"As opposed to...?"

"Méllonology," she said, not understanding the direction of his question. "The word is a shabby inversion of archaeology, the study of what is past and done. I don't study the future; I curate how we in the present wish to be interpreted by those of the future."

"I assume reliquus comes from the word relic," said Dan. He held out his hands, as if he were presenting her with a primordial terra-cotta bowl. "Doesn't your work encompass the intangible as well?"

"Of course," Katrin said. "An idea could also be an anachronism. An ideology could be out of step with its age, in a way that the future may misinterpret. It's infinitely harder to erase stray ideas than anachronistic relics though, wouldn't you say?"

"I wouldn't know," said Dan. "My job was to produce new ideas and ideologies, not to prune them as if they were a topiary hedge."

"Some people make messes," she said. "Others clean them up."

"Some people act," he said. "And others just watch and form opinions about it. Or kibitz."

"The job of a reliquus is not passive," Katrin said.

"No," Dan said. "It isn't." He inclined his head towards her. "Enjoy the view. Perhaps I shall see you at dinner."

"Perhaps," she said. "Katrin," she added, finally introducing herself. "Katrin fen Sabin."

"Doctor," Dan said, an acknowledgment, of sorts, of her status. He made a tiny motion with his hand, that might have been a wave, as he left.

Katrin was seated at the captain's table. She nodded at the politician, who was seated on the opposing side of the table, and then returned her attention to her plate. She did not want to appear too familiar with so disreputable a personage as a politician.

"How much longer will we be stopped?" the lady sitting next to her asked the captain. Katrin looked up, and cocked her head slightly to one side. She had been preoccupied with her work, and had not previously been aware of a stoppage.

"It isn't anything to worry about," said the captain.

Katrin had been introduced to him in passing at a previous meal. She thought that his name might have been Lesran.

"The manifold that pulls us through space is a property of the skin of our ship," said the captain. "Over time, it accumulates damage, tiny lesions, from the harsh environment of space."

"The ship is damaged?" asked Katrin's neighbor, sounding alarmed.

"The skin of the ship is made from a self-healing material," said the captain. "We're just giving it some time to regenerate, so that we have a smooth manifold. There's nothing to be concerned about."

"Do you know how long we will be delayed?" asked the politician, interjecting.

The captain shrugged. "A day, or two, perhaps," he said. "Space travel is eternally changeable, as I'm sure you're aware."

"First time," said the politician.

"You look familiar," said the lady seated next to Katrin, turning to Dan. "Aren't you..."

"Dhanen Morriña," said Dan. "Yes, I am."

"I suppose you wouldn't have had much opportunity to travel, at that," said the captain. He clearly had either been previously introduced, or was also familiar with Dan's name.

Katrin's neighbor stared intently at Dan. "What was it like being a politician?" she asked. "I'm Ansha, by the way."

Dan made a tiny facial movement that Katrin interpreted as being a wince. She didn't think anyone else noticed. "As you can imagine," he said. "It was rather lonely being incarcerated, followed by the unexpected strain of the election. The politicians were kept isolated from the main prison population, and the process of voting on critical decisions happened around the clock, sometimes with few breaks. It was stressful."

"You're obviously free now," said the captain. "Unless I'm illegally carrying a fugitive." He smiled, although nobody laughed.

"It's traditional for politicians to make a pilgrimage at the end of their sentences," said Dan. "A way of symbolically indicating atonement for our actions, both before and during our terms of office."

"Earth?" asked Katrin, joining the conversation for the first time.

"Yes, eventually," said Dan. "There's a route in a place called Iberia that is close to where my family originated. All things being equal, my goal is to walk from..."

"What were you originally incarcerated for?" asked Ansha, interrupting. "I voted for you, by the way," she added. There was a moment of silence, as the other diners around the table appeared to digest her tactlessness.

"I'd prefer not to talk about it," Dan said. He sounded more pensive than affronted.

Katrin spent several days intently focused on research for her next project, having her meals delivered to her room. The need for exercise, rather than boredom, eventually forced her to emerge.

The ship had a rotating, centrifugal running track, to allow passengers to exercise at a higher gravitational pull than the ship standard. When Katrin arrived, nobody else was using the centrifuge, so she set it to a few percent above Earth normal, and started jogging.

"I think you've been avoiding me," said Dan, unexpectedly. Katrin looked up, slowed to a walk, then stopped completely. Dan was standing on the ladder that led down from the hub of the centrifuge to the circular track.

"Either come down here, or go away," said Katrin. "I'm getting vertigo looking up at you."

Dan hopped down and made some casual stretching movements, using the ladder. "I was kidding," he said, lightly. "Although I doubt you'd want to openly associate with somebody as inherently disreputable as me."

Katrin shrugged, and then resumed running, at a slower pace than before. Dan waited until she had made a full circle of the centrifuge, and then started running alongside her.

"I wanted to apologize," he said.

"For what?"

"We got off on the wrong foot," Dan said. "I believe I may have been rude. My social skills are rusty, for obvious reasons."

"Not the only thing you need to work on," said Katrin, speeding up slightly.

"I'm a bit out of shape as well. I'm sure you understand."

Katrin made a snorting sound, but didn't respond.

"I need...," said Dan. "No. I want to ask you for your opinion about something."

"I wondered when you would get to your point," said Katrin.

Dan laughed. "You don't miss much, do you?"

"I try not to." Katrin stopped jogging, and snapped her fingers to slow the centrifuge.

Dan sat down on his heels. He appeared to be slightly out of breath. "I heard of you recently, in connection with an artwork," he said.

"The 'Golden Spiral'," Katrin said.

"Yes," said Dan. "Beauregard's masterwork."

"Supposed," said Katrin.

"You don't like it?" asked Dan.

"It's certainly imposing," said Katrin. The painting was a vast oblong canvas, more than ten meters tall, and almost entirely matte-black. A tiny swirl of yellow, intended to represent the galaxy, appeared off-center, near the bottom. "I was brought in because some critics believed that it falsely represented something our society believes about human boundaries, or our place in the universe," said Katrin.

"Inaccurately," said Dan. He furrowed his brow, clearly trying to understand the obscure gist of the argument.

Katrin shrugged. "I told them that they were a sorry bunch of navel-gazing, self-absorbed imbeciles."

"Really?" said Dan, smiling. "What would you have done if they had been right?"

"You mean, if I had concluded that the future would actually have misinterpreted how we view the universe, as a result of that amateurish waste of pigment?"

"That's a bit harsh," said Dan. "But, yes. What would you have done?"

"I would have had the painting destroyed, erased any digital representations of it," she said. "Arrested anyone holding illegal copies, wiped it from their memories."

Dan whistled. "You don't do things in half-measures, do you?"

"No," said Katrin. "That isn't my mandate."

Dan clambered to his feet. "You don't feel that it is extreme to destroy an artwork that some people consider a masterpiece, simply because it might give somebody the wrong impression?"

"We live in a silly, narcissistic era," said Katrin. "One that
is endlessly obsessed with how it will be perceived in time to come."

"So you acknowledge the problem," said Dan.

"Oh yes," said Katrin. "I just said that I believe that I have a mandate."

"For what?" asked Dan. "To do what?"

"I'm a curator," said Katrin. "I'm given great power to arrange how our society will be perceived in the future."

Dan started to say something, but Katrin interrupted him. "In doing so," she said. "I curate the present. That is the job of a reliquus. Yes, Dan, I can and do make choices about how to change society. I believe that is what you are asking."

Dan nodded, emphatically. "You could fix things," he said. "If you wanted to, you could fix the political process. You could even write your own profession out of existence."

"There are limitations," Katrin said. "There are trillions of people in the galaxy, and only one of me. It is quite possible for a reliquus to overstep her bounds. I can't change everything. Even with the power that is given to me, I can only do so much. People have to change themselves first, sometimes."

"Will you hear my petition, though?" asked Dan.

"Yes," said Katrin. "Not now though. I'm trying to exercise."

"Thank you," Dan said.

"How much do you understand of how our political system actually works?" Dan asked. He toyed with a ceramic mug filled with coffee. "I don't mean the big picture, everyone knows that. I mean the details of the process."

"Hmm," said Katrin. She looked around to see that nobody else was close enough to hear them speak. Across the dining room, she saw Ansha, the lady from the captain's table, staring at her, possibly resenting Katrin's private discussion with Dan. Katrin frowned back, and she turned away.

"There's an old parable," Katrin said. "An extra-terrestrial observes a human walking a dog on a leash, with the dog running ahead as far as the rope can reach. The ET asks the dog to take it to its leader."

Dan laughed. "Because it is in front?" he asked.

"Yes," Katrin said. "In my experience, most leadership is of the walking in front, but continually looking back for direction, variety. The precise mechanics are details that I don't usually care to investigate."

"I see," said Dan. "A subtle politician joke, ever so casually delivered by the de-facto sovereign ruler of the known universe."

Katrin snorted. "I suppose I deserved that," she said. "I actually don't directly interact with the political system very often. Most of my work deals with commerce. Or occasionally art."

"People have always understood the temptations of power," Dan said. "The people who are entrusted with making decisions on behalf of society traditionally had the greatest opportunity to serve themselves first."

"Corruption," said Katrin.

"Yes, but also other abuses of power, including holding onto it tenaciously, beyond all reason," said Dan. "Our political system is intended to remove the temptations of power entirely. We elect our political class solely from the ranks of convicted, imprisoned criminals."

"Who are clearly the best decision-makers available," said Katrin.

"The system relies on the so-called wisdom of crowds," said Dan. "Politicians are isolated, so that they have neither the ability to serve themselves, nor the temptation."

"You mean, you," said Katrin.

"Yes," said Dan. "I spent most of the past few years in a cell, in almost complete isolation, with only a terminal to communicate with the outside world. Matters requiring my decision appeared on the screen, and I could either vote or suggest amendments."

"Are you asking for my sympathy?" Katrin asked.

"No," said Dan. "That's not my point. The system is intended to avoid many of the potential pitfalls of power, while simultaneously punishing criminals by forcing them to make all of the tough decisions required by society. Theoretically."

"Theoretically?" asked Katrin.

"Yes," said Dan. "My observations led me to conclude that the actual results did not come from our collective votes. A cynic might say that the entire system is just for show, that the true punishment is never knowing if all of it was indeed an exercise in futility."

Katrin mulled this over for a moment. She leaned her elbows on the table, and steepled her hands in front of her chin. "I think I understand where you are going with this," she said. "I'd prefer if you said it yourself though."

"How will posterity view us?" asked Dan. "As naive fools, trying vainly to separate power from circumstance? As hypocrites, parodying justice, while the true source of political power is actually concealed? I'm asking you for your judgment."

Katrin laughed.

"I'm serious," said Dan, angrily.

"No, no," said Katrin. "That's not what's funny. I believe that you're trying to destroy the system in order to save parts of it."

"And you? What are you doing, then?" Dan asked.

"I'm trying to save the system by destroying parts of it," Katrin said. "What an interesting inversion."

"Is that all this is to you?" said Dan. "An intellectual game? A puzzle to be contemplated? This isn't just an injustice to the prisoners forced to participate in a broken system. It's an affront to our supposedly democratic society."

Katrin stood up, abruptly. "I'll consider your complaint," she said. Dan opened his mouth to speak, but she raised her hand. "I need to think about this," she said.

"What was your crime?" Katrin didn't turn her head.

"How did you know that I was there?" Dan asked. He stood in the doorway to the observation deck.

"The glass is reflective," Katrin said. "I saw you enter." She gently leaned her forehead against the window, contemplating the stars outside.

"Did you know that isn't actually a window," said Dan. "They can't have breaks in the drive manifold surface like that. There's a tiny camera outside, and this is just a screen."

"Yes," Katrin said. "Sometimes illusions can be comforting." She paused. "What was your crime?" she asked Dan again. "Why were you incarcerated?"

"You're perceptive," Dan said. "You've figured it all out, haven't you?"

"I think so," Katrin said. "You deliberately committed a crime, in order to be caught, so that you could then be eligible for election."

"Yes," said Dan.

"But how would that help you?" said Katrin.

"The victims of my so-called fraud campaigned tirelessly for my election," said Dan. "They claimed that they wanted me properly punished for the harm I did to them, the damage that I caused to society."

"You planned it all with them," said Katrin.

"Yes," said Dan. "I wanted to change the system from the inside."

"And did you?" asked Katrin. "Did you change anything?"

"No," said Dan. "You need to understand why I'm telling you this. I don't believe that you're nearly as dispassionate as you try to appear."

"Perhaps not," said Katrin.

"You're an idealist, of sorts," said Dan. "You appear to serve the system by adjusting how it will be perceived in the future, but you're really trying to change things in the process. I believe you're trying to change things for the better, not just to fit how you want the universe to function."

"Perhaps," said Katrin.

"We have a political system that is profoundly unjust, that obscures the nature of power behind a facade of penance," said Dan. "I believe that the future will judge us harshly. I believe that you have the power to change that, even if you say that you do not."

"You're trying to influence my decision," said Katrin.

"I believe that an idealist like yourself has only one of two choices," said Dan. "You say that you curate the present, in order that the future will see us the way that we wish to be seen. I believe that the future will judge us as hypocrites. Either you should change the very nature of our political system, or you should stop pretending to curate anything. Abdicate. Resign. Legislate your entire profession out of being."

"Political corruption is still a crime," said Katrin. "When you conspired to be incarcerated, when you rigged the campaign in order to be elected, you committed a second crime as well. One with serious consequences for our entire system." She nodded at somebody behind Dan. "I don't believe that I will be campaigning for your reelection though."

Dan turned around. Two guards stood silently behind him. "I trusted you," he said. "I thought that you were an idealist, willing to change the world for the better."

"I actually am an idealist," Katrin said. "I told you that, as a reliquus, I choose how society will be viewed by those yet to come."

Dan opened his mouth as if to speak, then closed it again.

"I can't fix all of our problems," said Katrin, "But sometimes I can eventually execute justice. I choose to portray our civilization as hypocrites."

Jeremy Lichtman is a software developer, based in Toronto, Canada. His story, "Bob the Hipster Knight", was a finalist for the inaugural Gernsback Competition at Amazing Magazine, *and will be published later in 2016. His fiction has appeared in several anthologies, including* Visions II: Moons of Saturn, *and* Visions of the Future *from the Lifeboat Foundation. Leave comments for Jeremy at* www.lillicatpublishers.com *under the Authors tab.*

For Exarch Aka, conduit between worlds, God lives deep within Dark Matter. As Aka prepares for death, he must struggle with fresh doubts about his beliefs, even as he rushes to teach his successor what he needs to know to guide his people home.

ONE LAST TALK WITH HIS GOD

By

Jeremy M. Gottwig

Aka smelled of death.

"It is true," he rasped.

"What is true, Exarch?"

Aka had not sensed the boy. He grasped through the air for some piece of flesh and found the boy's wrist. "Why are you here?" Aka pulled the boy closer. "Why?"

The boy's muscles tightened. "The Soro have chosen me to follow you, Exarch."

Without my guidance?

Aka dropped the boy's arm. "Leave me," he demanded.

"But I am told to learn from you. Before you..."

Aka could smell the boy's trepidation. "Before I what?"

"I do not want to say it."

"Then say nothing." Irritation flared with feeble intensity.

He felt the boy step away from the bed, but remain in the room.

"It is too soon," Aka wheezed. He withdrew into his mind and allowed his senses to descend through his bed and into the deck. He could feel the hum of the ship's engines. He could sense the flow of energy and air through the conduits and ducts. He could taste defects and decay in the ship's joints and bearings.

He could sense The Being, but he could not find it.

Do you hide from me?

Aka breathed deeply, allowing his senses to contract, until he could drift along the darkness of matter. His thoughts settled among the complex quantum synapses within that darkness. He inhaled The Being at its source.

You kept this from me.

-The choice is not yours.

But I am the Exarch.

-The choice is not yours.

The Being severed their connection. Aka tumbled through the void. His rage subsided. He felt for the thoughts of the Quiet Child and found her. While others slept, she stared into the stars and reached for The Being's boundaries. Aka often found her in such a state.

The Being continues into eternity. You will find no limits.

The Quiet Child turned and glared at him.

Aka gasped, woke, and sat up. His back spasmed and he grunted.

The boy came to his side again. "Exarch?"

Aka ignored the question. He caught his breath and attempted to climb out of bed. His muscles burned and abandoned him. Aka fell and the boy caught him.

"How may I help, Exarch?"

"You may go away and never return!" snapped Aka. Guilt and shame settled into his heart. "Help me to my chair," he commanded. Aka allowed the boy to bear his weight. He tugged himself along the edge of his bed until he could reach the handrail along the upper bulkhead, where he knew it to be. Aka paused and caught his breath. "The deck is cold."

"The deck is always cold, Exarch."

Aka smiled.

They skirted the bulkhead. Aka felt for familiar objects as they moved. His weak muscles had confused his senses. Had he been healthy, he could have navigated from one end of the ship to the other by doing nothing more than counting steps and detecting changes in the environment.

Aka smelled his chair. He lowered himself until he could feel the fabric armrest. "I can finish this task by myself," Aka insisted.

"Yes, Exarch."

Little-by-little, Aka eased himself into the old chair. His arms trembled but maintained their strength. Aka let himself fall the final few inches. The cushions caught him. Aka breathed deeply, his muscles aching as they relaxed.

Aka reached for The Being.

I have angered you?

Aka received no response. "So be it," he muttered, aloud.

He shifted his focus to the boy's breathing. "You should be resting like everyone else," he critiqued.

"I will sleep only when you sleep, Exarch," the boy promised.

Aka flipped a hand. "Then you will never sleep. It seems as if I have lost that ability. I suppose I should acknowledge that my age has finally caught up with me." After a long sigh, he added, "But it pains me to admit that I can no longer carry myself without the aid of another."

"The Soro's Voice told me that you are the eldest Exarch to have served aboard the Exodus."

"She is wrong. My predecessor, Kaim, lived much longer, but he abdicated once I came of age." Aka considered this and admitted, "As an Exarch, this makes him younger, but he lived well beyond his years." Aka again reached for The Being. He sensed rejection even as darkness began to gather around the boy.

Do not deny me.

-Your time has come.

This boy is a mistake.

The Being slipped out of reach. Aka descended deeper, but The Being evaded his tendrils of consciousness. Aka returned to his chair and nursed his anger.

He would need to find some other way to commune with his God.

After a deep sigh, Aka asked, "In this moment, tell me what you feel."

"I am concerned."

"Explain."

The boy hesitated. "I am concerned for your health, Exarch."

"I am near death. The state of my health is no longer relevant. Something else troubles you. What is it?"

Aka heard the boy's heavy heart pounding into the silence.

"As a child, I could sense The Being." The boy hesitated. "But it has been so long since I last felt its presence."

"And you are worried that you have lost this ability. You haven't."

"But aren't there others with greater acuity? I have heard you tell stories about those who could...."

"I know my stories," Aka snapped. He sighed and acknowledged the boy's fears with a nod. "There are others, but they are few." He left the next part unsaid: each generation seemed less tuned to understanding The Being's thoughts.

"Now. Close your eyes. Disable your senses one-by-one. It may not be enough to kill your synthetic systems. You may need to deny your organic senses, feelings, or urges. Perhaps you must deny yourself joy or sexual fulfilment. Or your ability to see. You must find that part of yourself that keeps you from sensing the darkness of matter. With each little death, reach for that shadow you feel in your dreams."

The gathering of darkness shifted.

"I know that shadow."

"But can you feel the whispers along the waves? Even if you are unable to understand these thoughts, I know that you can feel them."

"I hear nothing, Exarch."

Aka frowned. "There is nothing to hear," he reminded. Aka allowed his thoughts to drift toward the boy. The darkness threatened to recede, and he withdrew.

"I forced the Soro into this mistake," Aka whispered. He knew that The Being had influenced their decision.

You should have allowed me a voice. Or perhaps you wanted me silenced?

Aka had planned to select the Quiet Child as his successor, once she came of age. He intended to begin grooming and teaching her within the next Worion cycle. When the time came, he would present her before the Soro during Gathering and abdicate his position as Exarch. He knew that the Soro could reject her, but they would have been foolish to do so.

But he had grown too old, and she was still too young. In the meanwhile, the boy had become a young man.

I feel her even now.

Aka twisted his mind and found the Quiet Child observing him.

-You are dying?

Yes.

The Quiet Child lingered for a moment and then descended. The Being resisted her advances. She expanded her reach and grasped a retreating thread. Aka marveled as she entangled The Being and disappeared into its thoughts.

You cannot flee from her. Is that why you are afraid?

The Being didn't answer.

The boy gasped and started to cough.

Aka waited.

"I lost myself, Exarch," the boy added, once his coughing had subsided.

"You lost yourself, and The Being entered," Aka amended. "It has been seeking you."

"Then I can become like you?"

"Yes. I have never doubted that. I have watched you through your dreams, and I know that you feel the darkness of matter. I have seen your mind flow along that darkness, and I have seen you react to the consciousness that lives there. But it is not enough for The Being to enter you. It can enter any of the Soro. Even those with closed minds tend to open themselves while they sleep. An Exarch is different. You must find your way into The Being's thoughts. It may fight you."

"Why does it not give itself freely?"

Aka considered this a stupid question. "Why should it?"

"I do not understand, Exarch."

Aka leaned forward in his chair. "What is your purpose as Exarch?"

"To communicate with The Being."

"Wrong."

"To keep the Soro faithful."

"You are thinking too small. What is our greatest purpose as Soro?"

"To find a new home."

"Yes. And your ultimate purpose as Exarch is to point the way." Aka leaned back in his chair and sighed. "The Being is everywhere, but we are a lost people. We must believe that somewhere out there is our home. We must hope that this ship will continue to sustain us, and we must remain faithful that The Being will continue to guide us. You are the conduit between The Being and the Soro, but you cannot allow yourself to become merely a vessel. Without some sense of yourself, you will be unable to interpret what The Being has to say."

"I understand," the boy claimed, but Aka had detected a hint of hesitation.

"Do you? I remain skeptical. I believe that you aim to please. This is not your purpose as Exarch. We Soro are a complex people. We will attempt to sway you. We will question your interpretations and make you unsure of your own beliefs. You are well-liked aboard this ship, because you are amiable. Perhaps you should cast this part of you aside. Perhaps you must deny yourself companionship and the company of others. Perhaps you need to rebuild yourself as someone who commands respect. If you fail to earn influence aboard this ship, I fear we are lost forever."

The boy said nothing.

Aka allowed the weight of silence to linger. He added, "You must decide if you can do this."

"Do I have a choice, Exarch?"

Aka smiled. *There is always a choice*, he meant to say, but his body vanished as if ripped from his mind. He descended outward and inward. When he stopped moving, he found himself trapped in the darkness between stars.

126

Aka grasped for the safety of the ship, but his mind continued to drift through space. He could feel the darkness of matter, but The Being was nowhere to be found.

This is not possible.

Another mind touched his, and Aka sensed the Quiet Child. Her presence calmed and unnerved him. Aka searched the void, but he could not find her.

A thought rang through Aka's mind. It belonged to the Quiet Child.

-Why are you dying?

Because it is my time. Where am I?

-With me.

And where are we?

-Alone.

We must go back.

In one, violent motion, the void shifted, and Aka found himself back aboard the ship. He wanted to scream, but he had no breath. The feel of the chair eased his pain. Aka drew in a deep, trembling breath.

"Do I have a choice, Exarch?"

Aka's fingers clenched the armrests. His palms began to cramp. He wished he could open his eyes and disappear into the physical world. The experience had left him stunned and afraid, but one thought ascended to the forefront of his mind. "The Being was not there," Aka whispered.

"But the Being is *everywhere*, Exarch." The boy's voice shook.

"Yes," Aka rasped. He injected strength into his voice and added, "You paid attention during Gathering, it seems."

"I am a good listener, Exarch, and I will learn anything you teach me. But I worry that I will be unable to lead."

As Aka focused on the boy's words, the shock of his experience with the Quiet Child faded into a tremor along his spine. "Your's is not a position of leadership," he corrected. "Not as you imagine it."

His thoughts continued to trouble him. He wanted to seek out the Quiet Child. He wanted her to carry him back to that place between the stars. He wanted to find The Being waiting for them there. He wanted to prove her wrong.

And if she isn't wrong?

Aka forced the thought from his mind, but he could not bring himself to release his grip on the chair.

"You advise. You bring hope. You encourage the faithful. In all of these things, you must be strong. On occasion, The Being may require you to make demands, but this is not the same as leadership. A strong Exarch has great influence, but not even the strongest Exarch has control over this ship."

"And if I cannot be this person? Do I have a choice? Can I step away from my role as Exarch and allow another to take my place?"

There is always a choice, Aka thought, but he stilled his tongue. He knew that he could break the boy and then the Soro would need to choose another, which would allow Aka to inject himself into their deliberations. "Without free will, there is no chaos," Aka whispered in a voice too faint to hear.

"Am I a mistake, Exarch?" The boy's voice quavered.

Aka could not answer. His experience with the Quiet Child had left him with too many questions. He let out a tremulous sigh and released his grip on the chair. His mind entered the darkness. The gathering around the boy had expanded.

Aka hunted for the Quiet Child.

Take me back to that place.

His call vanished into the ether.

Aka flowed along the darkness and passed through the dreams of the sleeping Soro. He tasted every thread of consciousness. He recognized the thought patterns of those he had loved and guided. He relayed his blessings as Exarch and drew comfort from their grateful responses.

My time draws short.

The Quiet Child remained elusive.

Aka abandoned the search. He descended deeper and reached for The Being, perhaps, for the last time.

The Being refused him, but Aka sensed the Quiet Child along the fringes of The Being's consciousness.

Take me back to that place.

The Quiet Child emerged.

-Why?

So that I might understand.

-There is nothing to understand.

Aka ensnared her thoughts before she could depart.

Then carry me deep into The Being.

He felt the Quiet Child extract her thoughts from his.

-Why?

Because I must.

The Quiet Child wrapped herself around Aka and drew him into her mind. She forced herself into The Being. Aka did his best to ignore the pain. She acknowledged his anguish, but Aka sensed no empathy.

The Being tried and failed to pull free of her spines of consciousness. The struggle shredded Aka's thoughts. He lost his sense of self, until his mind could piece itself back together. When he regained composure, he felt himself closer to The Being than he had ever been before. The equilibrium felt unstable, but it held.

You were not there.

The darkness began to vibrate.

You were not there.

-You are no longer allowed.

You were not there.

-It is time for another.

The Being attempted to sever Aka from itself, but the Quiet Child tightened her net. Aka marveled at her strength. He hoped that age wouldn't rob her of her abilities.

The vibrations intensified, and Aka felt himself losing focus.

You are afraid?

The vibrations ceased.

-Yes.

She frightens you.

-No.

What frightens you?

-I was not there.

Then you are not everywhere.

Aka acknowledged this as truth and terror crept into his thoughts. He wanted to separate himself from The Being, but the Quiet Child maintained her grip. Aka knew that he needed to ask one last question.

Where are you guiding us?

-Searching the void. As you are. As those who have come before. As those who will follow.

Then we are lost.

-We are always lost.

The Being's words shook Aka free of the Quiet Child's net. He disappeared. Everything disappeared.

Aka drifted.

Voices brought him back.

Aka gasped back into his body. He focused on the sounds, but his mind failed to discern meaning or structure. His thoughts, the voices, and the sounds of the ship bled together into a simple static.

Death.

And Aka was back in his bed.

His memories remained a jumble, but he began to recognize sounds. He heard the deep rumble of the ship's engines. He heard heartbeats. He heard feet along the deck. He heard that repetitive squeak he had long since learned to ignore.

He heard the boy's voice among many.

Aka licked his lips. He felt the warmth of bodies as they drew near.

"Where is the boy?" Aka forced.

Every voice vanished but one, soft with concern.

"I am here, Exarch."

"Send everyone away. But stay."

Aka's mind tried to peel back his layers of memories as the boy ushered everyone out of the room. He could remember only fragments, but he remembered enough. Aka felt too weary to be afraid.

"We are alone, Exarch," the boy informed.

"I am afraid that my mind is now as broken as my body," Aka whispered. "I will not be able to teach you as I should."

"I will make my own way. If I can."

"No." Aka touched the boy's hand. He wanted to clench it but lacked the strength. "You must not do it alone. Not anymore."

"I don't understand, Exarch."

Aka again licked his lips. He knew he couldn't explain everything he had seen and felt, nor did he trust his interpretation.

"I am a flawed man," Aka said.

"You are our Exarch."

"That does not excuse my flaws. Nor will it excuse yours."

"Exarch, I remain unconvinced that I will be able to serve in this role."

"You wanted another life. As did I. But you will serve. You will do well." Aka caught his breath. "But you must find her. The Quiet One. Learn from her. Listen to her. Support her. She is fearless and strong. Allow no one to limit her. Not even yourself."

Seconds passed, and then, "I will do as you advise."

Aka withdrew his hand. "Perhaps it is better this way." He folded his fingers over his abdomen. "I can do nothing more. Find your way, Exarch. Bring us home."

And Aka opened his eyes.

Jeremy M. Gottwig is a librarian and programmer. He wakes at 4:30 a.m. every morning to write science fiction. As a result, he has a caffeine addiction. You can find Jeremy's work in **Nature: Futures, Mythic Delirium,** *and the* **Hides the Dark Tower** *anthology (Pole to Pole Publications). He is currently finishing up a book entitled,* **Chet Eubanks is Employee of the Year.**

Jeremy lives in Baltimore, Maryland, with his wife and young son.

Tana must face her fears when she and others of her crew board a mining ship that has gone dark. She discovers that sometimes the hardest fight is to do what is right.

SHIP OF SHADOWS

By

Sidney Blaylock, Jr.

The *DSRV Outrider* slid silently next to the *TMS Discordia*. Tana's hands flew over the control nodes while her eyes remained locked to the holographic image of the *Discordia*, as it floated wraith-like in the Outer Rim of the Galactic Spiral Arm.

Piloting a starship was no easy thing, but it was what Tana had trained for, had crewed for, and was now, finally, getting a chance to do. But a Deep Space Recovery Vessel (DSRV) would not have been her first choice for a piloting assignment; a DSRV was half salvage ship and half up-gunned frigate. Taking on contracts and towing lost or damaged vessels required enough fire power to fight off pirates, and sometimes even the use of the "heavy gear" armed combat suits buried in the holds. Tana only recently earned her Pilot Ranking and very few ships were willing to take on a Rank One Pilot. The *Outrider*, however, was one such ship.

"Back us off nice and slow, Ms. Reeve," the captain called out from behind her. "I want to get a good, long look at that ship's exterior before we clamp on."

Tana nodded and keyed in the commands. In less time than it took to blink, millions of subroutines activated behind the scenes and small micro-thrusters mounted along the hull of the *Outrider* fired, pushing it warily away from the ghost ship.

"I don't see any outer hull damage," said Junior Engineer Gray Jansen. Tana recognized the crew members by voice even with her concentration locked on her job. "No explosive decompression. Engines seem intact. But she's powered down and there's no spin. No grav or air. She's a ghost ship for sure."

"Anything to indicate why she's gone dark?" Captain Kalen asked Senior Engineer Melodi Song. Tana knew Jansen would be steaming inside, because, even though the captain valued the input of his junior crew members, he relied on his senior members' opinions to make the majority of his decisions. It wasn't necessarily the way she would have run things, but it did seem to cut down on a lot of cross chatter during crew deliberations. Tana felt her lip quirk. Melodi Song's personality was that of a mother hen who always wanted the best for her brood, and she considered all of the juniors, hers and other sections', as part of her flock. As an orphan, Tana reveled in the mothering that Engineer Song displayed, something she had missed in her life. Others, especially Jansen, bristled at Song's attention. Based on Tana's limited conversations with him, he seemed to feel that carrying out her responsibilities as Senior Engineer bordered on micromanaging him for things that he could handle perfectly well on his own.

Tana couldn't resist taking her eyes off her scan and sliding a quick peek at Jansen's face and, sure enough, it was screwed up like a star about to go nova.

"Nothing. Scan's good and she's clean. So far, all of our scans match the last known running profile that we have on her. She should be operational."

The captain stood watching the ship for a while, assessing the risks.

If Tana had been captain, she knew what she would have done—she probably would have risked her crew's ire by tagging it and leaving it for the company to recover. This recovery operation would net them all a sizable bonus, in addition to their standard fee, as the owners of the ship, The AVG Mining Consortium, had put in a priority request to locate and recover the ship.

Tana shivered. There was something very odd about this ship. What was a mining ship doing this far out in deep space? No planets or asteroids were out here, so there was no money to be had, no profit to be gained. No, the thing was just drifting out here, like a dead weight. Only the fact that the mining company's policy to quantum entangle all of their ships had made it possible to locate the *Discordia*. She might have been lost in the void of deep space for all eternity otherwise. Her sister ship, *Dementia*, had called in her position a day after the *Discordia* went dark.

She shook herself. *Get a grip.* Someday, she *would* be captain of a ship of her own. She'd made that promise the day she'd graduated from Pilot Training. This was deep space and space was neither kind nor merciful. Sometimes, one had to take risks in order to advance. To Tana, the key was to carefully manage the risks and never let them outweigh safety.

"Alright, Ms. Reeve, kill our spin and clamp on. Not a bump, if you please. I want us tied on as quietly as possible."

"Yes, sir," she said. The captain wanted her to not transfer any of the *Outrider's* inertia to the *Discordia*. Hard under normal circumstances, but without spin?

Tana took a deep breath and keyed the commands. Telemetry streamed on multiple displays. Her eyes flicked over the data, but she only took it in on a surface level. Engineer Song had once told her that a ship was alive. Not in the strictest of senses, of course, but like any machine inhabited by humans, it had its own systems and rhythms. Once you learned those, mastering it was easy. It was advice Tana had learned to live by. She keyed in commands at a furious pace, feeling more than seeing changes her commands were causing. The *Outrider's* spin slowed, then stopped. She heard the pinging sound of the proximity warning. She ground her teeth as the *Outrider* closed to its target; she wanted to kill the noise, but Captain's orders were to keep the ping active during any docking maneuver. When the two ships were close, she cut all engines and maneuvered the ship via thrusters only. At the last moment, she fired all thrusters, dropped the *Outrider's* inertia and clamped on using the station-keeping micro-thrusters. A small *woosh* of air was the only sound as the seal was made. She licked her lips, realizing her mouth was dry, as the electric whir of the docking bridge extending indicated the two ships connecting.

"Good job, Ms. Reeves. That's exactly what I was hoping for."

Captain Kalen keyed into the Comms system. "Richter, get your team ready."

There was a moment of silence on the comms before Richter responded. "Yes, sir. I read you. My team will be in our *heavy gear*. We'll let you know what we find. Out."

"Okay, so I can guess why you're bringing along the kid, but why are you bringing our only pilot?" Delmont asked as they walked down the barely lit corridor of the *Discordia*. "I mean, what if something happens to her? How do we get out of here without her? Something had to have happened to Richter and his team for him to miss three different comm-checks. Six people in power suits do *not* go silent without a reason."

Tana glared at the back of Delmont's yellow and black exosuit, but didn't say anything.

The Captain turned and locked his gaze with the Environmental Section Head. "She's coming because I said so. As for Jansen, I'd rather not go looking for Richter and his team inside a ship with no spin, no power, and no lights. I watched the same Holovids as you did when I was younger. I know how those stories end, and so do you. A lot of screaming and dying in the dark. First priority, Song and Jansen get the lights back on, then we find Richter, hook this tub up and get it back to AVG. And before you say, 'let's just tag and bag it,' let me remind you that our contract with AVG says that the commission goes down by forty points as a penalty, if we don't bring it in ourselves." He ticked off the points on his fingers as they walked. "Plus, they'll take out an additional cost, based on the retainer they have to pay another ship to pick up what we should have brought back in the first place. Say goodbye to our profits."

Both Tana and the captain knew why she was here. It was highlighted on her Pilot's Training Record: Top marks in Basic and Advanced CQC Training, Small Arms Training, Exosuit Training, and Ship to Ship Weapon Systems. She narrowed her eyes as she assessed Delmont's swaggering, lumbering style, noting at least three different ways that she could put him down, even though he had a distinct height and weight advantage. Captain Traver had access to her file, of course, so he knew it as well as she did. If he chose not to share well, then that was his business.

Her father and mother had been on the *Tritanium* when it had suffered explosive decompression, making her an orphan at the age eight. The station she was on at the time of the accident had been in a spiraling economic depression, although she hadn't known anything about that at the time. Very few on the station could afford to feed extra mouths, so she'd remained in the foster care system. Her good test scores had been her escape path and she'd taken it. She had made sure that she learned how to protect herself. Foster care had made her angry. Her parents had loved her and had cared for her, just because she was their child. From what she could remember, when they punished her, it had been fair. Not so, in the system. She'd been whaled on many times for things that were not her fault. At least, she had until she'd learned to fight back. She'd earned a reputation of being hard to foster and that meant very few families wanted her in their houses. In the system, she became recognized as either a commodity to get a larger food allotment, or an extra burden to be taken on reluctantly. That rankled inside of her. She had not allowed it to fester and corrupt her like some of her friends who jumped station on the first tug they found, but it still burned.

"Could it just be Richter's comms acting up?" asked one of the three Juniors from Environmental that Delmont had dragged out of their berths for the search. She could all but hear Jansen's voice in her head changing "dragged" to "scrounged."

Jansen shook his head, seeming to move in slow motion in the low-grav environment. His lip curled. "He went over in a combat suit," he said extra slowly, as if explaining to children. "They all did. Those things are like tanks with legs. Nothing short of a singularity should be able to get through them. And even if his suit's comms were somehow fried, how do you explain not getting anything from the other five suits?"

Tana watched Song give her protégé a disapproving frown. Tana had seen Station Security's combat suits popped by something as mundane as railgun fire. Tana had no doubt that sometime in the near future, Jansen would hear about it from Song. While she didn't actively dislike Jansen as she did Delmont, who had given her a hard time her first month shipboard, she knew Old Mother Song, wouldn't let him get away with such blatant condescension of his coworkers.

Her attention was diverted from that thought as something scuttled off to a side passage way on her left. She whipped out her gun, a small hand bolter, and trained it at the corridor. She wished she had something heavier in caliber, like a railgun or even a scattergun, although its spray pattern would be dangerous shipboard, but Richter and his team had the assault weapons with them, wherever they were.

"Captain," she said and waited at the head of the passage.

She felt Captain Kalen come up beside her. "What'd you see? Richter or someone from the other crew?"

She shook her head. "Something moved in there. Not sure what it was, but I definitely saw movement. There's something in here with us."

"Hah," came Delmont's barking laugh in her ear through the comms, "what a joke. She's jumping at her own shadow."

Tana saw the Captain about to say something, but Melodi Song beat him to it. "Shut up, Delmont, and listen." Melodi had her own bolter out as well.

All around them came small quick noises like the rustle of things scampering around them. A quick rustle there, in her right mic. Then it stopped, then it started again, but this time it was picked up by her left mic. Then another flared in both, but *above* her. Tana felt her pulse quicken and felt the familiar thumping of her heart. Rather than fighting the feeling, she felt her body preparing itself. She took a deep breath and focused. Everything seemed to move slightly slower and her senses seemed to expand.

"How far are we away from the Engineering section?" Captain Kalen asked.

"It's just up the corridor and down half a level," Melodi answered. Her voice cracked slightly.

The sounds that her suit picked up made her skin crawl. They were inexplicably *insect-like*. Quick, staccato bursts of sounds, like many legs hitting a hard surface.

"We should go back to the ship and get the hell out of here," Delmont complained. He whipped his pistol back and forth, like some action hero in a holovid.

They all turned back the way they had come. Tana knew what everyone was thinking because she was thinking it herself. None of them wanted to venture back through the long, dark corridors of the *Discordia* with those sounds of scuttling all around them.

Captain Kalen called out over the comms. "Richter? Can you hear me? If you can hear me, we're headed to Engineering to get the power back on. Be careful, there's something on this ship."

The silence on the comms was almost as unnerving as the shifting shadows in the corridor behind them.

"Got it!" Melodi Song called out. "I can have the core systems back online in about four minutes, including the phase drive." Her hands flew over several control pads in quick succession. "It's gonna' take about twenty minutes before I can stabilize her enough so that she'll enter phase space with us when we're ready to tow her." She keyed in a quick query. Several sub-nodes lit up in succession. She blew out a quick breath. "I might be able to cut it to five minutes if I bypass the lockouts. Won't promise *Discordia* will phase back in with us, though, if I do."

"Lose the lockouts, Song. I want to get back to the *Outrider* ASAP," Captain Kalen said. His gun was drawn and he twisted trying to scan into the darkness for incoming targets. The scuttling sounds had not diminished. If anything, they had increased. "I'm not liking this at all."

Tana's heart thudded, but she was in control. Her training had kicked in and she was in that zone she knew so well. The other Juniors, however, were on the verge of panic. Their shots would be wild and frantic. Tana stood behind them, well out of their line of fire.

Tana could smell the saltiness of her sweat from wearing the bulky suit, but even though there was really no need for it—the ship air was perfectly breathable—she didn't want to even consider removing it. There was a comfort to having the bulky suit. Even if it wasn't a true combat suit, it gave her an illusion of protection, at least. And that was all it truly was. The illusion. She'd learned it again and again. Feeling safe was an illusion. She'd learned that the moment her parents had died. The beatings, the feeling of hunger pains so unbearable that they bent you over, the anger at being left alone in the world, had all reinforced Tana's world view. Life was not fair. You had to fight back. You fought to survive, you fought to achieve, you fought to live, and sometimes unfairly, you fought even though you still died...as one of her foster brothers had found out. at the hands of a roving station gang. The key was to fight and not to stop fighting. Not for one moment.

Somehow, she was certain that Richter and his team were dead, and that the things behind the sounds were behind it. She was just as sure that she was going to have to fight once again.

Bring it, she thought, keeping her bolter low and ready.

"Jansen," Melodi Song said, "boot up the Control Module and let's see what we've got."

Jansen keyed a couple of commands into the Command Matrix and suddenly the power spiked. The drives spun up. The ship began to lurch as the spin was enabled and grav was restored. There was a high pitched screech as if thousands of mouths suddenly cried out.

The lights flickered on.

Tana, despite her training, felt her eyes widen. There were thousands of the spider-like creatures in the room. They filled every nook around Phase Drives and any of the control matrices and nodes connected with the drives. They looked quite a bit like spiders, except for their prismatic metallic skin that reflected, rainbow-like, under the harsh Engineering lights. Unlike spiders, they had ten legs, five on each side, and when they scuttled sideways, like Old Earth crabs, they resembled disembodied human hands.

Hundreds of them were standing over the desiccated corpses of Richter, his crew, and many of the apparent crew of the *Discordia*

One scuttled toward Jansen and he jerked backwards. He slipped on an exposed bit of cable and landed hard on his behind. As the spider-thing scurried towards him with its mouth wide, making that awful keening screech, Jansen scooted backwards trying to get away.

Delmont ran.

As the creature scuttled forward, its body flared brightly as if it burned with an inner light, then it went intangible, not quite invisible, but transparent enough to slightly see through. It repeated the process twice, each time flaring brighter and becoming more intangible. Then it disappeared entirely. There was an audible gasp on Tana's mics.

Almost as if she were back in Ship-to-Ship Combat Theory class, her mind's eye plotted the exact reemergence point of the spider-like creature. They were phasing, just like starships, on a straight-line vector. Having seen more than a million possible combinations during her time earning her Pilot's license, she could see exactly where the creature's phase vector would take it. Right inside Jansen's faceplate.

Tana tried to scream out another warning, but it was too late. The Laws of Quantum Mechanics, Newtonian Physics, Relativity and Fuzzy Phase States all conspired against her. Before her vocal chords could utter a sound, the spider-thing reemerged right where her mind had predicted it would, inside Jansen's faceplate.

Jansen screamed, thrashed, and clawed at the faceplate as the creature tore bloody chunks of flesh from his face.

Without thinking, Tana began firing at any spider moving towards her that flared brightly. Her shots unerringly hit their marks. The Captain had begun to do the same while screaming at the others to fire.

The other Juniors lost it. They began firing indiscriminately. Their shots tore through controls, systems, and dedicated simulation terminals, pretty much hitting anything *except* the spiders scuttling towards them.

Within seconds, spiders flashed all around. The juniors were down in almost no time. Bile rose in Tana's throat as she watched more and more spiders phase into the exosuits of the three juniors. They fell to the floor, thrashing like puppets with their strings being jerked wildly, while bulges surged and scuttled underneath their suits and blood leaked out.

Tana exchanged a quick glance with the captain. There were too many. Sooner or later, if they didn't move, they were going to end up like Jansen and the other juniors. He nodded and covered her. His shots kept the creatures at bay.

Song reached out to the lifeless face of her apprentice. Tana grabbed Song roughly by the arm and spun her around towards the door.

Out of the corner of her eye, Tana saw a creature scuttling directly towards herself. It was in the final stages of phasing. She didn't have enough time to train her gun. Her blood thundered in ears. It phased. Its movement was familiar enough to her to cause her to duck. Sure enough, the thing emerged in mid-air right where her head would have been.

With the grav back on, the thing was beginning to fall towards her. She brought up her bolter and squeezed off four shots, three of which connected. Each bolt tore through the silvery metallic body and exploded on impact. The spider-thing splattered to the deck, dead and unmoving. Greenish bile-like blood flowed weakly from its lifeless body.

Something in her mind clicked.

"Back to the *Outrider*!" Captain Kalen yelled. "Move!"

They tore back down the corridors of the *Discordia,* filled with shrieking, scuttling figures, firing every time one of the creatures began to move forward and start to phase. Not every spider phased. There didn't seem to be any rhyme or reason, but all of those that phased scuttled towards them first.

About halfway back to the ship, Tana saw one of the spidery creatures scrambling along the corridor's ceiling above them. It leapt toward the Captain and began phasing in mid-air. With absolute certainty, Tana knew where it was going to reappear.

"Duck!" she called out to the Captain, but he was too busy firing at a clutch of phasing spiders to hear her. The Captain screamed as he went down.

Senior Engineer Song cried out and tried to help the Captain, but Tana wrenched her along mercilessly. The Captain was already dead, other spidery creatures moving towards his body, phasing. Soon his corpse would join the others on this graveyard of a ship. Tana was determined that her and Song's bodies would *not* join them.

Heart racing, Tana pulled the Senior Engineer along. Tana's teeth were clenched as she scanned ahead, behind, and all around trying to make sure none of the creatures had a vector on her.

She bobbed and weaved like a drunk fighter trying to make her movements as unpredictable as possible. Song mimicked her movements, but the older Engineer's own weaving form was stiffer, less sure than Tana's lithe movements.

Somehow, someway, these spider-like creatures, these "Phase-Spiders" had evolved an ability to phase in and out of Newtonian space in the same way that starships traveled the stars. Phase Drives worked by twisting space, curving it upon itself until it created a wormhole-like effect. The energies for creating a wormhole were enormous, but the same effect could be initiated at the Quantum level, where the energy cost was much lower.   Once initiated, Phase Drives would effectively check the current "spin" of the atoms near it and at the transit point and "pull" the ship forward. A truism in Quantum Mechanics was that you could know the speed, but not the direction, or you could know the direction and not the speed. The only way around that was two fixed points: entry and terminus. Once you knew where it entered, you knew where it had to exit.

The Ship to Ship Weapon Systems class had included practice with ships in Phase states. Tana had become an expert at calculating terminus points in her battle simulation course. No curves, parabolas, and most importantly, no changes to velocity. Once the Phase Spider entered into its phase state, Tana's mind instantly plotted its exit point back into real space.

With her mind calculating various phase points for the incoming creatures, Tana drove them forward. Those spiders she could, she blasted before they entered their phase states, and for those that she could not blast, she dodged.

There! she thought, as she rounded the corner and saw the *Outrider's* docking boom clamped to the *Discordia. And no spiders!*

As she started to turn to Melodi Song, a face appeared in the *Outrider's* docking bay. Delmont.

Claxons began sounding. The boom was being disengaged!

Tana had seconds or they both were going to die.

She could make it back to the ship on her own, but not dragging Song. She could just leave Song. That thought flashed in her mind. No! Something flared in her like a sun burning hot and bright. She'd already lost one mother, her real one. She would not lose this one! She would *not!*

But the cold law of inertia told her that she could not make it back to the ship half-holding, half-dragging the engineer along.

Summoning up all ruthlessness, Tana keyed her mic.

"Stay alive!" she yelled at the wide-eyed Song and shoved Song back into *Discordia's* airlock and took off at full speed toward the closing doorway. She dove and slid.

She hit the *Outrider's* inner hull corridor with a thud, just as the hatch slammed down, missing her boots by mere inches.

She was up in a flash. From the *Outrider's* hatch viewport, Tana could see the Senior Engineer's wide eyes and could almost hear her screams as she tugged in futile desperation at the *Discordia's* airlock.

There was a half screech and sob from Song's comms and the face disappeared from the viewport. About a second later, two spidery creatures phased into view. They scuttled after her.

Tana slammed her fist on the bulkhead over and over, hot tears running down her cheeks like a broken-hearted child.

"Stay bloody alive, damn you!" she screamed into the comms.

There was no reply.

Tana finished keying in the code for the Ghost Protocol and turned from her station to face Delmont and the remaining members of the crew. They must have thought she was prepping the engines to leave. *Well*, she thought, *they're about to get a nasty surprise*.

Delmont seemed to believe that he was in charge. "So, that's it? Can we go now?" he asked, once she was finished.

She looked him directly in the eye. "Yes. Just as soon as I go back over and get Engineer Song."

He exploded, just as she had expected. "Are you out of your stupid mind? The old biddy's long dead by now! It's been what, ten minutes? No way she could have dodged those things that long."

"Yeah, well, you'd know, wouldn't you?" she said, her lip pulling into the same sneer that had been so effective for her as a teenager. "You lasted all of three seconds before you cut and ran like a little girl."

Delmont turned several shades of red. "I'm the Ranking Officer aboard this ship now," he bellowed. "And as your Commanding Officer, I demand that you get us underway right now!"

Tana jerked her head to the *Discordia*. "My former Commanding Officer is dead over there. My current Commanding Officer is still alive, otherwise the computer wouldn't have accepted her code, so you're not my C.O."

"Fine, you little snot. If you want to get yourself killed, be my guest. We can pilot this thing out of here using the ship's A.I."

"No, you can't. I've activated the lockout code. This ship isn't going anywhere without my counter code. Good luck with that."

She turned to leave the bridge.

A hand grasped her shoulder. "Why you little..." Delmont began, but Tana didn't give him time to finish.

She elbowed him in the ribs, and heard the satisfying *woosh* of his breath leaving his lungs. She spun, grasped his forearm with one hand, and his hand with her other. She applied pressure and bent his hand back until he was on his knees. She kept applying it until the inevitable happened and his wrist broke.

She let go and watched him writhe on the ground. Her face seemed devoid of all emotion.

"I'm getting Old Mother Song back," she said, not recognizing her own voice. She sounded dead inside. She knew she *would* be dead inside if Song somehow died before Tana could get to her. She turned to the rest of the crew. "It would also be unwise to try to stop me."

She left the bridge to refill her air and ammo.

Sweat rained down her neck as Tana fought through the Phase Spiders. She had reestablished the docking boom and enabled the lockout on it as well. She'd used Melodi's code, so there was no chance that Delmont or any of the crew could trap her again. Now she just had to stay alive herself.

"Melody!" she called out, "Head for Engineering. You've got to get the power off! I'll meet you there!"

She popped off shot after shot knowing that time was of the essence. She moved quickly, but not so quickly that she didn't take time to scan all directions.

Tana felt so stupid. The phase spiders had become agitated when the phase engines were activated. If the engines were deactivated, chances were good that they'd stop attacking. If they had just shut down the engines immediately, the captain, and maybe even the three juniors from Environmental, might still be alive.

Stop it, she snarled at herself. She was alive. Song was still alive...Tana had heard her sawing breath in reply. She just had to reach her in time.

When she got to the Engineering section, Tana was almost sick inside her exosuit. While she had luckily missed the corpse of the Captain, the corpses of the Juniors were plain to see. Their bodies were freshly chewed and great hunks of flesh and organs had been ripped from them. Their eyes stared up and their mouths were frozen in a rictus of soundless horror.

There was Old Mother Song! She was bent over the Control Matrix inputting commands.

Tana was about to call out when she noticed a phase spider scuttling towards Song and it was already phasing. A vision of Captain Kalen flashed through Tana's mind. "No!" she screamed and fired, but the shot was too late. It had already phased.

Song hit the Control Module then screamed as a bulge appeared in the side of her exosuit. Song went down and grasped at her side. The lights began to dim.

Tana had one chance—once the lights went out, there was no way she could see to make the shot. She focused on that small bulge quivering inside Song's suit, snapped the gun up before Song had a chance to writhe, and fired.

The lights went dark. Tana waited for the inevitable death in the surrounding darkness, but the sounds of the phase spiders quieted. Tana stood in complete darkness waiting for her death or for Song to expire from being shot. Tana knew that she would die from either outcome, one a physical death and the other a spiritual death. The faces of her mother and father seemed to swim in front of her face.

A moan from the corner brought Tana back to her senses. She turned and shined a light. Melodi winced. Tana looked down and saw that Melodi's right hand cradled her side, blood seeping from a deep gash of torn flesh beneath the hole in her suit.

Melodi opened her eyes and whispered. "You left me."

"Sorry. I had to."

"Why?"

Tana wasn't sure what she meant. *Why did you leave me, or, why did you come back for me?* In the end, it seemed to be the same question.

"Delmont cut us off," she said, as she gingerly lifted the injured engineer to her feet, looking around with the light the entire time. Now that the engines were not on, the spiders seemed to ignore them, although a few eyed them.

"I knew I could make it, but not with you. I had to come back for you. I *had* to." Tana couldn't say any more. Her throat closed. How could she tell this woman that her simple kindness was more than appreciated, it was needed? How could she tell her that she'd already lost one mother and had no intention of losing another one?

She hoisted Song up gingerly and they both moved out of the Engineering section back down the corridor. Melodi's arm was slung around Tana's shoulder for support and the engineer winced with every step. Tana, for her part, bore the burden of the engineer's weight, knowing that she would have precious little time to react if one of those phase spiders attacked.

The phase engines seemed to be the key, as they made it back to the ship without any further problems.

"Do me a favor and put that thing out of its misery," Song said, once they were safely back to the *Outrider.*

Tana gave her best salute. "Yes, ma'am."

She went to the bridge, entered the counter-code and fired up the weapon systems.

She backed off the *Outrider* to an acceptable distance and fired. Although it was primarily used for salvage, the *Outrider* was essentially an up-gunned frigate capable of dealing with anything up to a cruiser, if necessary. Its guns and missiles soon made short work of the large and ponderous mining ship.

Tana keyed the correct systems and Phase Drive came online. With a simple command, the *Outrider* phased out and Tana breathed deeply.

When Engineer Song—no, Captain Song—came back to the bridge, Tana made a quick report.

"Just so you know," Captain Song said, "Delmont's entered a formal complaint against you."

Tana's felt her jaw tighten, but before she could reply, she saw the Captain's mouth quirk into a smile.

"Of course," she continued, "seeing how he was the one who popped the boom and tried to trap us both on that ship, I've already given him his notice. He will be crewing on another ship as soon as we make berth. So, as Captain of the *Outrider*, I find his complaint has no merit as he is technically no longer a member of this crew."

Tana saw Song's smile widen and felt a grin light up her own face in reply. She was going to enjoy piloting the *Outrider* under Captain Song's leadership.

Sidney Blaylock, Jr. is a Science Fiction and Fantasy writer as well as a Sixth Grade Language Arts Teacher. He lives in Chattanooga, Tennessee. He has worked previously as a Library Assistant in the Reference/Information and Popular Materials Department of the Chattanooga Public Library, an Adjunct Instructor of English at the University of Tennessee at Chattanooga, and a Bookseller for Waldenbooks (where he bought many Science Fiction & Fantasy novels before they sadly went out of business).
You can find a complete listing of his works on his blog at http://www.sidneyblaylockjr.wordpress.com.

Sammy is a spacehound. Chased by Empire Patrol, Sammy finds himself in a very strange place—the Great Empty—a location where very few people dare go. This time, he may have gone out too far.

THE GREAT EMPTY

By

Preston Dennett

"Empire patrol are in view," said Zora with annoying calmness. I leaned forward and stared with anger at the viewscreen. It was patrol all right, a whole herd of them. I thought of all the laws I had broken, the borders I had crossed illegally, the fake certificates. I had to get out of there. I was surprised to encounter patrol way out along Karren, one of the few inhabited worlds situated along the edge of the Big Empty. Usually they weren't out this far. Before they could get a lock on me, I did what any spacehound would do: I jumped.

Right into the Big Empty. Forget everything you've heard or read or seen about it. Unless you actually go out there, you'll never know what it's like. It's more than just the fact that there are no stars out there, no dust, no radiation, just a vast nothingness. This is the bleeding edge of the Universe we're talking about. There is nothing out here. Until you find yourself in it, you can't know.

Looking out at it, I felt a wave of loneliness and despair sweep over me. What had I done? Why had I come out here? I knew Zora would be fine with it, but Viola was not going to be happy.

Right on cue, her small frame appeared in the doorway of the control room. Don't be fooled. She may be small, but every atom of her is packed with energy. Viola was born on Anfor, a pre-industrial edge planet. She is black-skinned, five feet tall and beautifully proportioned. Of

151

course, I am in love with her. Don't worry, she knows. I've made it very clear to her. Unfortunately, she has also made it clear that she's not interested. I don't get it. I think I'm a great catch.

"How dare you?" she yelled. "The Big Empty? Really? This is where you decide to take us? You said the deal at Karren was a sure thing. In fact, I seem to remember you promised. Now you run away and take us out here. Sammy, people die out here! This is crazy."

"Hey, give me a break!" I said. "We were being pursued. What was I supposed to do? I had to retreat. The place was crawling with patrol. There was no way we were going to get through."

"You know, Sammy, you've changed. Time was, a couple of patrol wouldn't send you running away. When I signed on with you, it was because you had a reputation for not running away. Yeah, I knew who you were. You don't think it was an accident that I knew so much about Zora, do you? I studied her line for a long time. It wasn't a coincidence that we met; I sought you out. I used to look up to you, Sammy. But lately, it's like you've given up." She looked at me with her large dark eyes, waiting for an answer.

When I remained silent, she stomped over to me and jabbed me in the shoulder. "The Big Empty? Really?" she repeated.

I spread my hands. I didn't tell Viola that it wasn't just one patrol that had spotted us, it was several. I didn't tell her how low I was on funds, and that unless something changed, I wouldn't be able to pay her. I didn't tell her Zora was about to be repossessed, or that we were wanted by half of the Empire worlds. "This is why I don't do trading deals," I said. "I'm a spacehound. I should be out there digging for Corlian artifacts, not running away from patrol."

"Well, we're not going to find anything out here," she said. "That's assuming we even make it back." She glared at me, then looked outside and shivered slightly.

"We'll get back," I said. "I don't know why you're so upset. This is not our first time out here."

She pointed outside. "Not this far, Sammy. You have to know how dangerous this is."

"At least we got away from patrol."

Viola looked at me with wide eyes. She clenched her fists and for a second, I thought she was going to hit me. Instead, she rolled her eyes at me and turned to look out the viewport.

Outside was nothing but utter blackness and one small white dot. It was hard to convince myself of it, but that one dot represented the entire known universe. The whole Big Bang. I doubt that Carpenter had any idea that his invention of the jump drive would lead to this level of exploration, all the way to the very edge of the universe and beyond, into the Great Nothing. Of course, way back then people could only speculate about the edge of the universe. They probably couldn't even conceive of actually traveling there.

Now, I'm not a particularly religious person, but every time I'm in the Big Black and I see that tiny white dot, I feel a little shiver run up my spine. You can't see something like that and not wonder what it all means. Or if there's any other white dots out there.

As I sat there in the control room staring at the white dot, pondering my fate and wondering how to soothe Viola and what to do next, a warning buzzer flashed on my console.

Viola looked up at me sharply.

It was the gravity indicator. The sensors had detected a gravitational field. Out here? I wondered, mystified.

"Zora," I said, "What the hell is going on?"

"A moment, please," said Zora, with her vaguely English accent. She sounded baffled. Zora was incredibly smart, with access to a lot of data. For her to take this long to answer was very unusual.

"It is a large mass of some kind," she said finally. "I have no reference. This is new data, Captain. One moment."

I shook my head with frustration. Zora sometimes has an annoying tendency to state the obvious. "What is it?" I asked, scanning my console. There were no electromagnetic readings of any kind.

"It's a black hole," she said. "I have activated the gravity shields."

"How can it be a black hole?" Every spacehound knew that even black-holes emit radiation and are easily detectable; we made our living digging up the Corlian treasures that had fallen into the gravity wells of black holes across the galaxies.

"Most black-holes are fed with new matter, Captain. Out here in the Great Empty, it has nothing to pull inside it."

"Are you certain?" I asked.

"That is my current assessment, Captain."

"Are you sure it's empty?" I knew the chances were small that there'd be anything way out here, but I'd hate to pass up a chance to make a big score.

"No, Captain. I cannot be certain unless we go deeper. I believe we have already fallen deeply into its well. I am sorry, Sammy, I should have detected it sooner. I had no reference. I am still in the process of analysis."

"Don't worry about it," I said. It was what made the Big Empty so dangerous. With no reference, it was almost impossible to tell where you were or if you were moving.

"A black hole? Are you sure, Zora?" asked Viola. "I mean, this place could be playing tricks on your sensors."

"I'm sure. Are we going deeper in, Captain?"

"Yes, Zora. Take us in, but slowly and carefully. And please keep an eye on the shields. We're pretty far out. I don't want anything to go wrong." Zora was a Carpenter Ship, and with her gravity drives she was able to move safely beyond the event horizon, the so-called point of no return from the gravity wells of black holes. However, even the gravity drives had their limits.

"Don't worry, Captain. I'm always careful."

I was surprised that Viola hadn't returned to the bottom of the ship. It was very unusual for her to be in the control room with me, but I wasn't about to order her to leave. I learned long ago, you don't order Viola to do anything. Besides, I kind of liked having her there.

"Good news, Captain. There's quite a bit in there . I detect several ships, but I am unable to identify the types. They are too deep in. Only one of them is still within the recovery boundary. It appears to be one of Corlian construction. Shall I attempt contact?"

"Do you mean it's still active?" I asked, looking at Viola with surprise. Was that a hint of a smile on her face?

"Yes, Captain. I'm reading life signs and multiple electromagnetic signatures."

"Yes, Zora," I said. "Make contact. And give us a visual."

I turned to Viola. "Can you believe this? A live alien craft! This is huge."

Viola was staring at the screen. "No, Sammy. It can't be. Look."

I stared in amazement. The alien ship was in perfect condition. I had only seen old hulks and wrecks. This ship was brand new. It was roughly the same size as Zora, just a small cruiser. But there were windows, and they were all lit up. I felt a thrill down my spine.

"Contact established, Captain," said Zora. "I am now in communication with the ship's computer. We have agreed to trade all our data. I presume that's acceptable, Captain."

"Yes, of course," I said.

"Are you crazy?" said Viola. "You're just going to tell them everything about us?"

"Yes," I said. "And they're telling us about them. Do you realize how valuable that information is? The entire human race has been wondering who the Corlians are...what happened to them. And we're going to be the first to find out."

"Not if they kill us first."

"They're not hostile."

"You don't know that for sure."

"Obviously, or Zora would have warned us. Right, Zora?"

"Of course, Captain. Actually, it was my idea, and it took quite a bit of convincing. They are considerably more advanced than Humans. They have concerns about your hostility."

"Ha, told you," I said. "How long will it take for you to exchange information?"

"We're finished, Captain. The Corlians are currently examining the data I sent them."

"Give me a short version of who the aliens are and what they are doing here. Oh, and I'd like a visual of what they look like."

The screen flashed and Viola gasped. I admit I had trouble believing my eyes. The aliens looked like weird cactus-like plants with a huge bulbous head covered with strange-looking protuberances. Eyes, I guessed. So much for the humanoid shape the scientists had insisted upon. The Corlians looked more like asparagus.

Zora explained that the Corlians had spread across the universe and found no evidence of other intelligent species. Skeptical that they were truly alone in the universe, they continued searching. Then finally humans were discovered. Because of our violent tendencies, they kept a close eye on us. When the Carpenter Drive was invented, they knew it was only a matter of time before humans would encounter them. And so, they decided to evacuate and find a safer place, free from the dangers posed by humans. They removed nearly all traces of themselves, leaving nothing but bits and pieces of junk. Those bits and pieces, I thought, had started the whole Spacehound industry. Old wrecks, tools, ruins of buildings...and lots of other stuff nobody understood—all of it left behind by the mysterious Corlians. They may have found it useless, but many humans were willing to pay a lot of money for a Corlian artifact.

Zora explained that the Corlians fled to the Great Empty because they knew of this black hole. With their superior ships, they were able to travel through them to a new universe. They left a few ships at the event horizon to keep watch, just in case humans should try to follow them. Those were the ships Zora had detected deeper in the hole.

"It's all in my files," Zora explained. "You can peruse it at your leisure. But I warn you, much of it is beyond my current understanding. In any case, we must leave shortly as we are within danger of crossing the recovery boundary. If we continue further into the gravity well, I cannot guarantee that we will get out. The Corlians are thanking us for the trade. I have already thanked them back."

This was all happening too quickly. I looked over at Viola. She was sitting at the console going through the Corlian files. I peered over her shoulder. She was studying the alien ships.

She saw me and flashed a rare smile. "They're amazing, Sammy. These ships can do anything. Compared to ours, I mean. They're much faster. And you can forget about recovery boundaries."

"Impressive," I said. "Hey, with Zora's memories, maybe we can even build one."

"That would be quite impossible, Captain, and is considerably beyond human capacities at this time. I can guide the process, but it will take a few hundred years."

"Okay, so they're advanced," I snorted. "I get it."

"Captain, we really must leave. I am taking us out."

"Thank you, Zora." Both Viola and I watched the screen as the Corlian ship began to recede.

I looked over at Viola and smiled. "Well, we did it. The big find."

Strangely, Viola seemed sad.

"What's the matter, Vi? This is huge. We're gonna be rich. This is what we've been waiting for. We don't have to worry anymore."

"So you're selling out, then? You're going to quit?" Viola's lower lip quivered and her eyes began to shine with tears.

"What are you talking about? Of course, not. I could never leave Zora. I love being a spacehound. I love being out here."

Viola smiled with relief. "Really? You don't know how glad I am to hear you say that, Sammy. I could kiss you."

Then Zora spoke up. "Captain?"

"Not now, Zora!" Damn that Zora! Couldn't she see that Viola was about to kiss me?

"Captain, it's very important."

Viola smiled coyly and said, "Go ahead, Zora. The Captain is listening."

"Before we leave, the Corlians have decided that they would like to offer you an opportunity."

Viola's beautiful eyes widened and focused on me. I smiled and raised my eyebrows. "Oh, yeah?" I asked Zora. "What kind of opportunity?"

"They would like to trade ships."

"Yes!" shouted Viola. "Tell them yes!"

"I already have," announced Zora.

"What?" I asked. "No way! Viola, you don't even know how to pilot a Corlian ship. And you, Zora! How could you? After all we've been through together? There's no way I'm going to trade you. Tell them no. I'm not leaving you."

"But Captain, I have ascertained a 98 percent probability that you would say yes. You don't have all the information."

"I don't care! I won't do it. You can't leave me."

"Captain, you don't understand. I'm not going to leave you. I can download myself into the Corlian ship. I can transfer myself entirely. I'm not going anywhere."

"Well, you didn't say that," I said, only slightly mollified. "Wait," I asked. "What's in it for them? No offense, Zora, but compared to their ship, you're a little primitive."

"They wish to study humans, Captain, and, suspecting that humans have many questions about them, they have given their ship as a gift."

"Aren't they worried that we'll follow them?" I asked. "I mean, humans are still a tiny bit hostile." The understatement of the year.

"No, Captain. It was pure chance that we were able to locate this black hole. It will be impossible to find once we return from the Black."

"Well, if they want to trade ships," I said. "And you're still coming with us, I guess I'd consider it."

"Then we're doing it?" Viola asked, looking at me expectantly.

"Are you sure you want to do this?" I asked her. "We've worked so hard on this ship. You're not even the least bit sentimental?"

"Pshaw!" said Viola. "Besides, just think what we could do with one of their ships. No recovery boundary, Sammy, think of it! Think of all those black holes out there, just waiting to be excavated. Who knows what's inside them."

"Are you sure, Zora?" I asked. "You won't leave me?"

"I would never leave you, Sammy," said Zora.

Viola rolled her eyes. "Do you two need me to leave?"

I glared at Viola. Maybe it was easy for her to give up the ship, but it wasn't for me. Zora was all I had ever known. And yes, she would come with us, but it wouldn't be the same in a different ship.

Annoyingly, as usual, Viola was right. With a Corlian ship, the possibilities were endless. All those black holes out there filled with who knew what kinds of treasures. Zora and Viola knew me too well. Of course I was going to say yes. Still, I wish they would have consulted me first, and at least give me the illusion that I'm in charge.

"Fine," I said. "Tell them we'll trade ships."

"Oh!" Viola squealed. To my utter astonishment, she jumped up, threw her arms around me and planted a kiss right on my mouth.

I promptly turned bright red. "Hey, what's that for?"

"That," said Viola, "is for not running away. You took a chance, Sammy. I'm proud of you."

"So all I have to do to get a kiss is give you a working Corlian ship?"

"It helps," she said smiling. She rose and began to exit the cabin. "I have some things to pack."

I waited until she was gone and then spoke to Zora. "I think she loves me, Zora," I said.

"Would you like me to give you the probability of this, Captain?"

I laughed. "No, Zora. Some things are better left a mystery. Now tell me more about this Corlian ship. What can it do?"

"You're going to love it, Captain. Let me start with how fast it can go."

I only half-listened. Instead, I was thinking about what people would think when Viola and I showed up with a working Corlian craft. All those worlds that had banned us would be begging for us to visit. Everyone would want access to our files. And this was only the beginning. With a Corlian ship, we could recover all kinds of artifacts that were inaccessible before. And I would be the most famous and successful spacehound in history.

Even better than that, I had just gotten my first kiss from Viola. The first of many, I was quite certain.

I leaned back in my chair, stared at the screen and watched the Corlian ship approach.

Preston Dennett has worked as a carpet cleaner, fast-food worker, data entry clerk, bookkeeper, landscaper, singer, actor, writer, radio host, TV consultant, teacher, UFO researcher, ghost hunter and more, but his favorite job is writing speculative fiction stories and books about UFOs and the paranormal. He has sold dozens of stories to various venues including Andromeda Spaceways, Black Treacle, Cast of Wonders, Grievous Angel, The Future Embodied *anthology,* Perihelion, Sci-Phi Journal, The Haunted by the Past *anthology,* Stupefying Stories, T. Gene Davis's Speculative Blog *and many others. He has earned eleven honorable mentions in the* Writers of the Future Contest, *and has also written eighteen non-fiction books and more than 100 articles. He spends his days looking for new ways to pay his bills, and his nights exploring the farthest reaches of the Universe. He currently resides in a crowded suburb outside of Los Angeles, CA.*

<u>*Speculative Fiction Stories by Preston Dennett*</u>
"Next!" *(reprint)* ~ Digital Fiction
"QuickFic" (forthcoming)
"Footprints on the Moon" (Reality Skimming Press) *(forthcoming)*
"Forbidden" ~ Sci-Phi Journal *(forthcoming)*
"No Good Deed" ~ Alternate Hilarities 5: One Star Reviews of the Afterlife
"Korba's Revenge" ~ Stupefying Stories *(forthcoming)*
"Stars Are Wild" ~ The Colored Lens, *(Spring 2016)*
"Tulpa" ~ Haunted by the Past, *(February 2016)*
"Valerie" ~ Frostfire Worlds, *(February 2016)*

"Reflection" ~ 4Star Stories, *Issue 16, 2016*
"Eye for an Eye" ~ Strange Changes *anthology, 2015*
"Sampson's Moon" ~ Silver Blade, *Summer 2015, Issue 27*
"Eyes of Fire" ~ Grievous Angel, *August 9, 2015*
"Dark Roast" ~ Coffee, Hot! *anthology, August 2015*
"Cloudburst" ~ Broken Worlds *anthology, July 2015*
"The Backwards Man" ~ T. Gene Davis's Speculative Fiction Blog, *June 2015*
"Go Fish!" ~ Kzine, *May 2015*
"Dust" ~ Allegory, *Spring/Summer 2015*
"Storm of Chance" ~ Bards and Sages Quarterly, *April 2015*
"The Caretaker"s ~ Frostfire Worlds, *February 2015*
"Wild, Wild Humans" ~ Faed Anthology, *February 2015*
"The Laughing Tree" ~ Liquid Imagination, *November 2014*
"The Phobos Monolith" ~ Cast of Wonders, *July 2014, Episode 130*
"Salvage Yard" (cover story!) ~ Andromeda Spaceways #59, *June 2014*
"Enter a Human" ~ Andromeda Spaceways #59, *June 2014*
"Len" ~ Black Treacle, *April 2014*
"Tears, Not of a Child" ~ Future Embodied *anthology, 2014*
"Next!" ~ Perihelion, *February 2014*
"Zombie" (cover story!) ~ Encounters Magazine, *2013, Vol 9*
"Can You Spare a Dollar?" ~ Aurora Wolf, *October 2013*
"The Dream Collection Center" (1st place winner!) ~ Midnight Zoo, *1994, Vol 4, Issue #1*

Travelling between stars is a journey of generations, not years. For their mission to succeed, 300 people aboard the space vessel Township must fulfill one self-evident assignment: procreate. But finding a suitable partner is no simple matter, particularly when the long-term isolation of deep space wears on the mind of a shy introvert named Mark.

PERCHANCE TO DREAM

By

Timothy Paul

Mark Averill shook his head clear, poured a cup of water from the insta-hot into his coffee maker and mumbled a disoriented curse. "The nightmare continues." *Did he say that out loud?*

Watching the black brew drip through a filter, he reflected on his childhood and recalled his last look at the rings of Saturn rising on Titan. He was eighteen when the enclosed city *Township* left the Solar system. How many standard years had passed since the tiered ship began its acceleration toward Alpha Centauri? Out here, chronometers only monitored time to provide a sense of order. Calendars, in the sense of charting the seasons, were meaningless, and concepts of day or night had faded long ago.

When his parents and sister died in a shuttle accident, Mark applied for the Alpha Centauri mission and was one of a very few who were recruited, while over twelve thousand applicants were rejected from consideration. Township Alpha-C would be the first attempt to cross between stars, and those chosen for colonization represented every ethnic group and nearly all of the 237 nations spread out across the solar system. No couples had survived the rigorous screening, yet over 300 people set out on the massive transport for an adventure that would see their great-grandchildren establish roots around a new sun–assuming the travelers found compatible mates along the way.

With a steaming mug in hand, Mark paced around his four-room habital. "It just keeps going," he mumbled. "Need to tell someone." Yet even as he said it, he cringed. Opening up to people was not something he did well. He downed a quick breakfast, dashed off to the engineering staff room and spent his entire shift debating whether or not to burden his new friend further with his continuing dream.

An introvert by nature, Mark's budding friendship with a shy, middle-eastern woman began about the only way it could have...entirely by accident. Several days earlier, the two had been gathering supplies in the harvest zones. With arms loaded and other things on their minds, neither paid any attention to the unexpected traffic jam at a scantly-used intersection. The resulting collision sent rice and beans down four separate corridors. Five minutes of frantic cleaning and embarrassed apologies had led to dinner and a cordial friendship. He smiled, thinking about the awkwardness of that first meeting and how they had grown close in the intervening days. Or had it been weeks?

Lost in his introspective dilemma, his shift passed, and he stood outside his friend's unit, still debating how much he would tell her as she opened her door. "Hi, Lalani," he greeted.

A wide smile spread across her face. "Hello, Mark," she said.

The familiar warmth in her eyes accentuated her greeting and for a moment, pushed aside all thoughts of his dream.

She reached out, took his hand and pulled him inside. "Dinner is ready."

Having little appetite, he picked at the organic stew in his bowl and stared as she dipped her spoon into the steaming broth. Trying to forget his troubles, he studied the decorative figures on her pantry shelf. He always loved the easy conversation they shared, but tonight he struggled to find anything to say. The pink walls of her dining space made him more anxious, and she seemed to notice his discomfort.

As if reading his thoughts, Lalani poked through his uncertainty. "I take it you had another restless night?"

"I'm sorry," he said. "I don't mean to...it's just unsettling. It's like a novel. You read a chapter, you set the book down, then you pick it up again at the next chapter. Dreams aren't supposed to do that."

"Hmmm. Well, the last chapter you told me about had something to do with radiation shields. So is this more about the shields, or some new problem?"

"More of the same," Mark complained. "At first it was just tedious, working through each detail of the repairs, helping technicians into enviro-suits. Talking them through the inspection grid once they're through the airlock. Inch by inch, they went over the hull until it was time for the next shift to go out."

"Sounds boring."

"On one level, yes. But it's hard to watch people dangle on a tether outside the ship when you're the one responsible for keeping them alive." Mark stopped short, still wondering if he should tell her the whole story.

Lalani poured him a fresh cup of decaffeinated tea, a rare commodity. "So, you're tense all through your sleep cycle?"

"I wake up feeling like I haven't had a minute's rest."

"You probably haven't." She dipped a spoon into her broth and took a bite. Her expression suggested she was deep in thought. "Mark, I know there are things the command team keeps confidential. Are there any mission-related issues you've been assigned that might trigger this dream?"

"Nothing. Not that I've been told about." He saw the doubt in her expression. "Really."

"Engineering's a critical function," she said. "Everyone aboard depends on you and your team to keep us safe. Maybe you're working through a worst-case scenario in your subconscious. I think the dream will stop after some crisis has played out in your mind. If you can identify what that might be, maybe that will put an end to it."

"Dream or no dream," he said. "There's a lot of things that could go wrong with this ship. I'm an engineer," he muttered. "I'm supposed to fix it all."

Lalani quietly folded her napkin and set it on the table.

"Sorry. I'm frustrated. I don't mean to take it out on you."

"I understand, Mark. But I think you should try to figure out why you're having the dreams to begin with." She began clearing away the dinnerware. "Maybe some time on the treadmill would give you an outlet."

He bowed his head and sighed.

She frowned. "Something is on your mind and you don't want to tell me. That's not okay. We're friends and I want to help, if I can. So tell me what happened this time that's made you so tense."

"My shift partner, Stephenson."

"Nicole?"

"You know her?" asked Mark.

"I've seen her a few times in the vegetable gardens."

Mark nodded. "I watched her die last night."

Lalani pulled her chair close and placed a hand on his forearm. "Mark, I'm so sorry."

"It was the end of a shift. She was helping a techy out of his suit. The guy had radiation burns along the whole side of his face. She was reaching for the treatment kit when he fell into her." Mark put his hand over his eyes and pushed into the sockets until the pressure was too much. "She fell against a tool rack. There was a trowel. It went straight into her heart."

"It was a dream."

"I know. It just seemed so real."

"How was the technician?"

"Corpsman said he had some serious burns, but should be okay."

Tapping a button on her wrist pad, Lalani said, "Nicole Stephenson."

After a brief moment, a sleepy-sounding voice answered. "Ensign Stephenson."

"Hi Nicole. This is Lalani Nayar. I'm looking for Mark Averill and wondered if you'd seen him since your shift ended."

"Sorry. I came back to my quarters and went straight to bed. Alone," she added, as if she felt a need to clarify something.

"Okay, thanks. Sorry to bother you."

Nicole disconnected without signing off. Relieved to know she was alive and well, Mark took in a deep breath. "Thank you, Lalani."

Like a poorly written denouement, or the lull at the end of a roller coaster simulation, the next few minutes were filled with an uncertain silence. Both he and his friend were avid readers and enjoyed discussing the classics from the past three centuries, so they settled into synopsizing their latest books. Genre was no obstacle to either of them, and a debate over which of the Bronte sisters was the superior writer lightened the evening.

"How would you feel about a glass of wine and a movie?" asked Lalani.

"That sounds nice."

She took his hand and led him into her small living space. Like many of the residential units aboard, a single padded chair sat in front of a low, oval table. Behind that, an entertainment center provided a variety of audio, video, and literary media for relaxation. Inviting someone into this space was normally an indication of intimacy beyond the level he and Lalani shared. Still, he wasn't about to read too much into the gesture. She directed him into the cushioned seat. While it was wide enough for two to sit comfortably, she brought in one of her dining chairs and sat across from him. Using a quaint, hand-held remote, she turned on the monitor, sorted through the video library and selected an ancient, Neil Simon comedy.

Five minutes into the show, Mark said, "I've seen this one before."

"Would you prefer something different?"

"No, no. I like this one."

She smiled. "It's one of my favorites."

Something more we have in common, he thought. Discovering they both enjoyed watching shows more than once did more to distract him from melancholy thoughts than the movie itself. By the time the program was over, he had settled into the plush chair as if wrapped in a cocoon. He hated to leave, so when Lalani invited him to come back for another movie the next night, he eagerly accepted.

Dinner was ready and waiting when he arrived. "How'd you sleep?" she asked.

"Uninterrupted and tedious," he replied, and he meant it. Arms and shoulders sagged, as if he'd worked two long days without sleep instead of one. "How was your day?" he asked.

She tilted her head slightly and gave him a Mona Lisa smile. "Off shift today. I rode the tube to the agri-pod and picked some fresh vegetables then slipped down and bought a bit of beef."

Mark wrinkled his nose. "You went to the stock pods? I've been there. One time was enough."

"Well," she said with a raised eyebrow and a twinkle in her eye. "I did come straight back to a hot shower and lots of soap, to get the smell out of my nose. Afraid I used up my weekly ration of purified water."

An image of Lalani standing in the shower stall touched his thoughts. He brushed them aside quickly. They were friends. Nothing more. Despite his resolve, as the evening progressed, his eyes wandered down from her face, each time the entertainment captured her attention. This time they'd chosen a drama filled with romance and espionage.

Over the next few weeks, evenings together became part of their daily routines. Occasionally, they would meet in Mark's habital, but his untidiness, along with the perpetual smell of machine oil, made for a less comfortable setting. When they weren't together, thoughts of Lalani often distracted Mark from his work. He had no idea how to express his feelings and she remained reserved, modest. Nineteenth century novelists might have called it cool, or aloof. That wasn't quite right. Proper, perhaps. After weeks of wondering if he should mention his amorous thoughts, an incident in one of his dreams brought an unexpected opening.

"It was after work," Mark explained. "I was tired and wasn't paying attention to the occupancy sign and I walked in on Karen Beatty changing clothes."

"That's an innocent mistake. Was she angry?" Lalani asked.

"Not quite the word I'd choose. She once said if I were the last man alive on this forlorn voyage, she'd shoot herself out an airlock rather than deliver my descendants for future generations."

"That was in your dream?"

Mark thought for a second. "Actually, that was something that happened awhile back. Unfortunately, that wasn't a dream."

Lalani chuckled. "And what is it she finds so offensive?"

"It's a mutual distaste. Started a year out from Titan. A dozen or so English-speakers gathered for a celebration. Admittedly, there was a fair amount of alcohol still aboard and we indulged liberally. Karen Beatty was the only woman there."

Lalani's eyes widened with alarm. "What did you do to her?"

"Not what you're thinking." He felt his face flush. "It would be more accurate to say she assaulted us. After four martinis, she'd found reasons to shed most of her clothes and cozy up to half the men there. It so bad that I gave her the name Karen Bed-Any. Once that spread through the ship, she couldn't find a man who'd spend ten minutes alone with her."

Lalani poured a fresh cup of tea for each of them. "So, if we are to spread humanity to a new star system, we're going to have to hope the two of you aren't left alone to make it happen."

"That's about the size of it." He took a sip of the tea and mustered up his courage. "Have you ever thought about hooking up with someone?" He wasn't sure if *hooking up* was an expression she'd appreciate and he regretted the question as soon as it left his mouth.

Lalani didn't blink. Instead, she bit down on her lower lip and drummed her fingers on the table. "You are the first man I've ever called a friend." She inhaled deeply, her eyes widened and tiny crow's-feet appeared. "I wasn't going to tell you this." She hesitated. "My preference for companionship has always been other women. To be honest, I've never been attracted to a man. Only way I was able to get on this crew was to pretend I was anxious to have babies and settle down. I never intended to follow through."

Mark tensed, trying to collect his thoughts.

"It's not that I've ever been with a woman intimately. That would have killed my parents. And after all they've done for me, I couldn't do that to them. So it seemed kinder to leave them behind, believing I would one day give them grandchildren. Even if they could never meet them."

Mark felt the familiar sinking feeling of disappointment in his stomach. Until Lalani came into his life, he'd never had a sustained relationship with a woman. And he just plain liked her. Who else could appreciate both Shakespeare and Bradbury?

"You have to know, Mark," she went on, "You're the first man, other than my father, whose company I enjoyed. Because of you, I can imagine I might someday take a husband."

While Mark wasn't quite sure what to make of her revelation, thoughts of a romantic overture evaporated, at least for the night. A murder mystery seemed a safe choice for the evening's entertainment. To his surprise, Lalani sat down next to him in the padded chair and did not push away when his arm slipped around her shoulders.

Over the next few nights, Mark forced amorous flirtations aside by devoting conversation to his continuing nightmares. He explained how one of the stockyard tenders had gone to the infirmary with the flu. He was given antibiotics and the rest of the crew was called in for vaccinations. However, the medical team hadn't accounted for the increased radiation or its effect on the vaccine cultures. More than half the crew was sick with an unknown virus.

"That's a strange thing to dream about," Lalani said.

Mark recognized the tone in her voice and appreciated her effort to ease his mind.

"What if all this is prophetic?" he asked.

"Prophetic? You mean like in your Bible?"

He hadn't thought of it before, but Lalani came from a Hindu culture. "Well, yes. I wasn't thinking of it quite like a vision from God or anything." He thought about that. "Maybe. Or maybe there's a kind of psychic resonance out here that crosses through space-time and sends reflections back out as dreams."

He blushed at the look she gave him. It did sound a bit crazy. Oddly enough, the absurdity of it brought an instant wave of relief as they both laughed at his idea.

"So, leaving out the prophetic part," Lalani said with a chuckle. "Tell me more about the dream."

He sighed. All too suddenly, the frivolous moment passed into darker thoughts. His mind returned to the anxiety running through the entire crew. Nobody in the medical section had seen anything like this virus. After a week, the labs still hadn't determined how long the disease might take to run its course.

Days passed, dreams continued and physical intimacy with Lalani never progressed beyond the occasional hug or holding hands while walking through the ship's gardens. The distraction of looking forward to their time together helped ease the horrors of his ongoing sleep issues. Nevertheless, when the dream progressed to a ship-wide crisis, they began a more earnest search for an explanation.

"It seems logical that I'm trying to force something from life into my subconscious. Why?"

Lalani shook her head. "I can't see a reason."

"And why would I choose to give the entire crew a fatal disease?"

"I thought you said some were immune."

"Five. Out of three hundred. Of course I was one of them. Can you imagine what it would mean if only five people were left on the ship?"

"How many women?"

"One."

A shudder ran across Lalani's shoulders and chest. "She would be one busy girl."

Mark nodded, suppressing a smile. "Karen Beatty."

Lalani sucked in her lips and raised her eyebrows.

"Even with only five people, the ship's automated systems would keep us going. We'd have a few maintenance chores. Especially on the stockyard waste removers. We could shut down most of the living blocks and channel that energy back into propulsion. Might even cut a few years off the journey. Once we reset the planting and harvesting robotics to accommodate a smaller output, routine maintenance would be the only chores left."

"At least you'd have plenty of time for reading. Perhaps you could try your hand at writing your own stories."

"Yeah, right," Mark chuckled. "I wouldn't know how."

Lalani nodded. "I have to admit something," she said. "When we first started meeting, I thought you were making it all up."

"What changed your mind?"

"You did. Watching you, night after night, I can tell when you're hiding something. I still think it has something to do with being out here. Not some mystical resonance like you talked about. And I don't think the dreams are prophetic. More like a kind of space weariness. Like claustrophobia. Maybe we're not meant to stray so far from home."

Twenty-four hours later, Mark sat alone in his compartment, dazed. His eyes fixed on a wall, oblivious to either color or texture of the bare, wooden panel. Unaware of time passing, he suppressed a lingering notion that he was supposed to be somewhere else. Someone was waiting for him. A sound intruded on his stupor. Three dull thumps. Four. A muffled voice shouted something he couldn't understand. A pause, then three more thumps. A draft swept past him, chilly and fresh like the air in the corridors outside his room.

"Mark?" A voice beside him said. "Your pulse is racing. What happened?"

Her words seemed to echo off a deep cavern. *My pulse,* he thought. *Lalani?* His dining room came into focus. Lalani knelt beside him. She held a cool cloth on his forehead and stroked his wrist. He reached out and stroked her cheek. "You're here."

"What happened?"

"It was so real."

"Your dream again?"

He turned his head to face her. "Where can it go from here?"

"Mark."

"She did it. Exactly what she said she'd do."

"Did what? Who?" Lalani asked.

"Why did I call her that name?"

"Are you talking about Karen Beatty?"

"There were five of us left. After the virus. It killed them all."

"You told me that. What more did you dream?"

"An explosion in the reclamation plant killed Corey. D'Mitri and Abdi were face down in the water when we finally shut off the main."

"We?"

"Beatty and me. Karen. Chamber was up to my thighs in wastewater. I was focused on the shutoff controls and didn't see them fall. Abdi's skull was crushed."

"Mark, I'm sorry." Lalani wrapped her arms around him. "What did you mean, 'She did it?'"

He felt the blood drain from his face. "It was my fault. I never imagined the whole crew would pick up that name I gave her. I didn't know anyone would take it seriously."

"You worked together?"

"Not in real life. I just pray these dreams aren't some premonition of what's coming."

"I wouldn't worry about that," Lalani said softly. "Just tell me what happened."

"It took another hour to shut off the water. We just stood there staring at each other and then it hit me. We were the only two people left on the ship." He started shaking as he recalled the scene. "I remember thinking, *I am so sorry for what I said.* She wasn't a bad person. And I was trying to find a way to apologize, but she just stood there, glaring at me. I was about to say something when she said, "Here's Karen Bed-any and nobody would have her." I did nothing as she stepped inside the nearby airlock and sealed the door. I watched through the viewport. She looked back at me, raised her middle finger and pushed the decompression button. Then she was gone."

"Mark!" Lalani held him close. Her arms were warm and he let his head fall onto her shoulder. Eventually, she got off her knees and helped him out of the chair.

"I was alone. Totally alone. Last human on a voyage to another star."

"Mark, listen," She said, stroking his cheek softly. "Your dream has gone as far as it can. You have to believe it's all over now. Even if it continues, all you'll dream about is long, boring days on a ship. No more nightmares of death."

"Can you imagine living out your life, alone on a ship the size of a city. Headed for a destination you could never reach in a lifetime? No colonies or outposts to visit along the way. Maybe somebody with navigation skills could turn the ship around, head back to earth. Astrophysics. Calculus. That's not me." He shook his head. "The mission would be pointless. There'd never be any children to carry on."

"Shhhh," Lalani said. "No more talking." She pulled him into the bedroom and took off his clothes. He laid down. Then she undressed and climbed in beside him.

A loud clang woke Mark suddenly. He sat up and listened. For the past eleven years he'd worked with every mechanical system on the ship. He knew the rhythms and harmonics of working devices and he often diagnosed problems and malfunctions based on sound alone. Following the intimacy he'd shared with Lalani, he felt well rested for the first time in months. His senses were sharp and he focused on the echoes of whatever hit the ship. Damage to the hull or interior systems might need immediate attention. As he sat up rigid on his bed, nothing critical reached his ears.

A faint drip, drip, drip broke the silence. Worst case scenario, a water main had broken a seal. Or maybe he hadn't turned off the sink in his hygiene compartment. Dressing quickly, he decided an inspection tour was in order and set off for engineering at a quick jog.

Racing down the main corridor of crew compartments, he became keenly aware of what was missing. People. Without looking in a single room he knew no one was in their living space. Engineering was vacant, aside from the machinery sustaining the ship's functions.

Pressing a com-link, he called to the bridge. "This is Mark Averill checking in. Are you detecting any malfunctions up there?"

Silence. His chest tightened and his hands began to shake, but he wasn't ready to jump to conclusions. He climbed up to the galley directly above his residence. Whoever had used it last hadn't cleaned up. A coffee urn had tipped over into the sink. That was clearly the noise that woke him. Trickling from the faucet was a slow drip. Urn must have struck it when it fell. He turned the handle and the water stopped.

Now his only company was the steady hum of the ship's engines. He remembered Lalani's words. No more nightmares. Long boring days alone. He glanced up at one of the ubiquitous chronometers that occupied every room and hallway aboard. Every room except Lalani's. He couldn't recall any time pieces in her habital. Only the blue walls. Or were they yellow? He couldn't remember.

Turning suddenly, he dashed out of the room and sprinted to the reclamation plant. The room smelled awful and signs of recent flooding were spread two feet up the walls. His eyes moved slowly across the wide room and his stomach churned as he saw the bodies of three other crewmen resting amidst the machinery. Across from where he stood, the airlock was sealed with the outer door open to space.

Stunned, he went back to his quarters. A sudden sob shook his whole body as he sat at his computer. Sweaty palms danced over the keyboard scouring through personnel files. All but five crew members were listed as deceased. His fingers turned to thumbs as he misspelled and retyped over and over, N A Y A R, L A L A N I. No record. No such person was ever part of the crew.

A haze engulfed Mark's thoughts as he struggled to identify an assignment or purpose. Most of the day was spent dealing with his fallen shipmates. He wrapped their bodies in preparation for burial in space. *They deserve a funeral*, he thought. Uncertain about their religious views, he dug out his Bible and read a Psalm before offering a brief prayer. A prayer that included Karen Beatty. The airlock she'd used would now claim the bodies of Corey, D'Mitri and Abdi. As he dragged them inside, he looked at the doorway to deep space in a way he'd never before considered.

Back in his habital, he updated four personnel records. For Karen Beatty, he logged a commendation stating that she sacrificed her life to save his. More dignified than suicide, Mark wasn't sure this was a total fabrication. With the log complete, he sent a transmission back to Earth and attached the file. They should know there would be no colony awaiting a second mission.

Physically exhausted, Mark was nevertheless unable to sleep. Would Lalani reappear? *You have to believe it's all over*, she'd said. Did that mean she was leaving him? Did it matter? Even though he and Lalani had enjoyed an amazing night of intimacy, he couldn't father a new generation with a dream. Even beyond the sexual encounter, what dominated his thoughts were the hours he'd spent in her company, sharing all the same interests and passions. Perhaps dreams would give purpose to his existence. But would she still be there?

Regardless of his choices, the ship would continue on through space well beyond his lifespan. With proper maintenance and adjusted settings, the stores, and farms would sustain him as long as he cared to live. There were no accomplishments to be made. No contributions to humanity. No legacy to leave. All he had left was dreams. Could he stand the tedium of his waking hours? Hoping to distract his mind, he went to his bookshelf, pulled down a thick anthology of short stories. As he tried to focus on Damon Runyon's off-beat characters, the image of an airlock filled his mind and he closed his eyes. Whether from grief or pure terror, blackness swallowed his consciousness.

When he regained awareness, he stood at the edge of the orchards in the produce module. Not sure if he was dreaming or awake, he wandered through the various trees and vines. "Lalani," he called several times. There was no answer. He moved on to the vegetable gardens, pausing at various climate control panels to adjust settings in order to reduce output.

"Lalani," he called again. No one answered. When he had gone through all of the farm pods, he returned to his residence. Thoughts of the airlock resurfaced. If this was a dream, he knew where he would find her. With butterflies in his stomach, he walked to her residence block and found the unit that may or may not be hers. He took a breath and knocked.

A minute passed. Two. Fighting back tears he turned away to leave, when he heard the door open.

"There's no need to knock, Mark," a soft, beautiful voice said. "Dinner's ready."

For the first time since they'd met, Mark was fully relaxed, able to appreciate her company in ways he'd never imagined. And when they made love this time, his mind was free from outside distractions.

The noise that woke him was that of a large book falling on the floor. Picking it up, he flattened *The Best of Damon Runyon's* bent pages and carried it back to its shelf. Following a warm shower, he began a long trek through the vessel. As the only crewman left, his chores would keep him well occupied. It may be a lonely existence, but all the companionship he would ever need awaited him in his dreams. And if, or *when*, life became unbearable, he knew how to work an airlock.

Timothy Paul. Count me among those who believe in God. With that as context, consider this question: if an immortal designer really did create the universe and everything in it, what was His budget? It's a question one can't answer without more information. What would the word 'budget' mean to a being who exists somewhere beyond the edges of our universe? The piece of a puzzle like this that sucks me in is speculation about that other realm and the struggle to comprehend something infinite or eternal.

Being merely human, we are constrained by finite minds. My passion is to challenge the limits of imagination without shattering the conventions of our physical existence. From sci-fi thrillers to the woes of hobbits, werewolves, aliens and leprechauns, I am drawn to stories that make the adrenaline flow or evoke the pathos of romance or tragedy. I love to immerse myself in a tale with a setting, event or quality that lies beyond the ordinary. Show me a conflict and I'll side with the underdog. Most of all, I love a story that makes me think. Lay out a mystery and you'll capture my attention. Take me into the Twilight Zone where I can devour the moral ironies or expand my finite comprehension of creation and beyond.

My tagline at timothypaulbooks.com reads, "In stubborn pursuit of traditional publication." Fellow writers will understand the difficulty of my chosen path and I've been privileged to contribute to each volume of Lillicat Publisher's Visions series. As my appreciation for the short story and flash fiction formats continues to grow, I am working on three novels. My first book began an adult sci-fi cycle. And while books two and three are inching along, I am developing a YA series about three young people stuck in a single moment of time.

Spectacular scenery, elaborate architecture, comic books and traveling to distant places are just a few of my favorite things. Topping my list is Saturday morning writing time with my beautiful wife and soul mate, D.A. Couturier.

Crafters serve humanity with their Craft. Crafter Almira, a telepath and telekinetic, lives a life of servitude, this time on a ship far from home. Tensions build within and around her, threatening to explode. Would anyone survive the impact?

IMPACT WARNING

By

Sarah Buhrman

The bright, silvery form streaking towards its destination destroyed the serenity of the deep space darkness far more than any distant star could have. The light from the pinpoint stars ricocheted off the shuttle in flashes of barely discernable light.

A low hum from the craft's machinery gave constant reassurance to its passengers. The low sound traveled the metal girding throughout the ship, checking in at each room, until it reached a small chamber with twelve doors built into the walls. Just behind the transparent panels taking up the upper portion of the stasis chambers, ten faces mimicked the calm of sleep.

In the women's dorm, laughter and music drowned out the hum.

"Happy annual, Almira!"

Almira accepted the chocolate-covered cupcake and a cup of hot cider, and blushed while Seren broke into an ancient traditional song. Crafters were a sub-human mutation, born to serve humanity with their Craft, whether it was telekinesis or telepathy. As a Crafter, Almira wasn't used to being treated so well for so long.

Almira licked up some of the sweet goo. "Wow, I can't believe I made it to 22 years old."

"Seven in space, too," Seren laughed. "It's enough to drive you crazy." She immediately stopped, a look of horror dawning on her face.

Almira forced a cheerful laugh, trying to lighten the sudden change in mood. She knew that Seren, like all humans, knew the stories of Crafters like her. Stories that said Crafters could not handle the emptiness of space and tried to kill their crew.

"No kidding. Doctor Uzumati would barely speak to me. And when she did, it was to snap an order. Boomer and Mav each told me all of their dirty jokes and raunchy stories. I thought I would never stop blushing, or laughing." She sighed. "Crawler and Jack should be better."

Seren laughed nervously, picking at the black jumpsuit that labeled her a military-citizen. Her eyes darted away from Almira's before she dragged them back to meet the Crafter's gaze. Seren obviously wanted to say something. She often wanted to bring up topics that were considered inappropriate to talk to Crafters about.

"What is it?" Almira asked. She shrugged, suddenly aware of the red of her own jumpsuit, the symbol of her less-than-human status. She pulled her fingers away from the opals embedded in her throat, conscious of the nervous habit she had of playing with them. "Just say it. You should know by now that I won't be offended."

Seren took a deep breath and swallowed. "Why do Crafters go insane? You know, during the Sleeper trips. In my classes, we were told it is a genetic flaw in the Crafters' DNA. But it doesn't quite add up, and no one seems to be able to give details."

Almira grimaced. Seren certainly knew how to pick topics that dug into the basis of Crafter servitude. Almira was a good Crafter. She hated the feelings of doubt that came up when she had to look so closely at the system that dictated her place. "I don't know about DNA. You'd have to talk to Doctor Yosu about that. But I can explain how the common stories are exaggerations of rare occurrences."

Seren settled in while Almira took a sip of her cooling cider.

"Seventy years ago, when Crafters were still a new discovery, people struggled to come to terms with our existence. The Crafters were just starting to be isolated from regular people."

"Tell me about it," Seren said. "I asked my third-level psychology professor about it. She wanted to know why anyone would need to know Crafter psychology."

Almira shrugged. "I don't know about that." She popped the last of her cupcake into her mouth and swallowed it down. "Most Crafters are telepathic, or 'Pathers. That ability increases exponentially during puberty when the Crafter's neural web expands even further. That web is what causes the abnormal brain functions that allow the Crafts, empathy and telepathy, to work. When you combine this with the hormones of puberty, well..." Almira shrugged.

"That makes sense," Seren nodded.

"Crafters were given no privacy back then, not even from each other," Almira continued. "They were probably overwhelmed by emotions...their own, each other's, and the humans around them. Several did go insane before modern procedures, like Seclusion Training, were put into place."

Seren thought this over while Almira went to refresh their ciders. "So," Seren said, as Almira sat back down. "What about during stasis? What happens then?"

Almira pressed her lips together, taking a moment to remember the details of Crafter history. "That was actually a single case. The Crafter was a poorly Trained mild 'Pather. His strength was in 'Kinetics. He was put in stasis for three years and his control was virtually non-existent while unconscious. He was exposed to stray thoughts from his crewmates, five military-citizen brawns who had seen severe combat. Three of them were diagnosed with post-traumatic psychoses later. By the end of the trip, the Crafter was probably just overwhelmed by it all."

Almira smiled reassuringly. "I, however, am very well Trained, so the chances of that ever happening to me is virtually non-existent."

Seren shrugged. "But at least this way you're available for emergencies. And you keep very good company. At least, I think so."

Almira grinned, waggling her eyebrows. "Speaking of company, I understand you and Lino are getting along very well."

Seren's smile softened at Lino's name and her cheeks grew rosy. "Actually, yes. Oh! And he did the sweetest thing. He put a dozen white roses in stasis for me while I was Sleeping." Her smile widened at the memory.

Almira grinned. "I know. He had to ask me how to use the plant incubator for them. Of course, I didn't know. It was so funny! We worked on it for weeks. It's a miracle we didn't grow giant, man-eating Venus flytraps."

Seren laughed, leaning back in her chair until she nearly fell over, while Almira mimicked the pleading look Lino had given her.

They were still chuckling when the Long-Distance Communicator beeped for attention. Seren answered it, wiping tears of laughter from her eyes. "Yes? Er...I mean, Proserpine III. Seren Conner, Biology."

The delay timer showed a three-minute wait until a reply came in. The two women killed time talking about Lino. Then, Seren followed the instructions to store a private, coded message for Commander Kurtis.

"Do you know where the name of the ship is from?" Almira said, suddenly curious.

Seren furrowed her brow. "Proserpine? Yes, it's Greek. The Roman counterpart is Persephone."

Almira brightened. "Oh, the girl who was kidnapped by Hades. The one who ate the pomegranate seeds and caused the whole six months of winter, right?"

Seren nodded and gave a feisty grin. "I guess they are hoping that this mission will bear some fruit."

Almira groaned at the bad joke and laughed.

Seren checked the transaction when it indicated its completion. "Non-urgent. Probably a mission update or potential impact warning in the next few years."

Almira nodded. They were always getting messages about course changes that didn't take effect for months or years.

Seren pulled Almira to her feet and dragged her toward the mess and lounge area. "Let's go watch a comedy-vid. I know a great one."

One year later, Almira pressed the button for the synth-coffee before she pressed the wake-up alarm for the men's dorm. The decade-long journey to the newly discovered planet Gaia was not even half over. Almira would sacrifice more than 25 years to the journey before it was all done.

Unlike the non-Crafters that made up the crew, she couldn't cheat time in stasis. And, as a Crafter, they wouldn't trust her to be on her own.

Almira was setting Dr. Dunstan Pearce's breakfast on the table across from hers, when he walked in, half dressed.

She glanced at his lean, well-defined torso and looked away quickly, hiding her blush beneath her shoulder-length auburn hair. She chided herself for not being used to the sight of him, after nearly eight months of just the two of them in close quarters.

She did like the look of his golden hues before he put on the black, military citizen's jumpsuit. It blanched out his highlights and made him look nearly monochrome. He was definitely not like the dark, suave Lino. Lino hadn't cared about Almira being a Crafter, so long as she was happy to listen to him gush about Seren.

Dunstan sat down to breakfast without a word, and Almira sighed silently. Eight months of this cold shoulder treatment.

Almira was used to people treating her with distance or disdain. Almira was one of the strongest Crafters, so she had been a bit pampered, but she still wondered how someone who expected her to keep him safe, and possibly assist him with sensitive research, could be so dismissive of her. Most of the others at least tried to get to know her, once they were sure that she wasn't going crazy.

The computer system gave an attention-demanding squawk. Almira jumped up, welcoming whatever distraction it could provide. She brought up the alert message on the small screen and caught her breath as Dunstan's face appeared over her shoulder. His warm amber eyes narrowed at the data provided.

"Impact warning. Looks like a rogue asteroid field," he said, not looking at her. "This wasn't in the charting uploads." He scowled at the readouts. "There seems to be some irregular movement with some of the asteroids. You might need to supplement our shields. Can you handle it?"

Almira answered his abruptness lightly. "Of course I can."

Dunstan finally looked at her, his eyes piercing her calm. He seemed to be assessing her for the first time. She shifted under his gaze and tried to look older than her 23 years. Finally, he gestured for her to begin.

Almira sat down and entered a mild trance state. Years of practice made it quick and easy for her. She expanded her mind, stretching her consciousness out.

She automatically drew in and pulled energy from the sluggish, unconscious minds of the crew in stasis. She knew it gave them "dreams," but it would not hurt them. The boost it gave her own mind more than compensated for the chance of a few bad dreams, that almost no one would remember.

Almira began gently moving the asteroids out of the ship's path, pushing them slightly to one side or the other. She felt a small tug in the back of her mind, an alert of sorts, but, in the effort to keep herself focused, she ignored it. She averted several of the huge space-rocks, though they seemed to resist her. A small frown crossed her lips and a crease appeared between her brows. She slowly diverted some of her attention to searching out the cause. The strain on her mind was becoming uncomfortable.

Suddenly, several of the asteroids began to veer towards the ship, gaining in speed. Almira panicked and, in her confusion, flung out with her arms as well as with her mind. She veered most of them onto a different course. Two of them she kinetically grabbed and threw away rapidly. One crashed into a third asteroid, hovering just out of the way. The impact crushed the two rocks together, causing their masses to merge.

Several seconds later, an explosion rocked the ship, pelting the shields with debris and causing the metal hull to groan metallically. The reactive burst nearly bowled Almira over, both physically and psychically.

Almira felt Dunstan shake her shoulders, yelling at her to gain her attention. His words slowly penetrated her strained mind. "The scans are showing high concentrations of nuclear material. If the asteroids crash into each other, they may reach critical mass and blow! The shields and hull won't be able to hold up under too many of those kinds of explosions."

Still in her semi-trance state, Almira struggled to respond coherently. "Don't move right. Swerve."

"That's right," Dunstan said, gripping her shoulders too tightly. He shook her slightly again. "I'm also seeing varying levels of ionized iron, magnets. They may be attracted to each other and to the ship. I won't be able to tell you which ones are magnetic and which are nuclear. There's too many to scan that quickly."

Almira dropped into a full-trance state, this time going so deep she disconnected from her physical consciousness. Her head rolled back on her shoulders and she slumped over, sliding off the chair.

Dunstan laid her flat on the floor, then moved to the monitors. To his surprise, the readings indicated an unnatural movement in several of the asteroids at once. He glanced over at her prone form and sighed in relief. "Keep it up," he whispered. "You've got to do this."

Almira's consciousness expanded to a painful level as she tried to detect the most immediate threats and move them away, countering the effects of the magnetic fields. She struggled to push the gargantuan rocks in intricate patterns, preventing collision after collision, with the ship and with the other asteroids.

Each time she avoided a collision by mere meters, she pushed herself harder, demanding more from her abilities. The stress, mental and emotional, dumped useless adrenaline into her body and ate away at her concentration. After only a few minutes, her jumpsuit was soaked with sweat.

The journey through the asteroid field took just under an hour. But by that time, her mind and body had no reserves left. Almira's eyes fluttered open only long enough to see Dunstan staring at her, with a look of concern on his face.

Dunstan gathered the Crafter up and carried her into her sleeping quarters. He laid her out on the bed and checked her vital signs. She was in a comatose state, but still alive. He sighed and brushed a tendril of dark red hair from her face. His finger traced the line of a pert nose. His eyes fell on her full lips. She was a beautiful girl.

Dunstan stood up, once again taken aback by this line of thought. He was loyal to the Commander, regardless of their differences of opinion in the matter of Crafter treatment. All that mattered was to get the job done, to complete the mission.

But Dunstan knew the Commander didn't care about Almira. He only cared about the principals of being the Link to the Crafter on this mission. He would do what needed to be done to make the Link complete with no emotion attached.

Dunstan looked back at the girl lying defenseless. He would not have her against her will. That would be completely unacceptable. But if she came to him willingly, it would be different. A smile crossed his lips, softening his features into a hopeful expression. A plan began taking shape in his mind, only to be interrupted by a warning beep from the vitals monitor.

Her blood sugar had plummeted in the last few minutes and her mitochondria were slowing energy production; her body was shutting down on a cellular level. Dunstan brought up her med files and found the appropriate data. A shiver ran down his spine when he read the disclaimer: Theoretical procedure. This had never been tested. He got the injections ready, and began working to save her life.

"I hope this is worth it, sweet."

Almira opened her eyes to the darkened ceiling of her quarters. She blinked several times to clear the crusted sleep from her eyes. Her first thought was of how warm she felt. It was nice, but unfamiliar. A sweet, musky smell enveloped her, creating a tingle in her belly. Then she heard the rhythmic breathing next to her. She turned her head and found herself nose-to-nose with the sleeping Dunstan. She shifted unconsciously and his golden eyes opened.

He blinked sleepily and smiled. "You're awake."

"Yes," she whispered. She had realized when she moved that she was wearing very little, and he was wearing even less.

"I was a bit worried there for a while. You were unconscious for a full," he glanced at the digital timepiece at her bedside "sixty-three hours and some odd minutes."

Almira resisted a disturbing urge to nestle up against Dunstan's warm chest. "I'm sorry."

He chuckled softly, wrapping his arms around her, squeezing her lightly in a hug. "Don't be."

A surface-scan revealed desire on Dunstan's part. Almira felt torn between a similar feeling for him and a sense that she needed to be true to Kurtis, her future Link. "What happened? Why are you...well...."

"You were freezing, getting hypothermia. This is the best way to alleviate that problem. It was due to your mitochondria shutting down. Your cells were going into stasis and you were no longer producing energy. I checked your med file. It said to give you a concentrated solution of sugar water and insulin, with a high-voltage shock for a booster." He cleared his throat. "It seems to have worked."

Almira relaxed into his embrace. "Mm-hmm."

He sighed. "You are definitely warm again."

She lifted her mouth to meet his as he moved closer. The pleasure of the light kiss was mind-numbing, but not enough to counter a stray thought of the Commander. She broke the contact. "I'm not sure this is right."

Dunstan looked hurt. "Why? Don't you feel...something for me? Am I not good enough for you?" His face turned ugly, for the briefest moment. "Am I not good enough for a Crafter?"

Almira froze. "N-n-no! It isn't that. It isn't you." She struggled to find the right words. "The Commander...the Linking...He would know, wouldn't he?"

An angry look crossed Dunstan's face, but was gone in an instant. "You're right. He would know." Dunstan shoved Almira away and climbed out of the bed.

A feeling of pain and loss washed over her. Most of all, she was confused. She knew what she wanted, and she was certain that Dunstan wanted her, too. She was supposed to obey all humans, with certain conditions. For example, she couldn't be ordered to kill another human. But this was a situation that wasn't covered in any of her Training.

"I'm sorry. If it's what you want, I will..."

"No!" Dunstan cut her off sharply. "You were right." He stopped when he saw her expression. He moved to the bed and caressed her neck, his fingers stroking the opals of her collar. "The Commander is possessive." The bitter, angry expression flashed across his features again. He turned away. "And this is the way it has to be."

Almira's temper flared. "What if I don't want it that way? Don't I get a say in it?" She ended abruptly, realizing the foolishness of what she'd said. Of course a Crafter didn't get a say.

Dunstan paused to face her at the door. She watched the emotions cross his face, until his expression settled into a determined look. "Ha," his sharp, bitter laugh caused her to flinch. His voice cracked as he spoke, but he forced out the words. "Since when have you had *any* control of your life?"

The door shut behind him, leaving Almira to her own bitter tears as she wept for her broken heart.

Anger surged up again. Almira felt rather than heard the metal bones of the ship groan. She could crack it open, spilling the crew and cargo into space and ending her pain with their lives.

The lives of Seren and Dunstan would be collateral damage to that end.

Almira took a deep breath and released the telekinetic push on the ship's structure. How could she sacrifice their lives for her need to be free?

She probed the microchips hidden beneath the opals at her throat. A tendril of pain warned her against using her Craft on them, her slave chains. She could activate them, and the pain might eventually kill her. But that would leave the ship and crew more vulnerable to the unknown dangers of deep space and the distant planet they were sent to explore.

Almira sighed and fell back against her pillow. Her fingers danced over the opals.

Not now. But she knew in her heart it would happen. One way or another, she would be free. She would break her chains, and the impact of a Crafter rebelling would be felt throughout humanity. But not yet.

The dark shadows of deep space swallowed the silver ship as it streaked onward to its destination. Its fragile hull shivered in the light of pinpoint stars.

Sarah Buhrman has been writing for more than 20 years. She lives in the middle of nowhere with two monsters (the kids), an ogre (the hubby), and whatever drama-llama is coming to visit this week. Sarah is the author of several books, including the Life 101 (How to be a Grown Up) *series, and has short stories and essays in several magazines, such as* **The Witches' Hour** *and* **Dreams Eternal**, *and anthologies, such as* **Pop Culture Grimoire: 2.0** *and* **Pagan Leadership Anthology.**

On a routine visit to a deep space listening post, a pilot discovers that the mundane is a matter of perspective.

OLDTIME STATION

By

Emma Tonkin

In the half-light cast by the navigation buoys, *Oldtime Station* was a gigantic cobweb a hundred kilometres across, set deeply into a nest of struts and thinner matter which wandered out into a sequence of Fibonacci spirals. It made Brewer think of the desiccated husk of a sunflower. She'd seen planetside arrays built for radio astronomy, but they'd been tiny by comparison, bright fields of metal reliant on local geography to keep their forms.

It took the ship a while to see the pressurized hub of the station through optical sensors, but the navigational systems picked it up on infrared. She let the computer plot a course and took a few minutes out, while it negotiated an approach with the station's systems. It was too early, really, to dress for arrival, but the Interstellar Export Service ship *D'Artagnan* had been in jump space for four days and she'd had little to do but binge-watch old news bulletins.

Doing so had been a mistake. The news was full of the colonisation of Wolf 1061—geological surveys, new settlements and the political drama and conflict of pioneer life. Once upon a time, she'd have reveled in it. After six years of watching other people walk on the first habitable alien world, including three years of dull routine as a qualified pilot, it was salt rubbed into an old wound. She'd followed the Wolf reports since college, just as they all had. Every now and then, an old classmate would wander into sight in the background of a news broadcast and she'd ask herself again how she'd managed to miss the party. She still imagined what it would've been like to be first into orbit, first onto the stony ground, first to leave her booted print on what turned out to be an empty shore.

Brewer kept a scrapbook from her childhood in personal data storage. Signals from space, however mysterious, hadn't appealed to her childhood sense of adventure. *Oldtime Station* had merited a single clipping, sandwiched between a dozen articles on the nascent science of asteroid farming. Even so, it was pleasant to have a reason to force herself out of her lingering sense of failure. She shook her head to clear her thoughts, then she began to persuade her thistledown hair into an ordered state.

The station took over half an hour to respond to her call. When it did, having almost forgotten the line was still open, she'd fixed herself a drink. She coughed, sending droplets of iced tea into the air.

"*D'Artagnan*," said an amused Midwestern voice. On video, station control was male, with warm brown skin and a faded blue shirt. "We have coffee, if that'd suit you better?"

"Thanks," she said. "I've sent a delivery manifest through. How's it look?"

"Not bad. Be advised, though, we're out of mints."

"We have two hundred chocolate ice creams in the cargo hold, if you have a sweet tooth, *Oldtime*." She was smiling.

"I'll keep it in mind. Looks like an ETA of five hours, *D'Artagnan*. You'll be in time for dinner."

The station manager met her at the cargo hatch, where he waited politely until she came to terms with the station's idea of *up* and *down*, rotated accordingly, and anchored her magnetic soles.

"Welcome to *Oldtime Station*. Don Norfleet." He extended his hand. "I run this place." Solemnly, they shook hands.

"Rachel Brewer," she said. "Sorry for the wait. Trade Station engineers found some diagnostic problems on the *Darty* before I left Earth orbit–nothing serious, but I'm three days behind schedule."

"No problem. It's good to see you. We have a lot of observations to shift back to Mars."

"Can't you radio the data home?"

"We have a bandwidth issue. We produce it faster than we can broadcast, so we batch it up once every six months or so and send it back with the post. Also, it's true about the mints, though we aren't going to starve. Apart from anything else, we have enough lasagna for a lifetime. Neither Jay nor I care for Italian food."

"Are there only two of you? This place is..." She gestured around them at the domed spaces.

"Huge? It is. But it's old. It's been here nearly fifty years."

She considered him thoughtfully. He might have been in his forties. "And you?" she said.

"I've been here ten years, off and on. When I joined, there were eight of us and we were very understaffed, even then. Our chief technician, Hervé, left for Wolf 1061 at the start of the colonisation effort. The Hendersons went to Mars, though we still work together on signal processing. Computing hardware is hard to upgrade out here. We do what we can and send the rest to them." His sharp gaze met hers. "Tell me, Captain Brewer, do you know what we do out here?"

The subject had come up in class, part of an impenetrably dry discussion of information theory. Something about extra-terrestrial radio signals, high-entropy, complex and incomprehensible. A word popped into her head. Faced with Norfleet's appraisal, she took a chance. "Xenoarchaeology," she said. "You listen to the stars."

He smiled. *Bingo.* "Something like that. Want a tour before dinner?"

The cargo process was largely automated. Who knew if she'd ever have a chance to tour a spiderweb again? "Sure."

195

"What's your opinion on television?" he asked. She must've looked a little revolted, because Norfleet took a deep breath and started the tour.

She followed him into the cargo hub. Six large rooms were set up with miniature train-tracks and dense rows of railed shelving. "All this is primary data storage," he said.

She thought about it. "Why did they build all this in deep space? I'd think it'd be faster and cheaper to build it in Earth orbit. The transportation costs alone must have been insanely expensive."

"Politics, at first," he said. "Back in the day, jump drives could barely reach a lightyear. *Oldtime* was intended to act as a waystation."

It must've become obsolete almost before it was finished, she thought. "So it was just...a place to go?"

"Pretty much. The inclusion of the radio equipment may even have been an afterthought, but if so, it was a good one. If you're going to build something this big, it makes sense to do it outside the Kuiper Belt. The density of deep space is over a dozen orders of magnitude lower. Something could fall out of the Oort cloud in our direction, but it's not likely."

It sounded plausible, apart from the staggering cost of deep-space construction. "That can't be the only reason to build this out here," she said.

"Oh, it isn't," said Norfleet. "There's a lot of electromagnetic pollution in Earth orbit. When you listen as hard as we do, you hear a lot of noise."

"That bad?"

"And then some. Classical radio telescopes registered interference every time a janitor put his lunch in the microwave. The Dish is a whole lot more sensitive. If we'd built it in our own back yard, we'd hardly have been able to hear ourselves think. Out here we can barely pick signals from cosmic background radiation, but there..."

She bit her lip. "What about my transmissions?"

"They caused interference on about half-an-hour of our observations," he said, "but it's worth it. We've got to eat, right?"

She was still wondering about the train-tracks, when a high-pitched whine caught her attention. An articulated robot arm came whistling down the track, holding a green cartridge, and zipped past them into the last of the storerooms. She watched it position itself perfectly before the racks, extend upwards towards the ceiling and slot the cartridge into place. It shook itself back downwards into a compact shape, then made its way back past them.

"Where's the robot going?"

"Analytics. I'll show you."

Analytics proved to be a large cylindrical station module containing a dozen workstations, a few of which were in partial or complete states of disrepair. A slightly disreputable-looking blue teddy bear was wedged beside one screen. Brewer smiled.

"Benjamin here's a quiet guy," said Norfleet, deadpan. "Doesn't talk much, but he's got an unbeatable attention span."

Brewer launched herself towards an observation window beyond the blue bear's console. "What is there to see out here?" Above the rim of the saucer's spidery struts, there was nothing but a sprinkling of distant stars.

A woman's voice said, "More than you can possibly imagine." The station's other inhabitant waved from the far end of the room. "Good to have a dinner guest, Captain. We don't get many visitors out here anymore."

Brewer waved back. "I take it you're Jay?"

"That's me. Jacey Gailis. I used to be senior scientist on the Dish, but I haven't had a research assistant for three years. Don, if you want to start dinner, I'll show our guest some TV."

"She's not a fan," Norfleet said solemnly.

"We'll see," said Gailis. Norfleet sketched a little salute and left.

Gailis switched on an unoccupied console. "So now that you've met the team...here's what we do."

A hand-drawn 2D animation flashed onto the screen. Something mantis-like with an enormous head hopped into a desert, leapt into the air, did a flip and fell onto its back, antennae bent into a triangular waveform and legs pedaling helplessly. An orange thing that looked a little like a cactus stood up, opened a comically massive set of jaws, and swallowed the mantis-thing whole. A few bubbles floated from the cactus' mouth, making Brewer think of her iced-tea mishap that morning.

She grinned. "Did you draw that?"

"Nope. We just decoded it."

Brewer's eyes widened. *Alien TV?*

"It's straight off the Dish, broadcast from the approximate direction of Kepler-452b. We don't actually know whether there's still anybody making cartoons there. This signal's about fourteen hundred years old."

Gailis typed, and the image faded. Something new came up. This time it was black-and-white. Two pale grey things that looked a little like cacti were standing at a work surface. One, apparently wearing an apron, was mixing something in a bowl. They really did have a lot of teeth. "We think this one's a shopping program. Or a cooking program. Or maybe chemistry. It's a little hard to tell. We've never caught a live-action program involving eating. Maybe they have a social taboo."

Brewer shook her head in wonder. "I had no idea. I mean, everybody knows we found signals—but this?"

Gailis shrugged, palms up. "Decoding alien TV is hard, especially when you don't know what you're looking at. Decoding a highly compressed video format from scratch is generally a pain in the butt, anyway. We've been collecting signals for decades without knowing what they contained. It took a long time before we got past that point."

"How did you manage it?"

"We got lucky. Specifically, we got Jacintha and Mal Henderson. She's a cryptographer; he started his professional life as a cognitive scientist. Don't ask me how they did it, but they worked it out."

"This is really big! Why didn't it make the news?"

"It's big all right, but six years ago, our discovery coincided with Wolf 1061, which was bigger. A decade ago, technology reached the point where we could realistically get to our neighbouring planets within a month and go home. The first Wolf mission was reported just before we got our first signal decrypted, and Wolf caught a lot more media attention. We even *lost* staff to that one. I wouldn't be surprised if it was Wolf that persuaded you to join the Service."

It hadn't been, actually, but Brewer let it go. That had been a combination of following a boy to college, losing him and discovering that piloting was more than a consolation prize. She'd been in her second year of training when the first Wolf mission reports had hit the news. She wasn't sure whether to be pleased or irritated that Gailis had misjudged her age.

Gailis went on. "You have to realise that most people wouldn't care about dead aliens any more than they'd care about a video feed from tenth-century China. Maybe less. There's human interest in the Liao dynasty, for example, and a lot of evidence, but very few people read textbooks or make documentaries about it."

"They'd care about live aliens," Brewer said.

"Very astute, Captain. Live aliens have a purpose, a cause and effect. If we could talk to them, it'd mean competition, trade, or war. With no aliens to argue with, we have to establish colonies of our own and argue with them instead. It'd take a lifetime of study to get anything useful from the signals we have here. Most people wouldn't see the point."

Brewer nodded. "Still," she said, "it's a pity."

Gailis looked at her sharply. "When you got this assignment, you wondered who you upset to get such a tedious posting, didn't you?"

Brewer's face flamed red. She was relieved when Norfleet came back into the room.

"Come on, you two," he said. "Dinner."

It turned out to be lasagna. In combination with the grape juice she'd brought from Earth, it was actually pretty good.

The *Darty* was loaded and ready to leave, by the time she awakened. It was eleven o'clock station time. Brewer had dreamed of orange cacti with large teeth and multijointed arms. When she woke up, she wasn't sure whether she wanted them to be out there or not. Kepler-452b was still a long way away with current jump technology, but they'd been broadcasting cartoons when her ancestors had been fighting Vikings. They could be anywhere, by now, or nowhere at all.

The thought made her irritable, so when the *Darty* complained at her again about engine diagnostics, she was more annoyed than concerned. It wasn't the jump engine, anyway: just one of the short-range thrusters.

She raised comms. "*Oldtime*, be advised I have a red light on my starboard aft thruster. I'll modify my departure accordingly." There were five thrusters in total. These days, spacecraft were designed with redundancy in mind.

She made the necessary commands and started the firing sequence. The systems hummed gently. As it always did, the sound relaxed her a little, drawing her away from the events of the previous night.

Something whined and choked. The *Darty* lurched as all five thrusters cut off. Her screen showed her nothing but miles of spiderweb, slowly growing larger. They would collide. She undid her harness, pulled on a spacesuit, strapped herself back in and tried the controls again. Most were dead. Number three would fire, but did so in brief staccato bursts. She activated it anyway. Then she called the station.

"*Oldtime*, engines are out, thruster three intermittent. I'm drifting into the Dish."

There was nothing for a moment. Then Gailis swore violently into the microphone, hurting her ears.

Norfleet's voice broke in. "*D'Artagnan*, what is your velocity?"

She looked. "Um, slow. Maybe ten metres per second."

"Roger. We're tracking you. *D'Artagnan*, be advised you need to lose some speed. Fire that engine. I'll tell you if you're overdoing it."

She said, "*Oldtime*, I'd sooner land in the Dish than drift away."

"That's our plan too, Rachel, but you have to slow down. At this speed, you'll go through, and take some of the Dish with you. So you need to fire that thruster."

She did. The *Darty* lurched again.

"Okay. Three seconds more, *D'Artagnan*, and you should be just fine."

She counted it. One little elephant. Two little elephants. The *Darty* was starting to rotate in earnest now. She switched the engine off, waited for the net to swing back into view, switched it on again, off again. Along with the rubbery smell of the spacesuit, which she'd never expected to use and hadn't thought to air, the motion was making her feel a little dizzy.

Norfleet was saying something. It didn't matter what. At some point, number three engine had stopped responding, but she kept pressing the button anyway. It was something to do, as she watched the net grow in front of her.

The crash was slow and stately and probably the most frightening thing that she'd ever lived through, including the near-vacuum helmet drill they put candidates through during qualification. At least then, there'd been somebody ready to abort the drill if anything went wrong. She hadn't really been risking anything more dramatic than bruising, bloating, and an embarrassing lack of bowel control.

The Dish rippled as the *Darty* hit it. The web spread out around the ship in a soundless shriek of tortured metal and caught on the *Darty*'s stubby wings. To Brewer, it was utterly confusing. An air-pressure warning went off in the cabin. She unlatched her harness again, went mechanically to the locker and snapped open the ultrasonic air-leak detector. Finding the indicated areas, she slapped patches over each. Eventually the alarm stopped.

She tried the radio. "*Oldtime?*" Nothing. Maybe the antenna was gone. She switched to the suit radio. "*Oldtime*, are you receiving?" Silence. Then she remembered the conductive pad by the airlock and tried again with her palm slapped to the plate.

She didn't even have to transmit. Norfleet's calm, deliberate voice spoke straight into her helmet. "...in the Dish. Repeat, *D'Artagnan*, you are now stationary in the Dish. Disengage all engines. Acknowledge."

"*Oldtime*," she said. "The *Darty*'s lost radio. I'm on suit power. Do you receive?"

There was a note of relief in his voice, she thought. "*D'Artagnan*, we receive. Listen, do you have tethers onboard?"

"Yes," she said. "Duct tape of the universe. What do you want me to do?"

"Great. Listen, the *D'Artagnan* is most likely caught in the Dish until someone comes to fish it out, but we need to get you back to the station. Someone will come to find you when you don't make it home on time, but, in the meantime, I think you'd be more comfortable here than there. And I'm not sure how much slack you have in your air supply. You vented a lot of atmosphere just now. So I suggest that you tether the ship to a couple of struts, so we know for sure it won't drift away. Then we'll figure out how to get you back to *Oldtime*."

She tried not to hyperventilate. "How far is it?"

He paused. "Three hundred metres or so. It's not as bad as it sounds. You're on the Dish. We can get you to a maintenance hatch. Then you just follow your nose to the nearest rescue station. From there, we can pick you up."

She thought about it.

He said, "We'll bring you hot chocolate. I promise."

"Well," she said. "Okay. Promise me one more thing, though?"

"Anything, *D'Artagnan*. What did you have in mind?"

"Lasagna. Tonight. Again. This time, we defrost some garlic bread."

He laughed. "All right, *D'Artagnan*. Call us once you've found the tethers. Get yourself a fresh air tank. It really isn't far but I'd feel better knowing you weren't running on fumes."

In the end, it was a nightmare. The Dish wasn't made for wandering tourists. The structure was paper-thin and shook as she crawled. Twice, the tethers she placed pulled away, the supports she chose snapping away in the darkness. She'd forgotten the twilight of deep space. Unlike the Darty, her suit had no floodlights, just a simple shoulder-mounted torch for detailed work. The designers had clearly never imagined that it would be used between stars. As she crawled, she dictated letters into her suit radio to send to everybody she could think of who should have prepared for this situation, listing every shortcoming that came to mind. She addressed them to her suit's designers, the Service, even the *Times of Terra*.

She wouldn't have made it, if it hadn't been for the beacon. Someone had popped open the maintenance hatch and tied a flare to the external ladder. She crawled into the airlock, smacked the contact patch, and shut her eyes, listening to the popping sounds of pressure equalising around her suit.

Gentle hands manoeuvred her from the lock and opened her helmet. She opened her eyes cautiously. "Jay?"

The scientist patted her shoulder. "Just so you know, this doesn't mean you're forgiven," Gailis said, handing her a pouch of hot chocolate. Brewer wrapped her cold hands around it and laughed until she hiccuped.

The best things about *Oldtime*, Brewer decided that day, were the availability of air, food, water, and unbelievably luxurious hot showers with vacuum drainage and shower curtains. The downside was the silence. Other than the antenna, there really wasn't much to do.

She managed almost a day of quiet downtime in the cabin she'd used the previous night. It had probably belonged to the long-lost Hervé. The walls were plastered with artists' impressions of alien worlds, too many moons and suns hanging in the sky. Once she'd started to notice them, she found it difficult to look away. She spent too long there, imagining her boot prints in the yellow sand, before she shook it off, dressed, and went for a walk.

The whir of the tape robots made Analytics easy to find. Brewer paused at the door. Both of the scientists were there, each watching a screen. She gave an awkward little wave, entered and found an empty workstation.

The system wasn't as complex as it had seemed. She'd worked with worse interfaces. She found a channel and settled down to watch TV.

Three days in, she began to appreciate the entertainment. On one of the cactus-creature channels there was a program that recurred daily. After two sessions, it had begun to look familiar. So she requested the back catalogue and binge-watched a dozen episodes in a row.

After a few episodes, she thought that she was beginning to identify individual attributes in the cast of actors: twigs, crags, casts to the teeth, patterns and textures in their skins. She drew character sheets, giving each cactus a name and writing a list of their appearances. She drew storyboards. Regretting the lack of an audio track, she created specimen scripts for episodes of the series.

One of the creatures, more striped than the others, was laughably clumsy. It seemed to generate most of the drama. Brewer wondered if a watching cactus would've thought its antics as funny as she did. Interpreted through her eyes, she concluded that the show was, essentially, *I Love Lucy*.

It wasn't clear whether Interstellar Export Services had noticed Brewer's absence at all. Rescue arrived twenty-seven days later in the form of the *Akunin*, a Russian Federation ship designed for deep-space support operations. The *Akunin* had been chartered by Union Observatories, they explained. UO was the non-profit that operated the station. Perhaps it said something, that a few weeks without a data delivery had triggered an investigation, whilst Brewer's own employer, IES, was apparently happy to assume that she was safe, sound and sightseeing.

In the meantime, she'd been back out onto the Dish twice for repairs. The *Darty* was now floating free, tethered to the sturdiest available nearby support strut. She'd been too cautious to try the engines again.

The UO engineer volunteered to conduct brief field repairs on her damaged ship. The radio antenna was simple enough, but the thrusters resisted his efforts. Tutting regretfully, he diagnosed a fuel supply interruption, which as far as Brewer was concerned was Swedish for "it's broken."

In the absence of any other realistic option, he suggested that they tow the *Darty* manually into jump position. Brewer was a little relieved. It continued to bother her that Trade Station had certified a damaged ship for a deep-space mission. She felt too little confidence in the thrusters to put her faith in them again until they'd been thoroughly overhauled.

Brewer made Norfleet and Gailis promise to send her updates. "I'm sorry I damaged the Dish," she told them, again, when they hugged each other goodbye.

"Thanks for your work," Norfleet said.

"I don't want to miss a single episode," Brewer told them. "I want to know if Stripy ever makes it back into Spiny's good books."

Norfleet grinned at her. "We'll make sure you get access to the archives on Mars. Everything we've decrypted is available there. Share them as widely as you like. I think you're the best ambassador we could hope to have."

"Maybe I'll come back," Brewer said. "Someone's got to do the *Oldtime* run, right?"

"We'll have dinner again someday," said Gailis. "But I'm warning you now, no more Italian food."

Back on her ship, Brewer sat in the cabin, waiting for the Union captain's command to engage the *Darty's* jump drive. She was watching the ghostly outline of the Dish turning in the endless night. She thought about little orange creatures with spiny skin and too many teeth who made bad cakes, understood the art of the pratfall, and apparently thought that belching was an endless source of humour. She wondered if they were still out there.

"Either way," she told the silent darkness, "for now, I'm going home."

Emma Tonkin is a data analyst and researcher who has found it increasingly difficult to resist the compulsive tendency to write science fiction. The recent advent of design fiction as a practical human-computer interaction methodology was the last straw. Not only is science-fiction commonly used in the design process, but it is now officially considered as A Good Thing. Having given in to the urge, she has recently had a short story accepted in **Mad Scientist Journal** *and looks forward to spending a lot more time in her own universes.*

She lives in the south-west of England in an appropriately sparse garret and has occasionally considered developing a doomsday device in order to shut everybody up so that she has more time to write. For now, her lunch breaks tend to involve around a thousand words per day.

After a voyage spanning generations, a world ship arrives at the center of the galaxy. An alien ship emerges from a nearby white hole and launches a probe. Unable to find a common language, the humans fear the worst. How can a painter and his mathematician wife decipher the aliens' plans...and what could they be?

THE CENTRAL SYSTEMS

By

Mark P. Steele

Luyak and the other spectators watched as the light of the nebulae ahead was eclipsed, occulted by the blackness that loomed before them. Though vortices and clouds of debris surrounded the huge body in the galaxy's center, that great object still blotted out everything behind it. It was as visible as darkness could be to all on the observation deck.

Far from any sun, nothing could maintain itself this close to the central gravity well, but would be pulled apart and absorbed by the massive black hole at the galaxy's center. The celestial objects orbited in various patterns, with comets, supernovae, and quasars, all weaving an intricate pattern around the central core.

Luyak was aboard *World-Ship Scorpius*, which had traveled from the outer part of the galaxy at a fraction of light speed for many millennia. The Archivists had tracked the ship history over the journey, but many items had been lost over time. Even with crystal holographic technology, the computer systems had only so much storage space. The Archivists believed the records of the trip, and the star systems that they'd visited, to be more important than the individual lives of those on board. The people who were born and died mattered only if their lives affected the ship and its journey.

Luyak was in the observation deck toward the front of the ship, just behind the network where pilots and navigators did their jobs. He was not well versed in technology, his family being from the artistic social allotments on board. Rarely did he, or any of the others on board, think about their origins, but today the Archivists were reminding them.

One of the vital issues of the late twenty-first and early twenty-second centuries was Earth's burgeoning population and finding ways and reasons for people to migrate. But taking resources away from the depleted home planet was not an option. Even though faster-than-light travel had never been discovered, the Earthers built ships, using the resources of the asteroid belt and the other planets, and sent them out into the galaxy. The first Earth colonists had headed for Alpha Centauri. But those of more adventurous natures didn't stay there long, and found other places to go. *Scorpius's* journey had started from the star system Antares, many generations ago.

All this was ancient history to Luyak. He touched the stud on the implant behind his ear, to turn up the volume on the announcements being made concerning this historic event. This was the end, though in some ways the beginning, of their mission.

Luyak watched the outer reaches before him, his artist's mind speculating on the possibility that they might be inner reaches, since they were so close to the galactic core. Regardless, the beauty he saw would make good paintings. His renderings of interstellar wonders were his most popular subjects. His heart was really in the ones of the flora and fauna on the ship, which weren't nearly as popular, but he had to keep his clients happy.

The *Scorpius* had traveled for thousands of parsecs to get here, and there had been many stops, the first being Alpha Centauri, and some detours along the way. The vast distance from Sol in the Orion spur, on the outer edge of the Sagittarius arm, to this inner area around the galactic core--still more than 1000 light-years from the center-- had given the descendants of the Earth almost uncountable generations to see and learn about this slice of the cosmic reaches.

Of course, Luyak normally didn't think much about these things. Some he'd learned back in school, but much of it was being reported by his implant, and to the many others gathered to witness what was to occur.

"Luyak! Luyak!"

He turned toward a familiar-sounding voice.

Across the spiraling sector of the observation deck, he could see Synteesia, whom he'd known back in school. It had been years since their graduation. And in a city where 10,000 people lived and worked, it was easy at times to lose track of others. He smiled, and waved.

The deck swarmed with far more people than usual. Luyak came here quite often for solitude. The lesser gravity of this section of the ship made it somewhere one could escape the stresses of life.

Most people came for the avian sector, where, with the right equipment, the light gravity allowed humans to fly like birds. But he'd never tried that. The webbing strung across the section to prevent flying into the higher gravity sections, where people lived, always seemed claustrophobic to him, especially in an already tightly confining ship.

His implant was saying that, if they'd been traveling at light speed the whole time, they would have taken over fifteen millennia to get here. Luyak turned the sound down, and unbuckled his safety harness. He wasn't concerned about the information at this point. Right now, he'd rather see this young woman he used to have a crush on.

He guided himself along the navi-rails lining the walkways to where she was. While refreshing, the low G here created new ways one could harm one's self. Luyak had learned the navigation skills to maneuver on this observation area.

"Syntee!" He gave her one of those good-friends-but-that's-it hugs so common among the few their age. He pointed out toward the central core. "Do you see how beautiful that is?"

She nodded. "I remember—you were always looking at the world through artistic eyes. And you still see the world that way?"

He laughed. "Yes. I'm a painter now."

She smiled. "I'm not surprised. I ended up becoming an Analyzer."

He nodded. "You always did like mathematics. I guess that puts us outside the mating pool?"

She looked at him a moment. "I suppose. You know how strict the genetic screeners are."

Surprise came over his face. A remark like his was usually taken with either disdain or happiness. For generations, the genetic selectors had used social relationships to add to the suitability indexes. Subtle inherited genetic factors through the generations had led the eugenic hierarchy to include this factor in their calculations.

The ship had left the Antares system with a crew and colonist complement of only 2000. Its mission was to head for the galactic core, while examining and exploring star systems along the journey.

Some star systems were barren, something common in the galaxy. Some had life forms of varying levels of sentience. Those evaluated as potentially capable of, or at, the right levels of civilization were left alone and outside of observations. A few societies were at the same level of technology as the *Scorpius*, and a few were better.

Though there were times when conflict between the galactic civilizations was inevitable, some still were willing to share and trade information between species. And, during the long voyage, the scientists on board the ship had made their own advances.

Using the resources of asteroids, comets, barren planets, and other space bodies orbiting star systems they visited, the world-ship and its technology nearly doubled in size. Its population grew from 2000 to 5000, and eventually to 10,000.

Planets ripe for colonization were occasionally found, and some of the populace stayed on them to build human cultures. Though volunteers, the colonists were only allowed to leave based on the skill combinations that the leaders determined would not put the rest of the world-ship at risk. The decisions, in some cases, involved what primitive cultures of the past might call conscription.

They made the journey from Antares into the Sagittarius constellation, through the space between the Orion spur and the Sagittarian arm itself...and, within that, the Omega, Trifid, and Lagoon Nebulae. After passing through the Eagle nebula between the arms, they entered the Scutum-Centaurus arm.

Finally, on the last leg of the journey, they entered the Norma arm. They passed the five-kilo-parsec ring within that, where their journey confirmed the belief that no beings of an earth-like nature, or any other that they could detect, would be found.

No attempts were made to establish colonies within this inner ring, even though the technology of the *Scorpius* was designed to keep its inhabitants alive, and thriving in that zone.

Luyak and Synteesia looked out at the galactic center, while the implants droned on. The screens showed enhanced and screened visuals of the galactic core, with the systems orbiting around it.

The central black hole was surrounded by clouds of dust, flowing around it in a pattern that looked like a great doughnut. Jets of gas bled into the area from its poles, above and below the plane of the galaxy.

"Isn't it beautiful?" He looked at her, and smiled.

"Yes. My calculations on its orbits and behaviors don't give any sense at all of what it really looks like." She reached to her hair, pulling back the part flowing over her shoulders. "Have you painted this yet, Luyak?"

"Many times, but it hasn't ever been like this!"

He studied the whorls, and colors that the computer-enhanced images were displaying to the voyagers.

The ship slowed as they approached closer to center. Then the side rockets began firing. The image gradually moved as the ship rotated, until it was on the left part of the screens.

The maneuvering was finished—they were now in orbit around the central systems.

Scientists on board studied the central core closely for the next few months. Luyak and Syntee began seeing each other outside of work, and eventually became pleasure partners. They moved into the same quarters soon after that.

Luyak did his work at his home residence, but also displayed his work live at a gallery that was open to all. That place soon began showing his new works with a much more intricate, and colorful, vision of the central core than his earlier work. Business was booming for the first time

in his life. The economics of the ship were not something that the twenty-first century could have predicted. All of the citizens had an equal part in the survival rations, including at least a minimal berthing and clothing allotment. But there were many things beyond this that the inhabitants needed or wanted. And there were means to obtain the social items so desired.

There was no official hierarchy, but those responsible for the craft's guidance and maintenance were still of such importance that their needs were paramount. Those, like Luyak, with skills not considered needing wide cultivation, had to fend for themselves when it came to the more luxurious artifacts of human culture.

Luyak's work on the black hole images became very popular. Between prints, synthesized, electronic images, and the holographic projections, his work was soon displayed in many places around the ship.

Syntee's work also became more noted during this time. She analyzed new data from the core with a skill that the multi-Centenarians witnessed with envy. For a Younger, she had an extraordinary skill in mathematics and computer modeling of the core.

The two of them were still together after several decades, something quite unusual for pleasure pairs. The breeding couples—whether they made children naturally, or used the chambers available—generally separated after their allotment was made and raised. There were usually two, though at times those were with different mates.

Things settled down on board the ship, and the research went well. Occasionally, small data buoys were sent out at fractions of light speed toward Earth, though everyone knew the effort was probably useless.

The buoys were programmed to pass through the areas of human colonies and allies on the way to Earth, giving them the opportunity to download the data for their own use. But there was no assurance that anything would happen. It was all unknown, with the distances and time involved. Not only was it difficult for the buoys to reach the area where the most recent colonies were, there was no guarantee that when the records arrived there would still be life.

But then the alien ship appeared.

The last part of their research in the area had been at Kepler's Supernova. The world-ship had been monitoring the bodies orbiting the central black hole, while maintaining its distance from all of them.

The protection fields around the ship had been well-designed before they started the voyage and had improved over the generations. Though the earliest model of the ship could not have survived beyond the inner rim of the black hole, the advances made over the millennia had developed in the directions necessary for their mission's completion, and for the survival of the ship's inhabitants.

In ages past, cosmologists theorized that supernovae were baby black holes that would gain an event horizon when their collapse reached a critical point, at which time they would start absorbing the matter and energy around them. But some scientists in the early twenty-first century theorized that supernovae were the mouths of white holes, emptying into the surrounding parts of the universe around them, until their polarities reversed with age and they became black holes. The opposite of black holes, white holes created matter rather than destroyed it. The

Scorpius' research had already revealed that some of the supernovae in this case were, indeed, white holes.

So it was greatly surprising to them when the alien craft emerged from one of the supernovae orbiting the black hole.

Their data kept track of all the orbiting bodies around the black hole, and the telemetry from the new craft revealed that it contained life.

After some time, the other ship matched its intrinsic velocity to that of galactic center and eventually started on a course toward the *Scorpius*.

Syntee was tense and irritable during the sleep-interval after the discovery. Luyak tried easing her mind by massaging her back, but it didn't work. Neither did his efforts to try to distract her with small talk, and the events of his day.

Finally, he changed his approach:

"So, I take it there's chatter about these aliens at work?"

She nodded. "Of course. We've been analyzing the telemetry readings and energy signatures from their ship ever since it first appeared. We have to determine their intentions before first contact."

He nodded. "That's an important job."

She sighed, standing, then turning toward him. "What if we're wrong? If we decide they're peaceful, and then they attack us, we may not be ready. And if we prepare for war and they detect it, they may go on the defensive...and then we may end up coming into conflict, regardless. We weren't born when the last war with aliens was fought, and I don't know what to think!"

"What is it you do think?"

She shrugged, throwing her hands out wide, exasperation on her face. "I don't know! Were anyone to detect our ship's capabilities, they'd detect high levels of assault technology. We've learned to be prepared for conflict."

He nodded. "And some of your co-workers served in the last conflict?"

"No. It was so many generations back that all we have is the records. It was more than just a conflict. From what those records show us, it was more like an all-out war. The beings in the Eagle Nebula were one of the oldest, and most advanced, that we encountered along the voyage. If we hadn't been able to slip away..." She shuddered.

"And what makes you Analysts believe this may be the same problem?"

"The life-sign monitor readings we get from the other ship are very similar to the readings of the Eagle Nebula inhabitants. And the technology is also very close. It's enough to make us want to take all due precautions."

"And if they're not?"

"Then the officers in charge of our weapons array may start a war we could have avoided."

He shook his head. "Damn. No wonder you're upset! Is there anything you can do about it?"

She shook her head. "Not a thing. We just have to wait it out, hope both sides keep their wits about them, and that neither starts a fight."

The standoff continued for a few weeks. As was expected, the telemetry indicated that the other ship was using quite different devices to scan the Earthers. No openly aggressive moves by either side were made, but no known attempts to communicate were received from the other ship either.

After a while, by all sensor relays on board the *Scorpius*, the others ceased their examinations. The ship from Antares stopped its own probes soon after this in what would hopefully be interpreted as a sign of peace.

Then a small capsule emerged from the other ship. The readings when it was scanned indicated no life forms...no weapons capacity. The object was slowly brought to the ship by a tractor beam. A team of Analysts examined the device, and its contents.

It wasn't very different from the type of material probes that the *Scorpius* had used for millennia. The construction was of slightly different materials, but the necessities of outer space usage ensured similar manufacture. Its contents, however...

When Syntee came home from work the next day, she was accompanied by one of the Analyzers' cloaked superiors. Luyak looked up in surprise as they entered.

"Luyak? I am Cirdron, First Analyzer of the Prime Division." He extended his hand in a gesture that had survived the ages.

Luyak took his hand. "Good meeting you, First One. To what do we owe the honor of this visit?"

Cirdron sighed, slipping the carrying bag off his shoulder. "Get right to the point, don't you, Luyak? I understand that. I seldom visit those I work with. Always considered it bad policy."

The First set the case on the table...an elegantly polished work of what appeared to be marble...and opened it. There was what earlier generations would have called a laptop inside—though it was slightly different in form.

"We're not sending any of this through the web. Security is tight right now. All is on a need-to-know basis. You might say," the man said, smiling, "you're being deputized into your analog's department. Any issues, or objections?"

Luyak glanced at Syntee, then looked at the other man in surprise. "Sir...I'm not mathematically inclined at all. I've barely used any math not needed for setting proportions since graduating. What use will I be to you people?"

The First nodded. "That's exactly why we want you. The skills you have are very rare...and, right now, we need them."

He pressed a few keys on the board attachment of the deck, then paused. "So do you agree?"

Luyak nodded. "Of course."

Cirdron pressed one final key, and a series of images began flashing by on the video screen. "These were in the device the aliens released." He stood back, and let Luyak watch the flow of images.

The young artist whistled. "These are drawings...paintings...other art images of types I don't quite recognize." He turned toward the other man. "They sent you art?"

The First nodded. "Both hard copy, and in a device that they sent. It took us some time to decode the device's files, but—assuming that it was picture files we had to work with—we were eventually able to access them. The basics of computers...other than the differences between the crude binaries and the trinaries we now use...ensured quick work on that.

"But the meaning of these images—" Cirdron shrugged his shoulders. "That's beyond our understanding."

Luyak slowed the display, reversed it on occasion, and studied the art before him. He looked over at the First with a puzzled expression on his face, and then sat before the ongoing stream of art.

"So you mathies don't understand. What is it you want from me?"

"We need to decipher what they're trying to tell us. The images are all peaceful—tranquil—by our standards. But what there is other than that, we don't know."

Luyak nodded. "So you need art interpretation?"

"In a manner of speaking. We have records that there were cultures on Earth which used pictorial symbols for communication rather than alphabetic coding. The Egyptians and the Chinese were the two leading cultures that used that form of communication."

The young artist paused the readout on one image, and nodded. "I did some studying of those in school, and since then in the records. The Egyptian stelae and the Chinese scrolls were two of my favorite subjects during my early years."

"We know." The First smiled. "That's one of the main reasons you're being offered this assignment. Given the items that they sent us, we believe that they have peaceful intentions. But we need to learn to communicate with them...understand what it is they're trying to tell us."

"And that's where I come in?"

Cirdron nodded. "Exactly. We know that there were ways during the pictograph eras around Earth that numerical values—essential for any of our research—were communicated. But it will be difficult to identify any of that until we understand the basics of their writings."

Luyak studied the images closer, slowly scrolling up and down on the screen, then brought his own unit out. "May I copy these files?"

The First nodded. "We want to keep them off the net, and I believe this residence has a suitable security rating." He looked over at Syntee with a questioning look, and she nodded.

"It was updated a few days ago, First."

Luyak looked at the two with questions in his eyes, then returned his gaze to the screen with a slight smile.

"I guess you have an Artist working for you, Analyzers."

The work over the next few months was intense. Luyak had never bothered trying to interpret the meanings of images before, simply making them. He let people feel the meanings for themselves. The pictograph communication these aliens were using was something new, but something rooted in the origins of communication, even on earth.

The two ships orbiting the central systems of the galaxy traded communications with increasing frequency. Electromagnetic communications—not just physical ones—were eventually transmitted when the proper interfaces were constructed. These aliens used a different means for that type of communication than radio, the base of communication for the Earth-like beings of the galaxy. The electromagnetic spectrum was vast, and the data ascription complex, but headway was made.

Luyak was working with his analog rather early in the research. The personal rapport they'd established over the years enhanced their understanding of the communications from the alien ship, though he had little formal background in mathematics.

The data that the aliens provided them revealed parts of their story and some of the technology that they used.

These beings had come from a region that resembled the far side of the galaxy. Though there was debate as to whether or not the white hole was connected to a receiving singularity in the same universe, the pictorial records were still clear.

The Zannabites had evolved a technology that the crew of the *Scorpius* had never used, or even considered. Once the right translation point was reached, the mathematics were found to be parts of equations that had been known by the Earthers for millennia, although not generally used.

The black/white hole dichotomy had been one of the major parts of the Earth ship's research and analysis. Mathematics and theory indicated that both might be paired, the way the wormholes were paired. But wormholes were paired as two-way hyper-spatial conduits, while the black/white hole combinations were one-way conduits, unless one considered a polarity switching possibility. No species known to the colonists had discovered wormholes, but there had been some black—and a few white—holes postulated and identified.

The *Scorpius* crew went over the data from the Zannabites quite thoroughly, once the numerical Rosetta stone had been discovered. Luyak spent less time on the analysis after that, and more time painting. The objects that he worked on at this time were now interpretations of the white holes where matter was ejected into the universe.

A bridge was built between the *Scorpius'* main hull and the Zannabites' smaller ship. There was plenty of material circulating around the central core for constructing this link, and for extending the dwelling portions of both ships.

Much of Luyak's art now went over to the aliens' ship-home. He brought many of their works over to the Earth ship as well, and found good placements for them.

Syntee eventually came home with some news. She was excited, and threw her arms around Luyak.

"We've done it, my fancier! The equations got solved!"

He hugged her and then stepped back, curious. They had been together long enough that such displays of affection were not as common as they used to be, though their love—if that antiquated word was accepted—still seemed as strong as ever.

"What might that be? I must confess that it's been so long since I helped make connections to the alien allies that I've forgotten some of the Analyzers' objectives."

"Oh." She grinned. "The evaluation plans for traversing the black holes!"

He laughed. "How could I have forgotten that?" He steered her toward the couch, where she sat down, and stepped over to prepare a drink. "Tell me, now, what exactly is this about?"

"It was surprising to begin with when they came through the white hole. The problems of mass at the singularities, and the Schwartzchild radii—oh, never mind. The first point is that they solved the equations to stop being crushed to death as they passed through the hyper-spatial conduit."

He nodded. "I remember that. It was one of the main reasons I had to help decipher their written language. You remember when we theorized that it was their pictographic written vocabulary that helped them imagine the solutions to that complex?"

She nodded. "Yes. We were right about that. That portion's been mostly solved for a while now."

"Well, thanks for keeping me informed!" He grinned, and they both laughed.

"The second problem is what's got me excited. We could never figure out, with the initial sets of data, how the Zannabites had known they would exit here, and not in some other region of the galaxy. We thought at first that they may have entered without knowing where they were headed. But, after we achieved the proper level of communication, their own leaders quickly let us know that was not the case.

"Their species took a slightly different theoretical view of the warp conduits. The mathematics used back on

Earth did give us a clue, once we figured out what they were trying to tell us."

He set the drink before her, and moved behind her to rub her shoulders. "Go on," he said, as his fingers moved across her no-longer-young muscles.

"The theories were odd back then. There were differences in them between two different types of black and white holes...the rotating, and the non-rotating."

He laughed. "Yes, I remember some of us joking about the sit-and-spin idea back in the science classes."

She tried looking offended, and gently swung a mock fist back toward him. "Oh, hush, we don't need to get into that!" The smile crept over her face despite her best efforts, and she relaxed again.

"Well, what should we get into then?" He kissed her neck, his fingers still gently caressing her muscles.

"Mmm...let's go there in a bit, analog dear." She leaned forward, lifted her drink, and took a sip. "Right now...you remember someone called Einstein?"

He nodded, stepped back, and came around. "Wasn't he the one that figured out we couldn't go faster-than-light, then left the...um...loophole about the black holes?"

She nodded, laughing. "Yes, exactly! And it's his wonderful theory of Relativity that makes the difference here. You remember anything about that?"

He shrugged. "I don't really. There didn't seem to be anything in what little I remember to inspire my imagination." He bent down again to kiss her neck.

"Oh, you." A grin on her face, she grabbed a pillow, and tossed it at him. "I can never tell when you're giving me a line, or not!"

"So, presume I don't know, and try to tell me."

"Well, you remember what I said about rotating and non-rotating black and white holes?"

He nodded. "Yes, kind of like tops, right?"

She grinned. "Quite similar, yes. Well, in theory, the rotating ones are connected to one with the opposite polarity—one rotating black hole leads to one rotating white hole, whether in this universe or another."

He chuckled. "Now it's sounding like one of those water hoses in the old records we have."

"Exactly! Water, if I recall the vids you're referencing, enters one end—the black end—and comes out the other—the white end."

"Pretty clear. Now, what about those others...the ones you said didn't rotate?"

"In those, the singularity at the center is a place where all moves out of, or into, existence. Matter and energy are created or destroyed."

He stood silent a moment. "That...I think that violates one of the basic principles of physics?"

"Oh, it would, if it happened within the universe. But, since it's outside...beyond the event horizon...then it really doesn't count."

He sighed. "I don't quite get it, but...it's like how the universe was created, so long ago?"

She nodded. "Yes. Perhaps, eons ago, this black hole we're orbiting was a massive white hole, and gave birth to the matter of this galaxy."

He shrugged. "And this is important to us now because...?"

"It's all about the relativity! See, when Einstein, so long ago, came up with these theories, he said that there weren't any objective frames of reference...that all were relative to something else. Like our ship passing through space has its own co-ordinates, but the planets we passed each had their own frames of reference."

"Sure. Like the frames on my pictures. Some folks want me to choose, others want to put their own on them. The choice is relative, depending on the person who wants the painting."

She laughed. "I hadn't thought about it that way, but you're right." She stood, and took her cup over to the drink-maker. "Want one?"

"Yes, please."

She refilled her own drink, and made one for him. She set them down before sitting, and continued.

"So, if we're looking at a black hole, and we see it rotating—the axial component being something that we can detect as the spike coming from the central core shows—then that's what our frame of reference is telling us.

"What if we choose a reference frame that, according to the one we were using, rotates at the same rate as the black hole?"

He sat a moment, taking a sip of the drink. "Huh." Leaning back, he rubbed his eyes. "What you're saying is that, by choosing relative frames of references, the black hole is both rotating, and not rotating?"

"Exactly!"

"So the black hole both accesses a white hole and reaches to where all is annihilated?"

"That's the point."

"And what happens if you choose a frame where it's rotating at a different speed?"

"That's exactly the technology that the Zannabites developed! They were able to take enough readings on the galactic core to detect the presence, theoretically, of the white hole from which they arrived. And they calculated what angle and speed that they'd need to use when entering a black hole near their main space to arrive at it."

"Brilliant." He laughed. "You know you've totally lost me now!"

"Oh, my analog, don't try to hide your awareness." She laughed. "Some of the references you made when studying their pictographs showed much insight."

"Well," he said, "I may have insight, but I don't see why all this is so important now."

"We finished this stage of the calculations, and the engineers have finished the vessel. Tomorrow it will be announced...the first of a series of data capsules will be launched toward the Galactic Core, and will accelerate to a far larger percentage of the speed of light than we could ever do.

"The capsule will give all the data on how this technology works, and a mapping of all the known—and suspected—black and white holes we've accumulated in the millennia of the *Scorpius'* voyage. We're sending it to the white hole that we've identified as being closest to Earth.

"After that, we'll be preparing and sending similar capsules to space near each of the colonies, and the allies that we made on the voyage, giving them similar information.

"When they get the information, and make the ships that can endure the voyage—assuming, of course, that any on Earth are still alive—they can make the journey, through the nearest black hole to the white hole that we have near here." She lifted the glass with a grin, and finished the drink.

He laughed. "So we really will be in the center of things, when all start traveling here." He lifted his glass, and finished his drink as well.

She set the glass down, and coyly put her arm around him. "It's more than that. To prepare for the visitors that will be coming our way when the time is right, the engineers are going to be greatly expanding our world-ship. The population will have to increase, and..." She dropped her eyes, blushing slightly, and her voice became very quiet.

"The geneticists have authorized our...children. And with the increase expected, we will be allowed to have more than two. We might be getting older, but..."

At those words, a wide grin came over his face. Grabbing her, he pressed his lips to hers, then swept her up, and carried her off to their sleeping room.

The capsule went off without incident, soon followed by others. Luyak and Synteesia did have their children. And the ship grew, its population increasing, as it did.

In time, the first of the Earthers came through the black hole closest to the original solar system and emerged from the white hole near the world-ship. As time went by, others arrived from other points along the line drawn between Sol and the galactic core. Some stayed, others used the world-ship as a way-station to travel to yet other parts of the galaxy.

By then, the theorists were working on the idea that the central black hole might be used to travel to other galaxies, if dealing with the huge differences in intrinsic velocity between the huge bodies of celestial objects could be solved.

Of course, Luyak and Syntee were long gone by then, even with their lives spanning far beyond that of twenty-first century humans. But a large percentage of those aboard *World-Ship Scorpius* were their quite active descendants. Many traveled to other worlds, others began space voyages to unexplored reaches of the galaxy, and some were working on a communication system, using the mini-black and mini-white holes of—

But that is a different story!

Mark Steele has been involved with comics, science fiction, and other such literature most of his life. He attended a liberal arts college at the age of 16, and soon entered the health care field, where he's spent much of his time since then.

His publishing accomplishments include: writing and some inking on a comic book adaptation of Shea and Wilson's ILLUMINATUS! Trilogy (the first self-published issue now available on-line) from Apple products and Rip Off Press; and a translation of "Daughter of Fantomas", the 8th book in the pre-WWI series, from French to English for Black Coat Press. Most recently, Mark has developed a comics series set in the late 1930s and a series of internet TV shows for a private company.

Mark has also been a Pastor for an Earth Spirituality Church filed with the State of Michigan.

His current upcoming prose works include publication in the online InfectiveINk web site, science fiction for Lillicat Publishers, adventure for Visual Adjectives, and a heroic adventure tale set back in 1939...at one of the first World Science Fiction cons.

Across the abyss of inter-stellar space, humanity joins with alien life-forms in defending the Worldship, a gigantic, ancient spaceship drifting for eons between the stars. The cosmic mystery of the Worldship may offer a new future for humanity, or its destruction.

JOINING

By

Tom Olbert

Jorrin pulled up desperately, his space fighter spinning to avoid the crackling wave of blue lightning and immense ebony shards that was the Swarm. A dark marvel in the interstellar void, the Swarm appeared one moment like a splintering, black, crystalline planet, and the next, like waves of shimmering black/silver matter reforming into arcing tendrils, growing miles long as they artfully intertwined.

Jorrin grit his teeth and pressed the firing button. Twin particle beams lanced out from the prow of his fighter, blasting the key points in the Swarm's formation, which the A.I. net targeted. Blue bolts flashed across Jorrin's vision as his fighter passed between the monstrous streams of the Swarm. The colors danced across the mutating crystalline lattices deceptively, almost intoxicatingly beautiful. He aimed and fired again and again, the machine net guiding his every move. Beauty shattered into fragments of beauty, light and color splintering across a disintegrating sky.

His squadron's fighters slipped into attack formation in coordination with the Kyll and Zaarth squadrons. The Swarm was a continuous stream of matter, hurtling with purpose and direction towards the immense sphere of the *Worldship*. A starship the size of a star, the *Worldship* moved through the galactic void, silent in its opaque majesty. The Swarm branched out into nightmarish streams. Like immense tentacles, they tried to slip through the *Worldship*'s encircling layers of defense fighters and A.I. orbiters. Flitting motes of light, the fighters blasted the branching tentacles to bits.

Jorrin gunned his thrusters, his fighter advancing in the three-pronged assault formation, as what remained of this incarnation of the Swarm reformed for its final assault. His heart raced. Tentacle-like formations, surrounding an immense maw of crackling blue and silver lightning, opened wide enough to swallow a dozen space squadrons.

"All fighters, concentrate on designated nexus-points," the cold voice of Rutann, the coordinating A.I. intoned. All three squadrons converged with flawless unity, Rutann's robot defense units blasting downward in coordination.

Jorrin fought to keep steady as he closed on his target and fired, the Swarm formations shattering in blue fire. He winced and lowered his shades as a million flaming shards hurtled towards the squadrons in one last, desperate onslaught. Fighters disintegrated around him, consumed in the web of crackling energy streams spread out between those oncoming shards. The dying screams, human and otherwise, of his brother and sister space pilots shrieked through his ear phones. Those screams were like skewers to his nerves, but Jorrin would not allow himself the luxury of switching off the audio. He owed it to his comrades to bear witness to their last moments. His blood boiled with hatred as he remembered the Swarm attack that killed his parents in Cartagna when he has nine.

Switching to manual, he weaved and dodged, blasting the shards as they lined up in his beamer sights. Enveloped by three huge fragments, a blazing white mass of energy between them, he was hopelessly trapped. No way to clear out of the way in time. He swore in rage, tears in his eyes. *Spirits of the Ancestors, accept me*, he silently prayed.

"Jorrin, come to 1-1-0," Kryzgh's inhuman voice slipped in over Jorrin's comm beam, the computer translating his Kyll friend's screeches into comprehensible human speech. Jorrin obeyed the order and came about, firing as Kryzgh's fighter swooped in from above, blasting downward into the Swarm fragment. The dual particle beam burst shattered the nexus of the fragment, energy streams cracking wildly.

Kryzgh's fighter broke up in the energy blast. The Kyll's pilot pod ejected and spun wildly. "Kryzgh!!" Jorrin yelled at the top of his lungs as he quickly altered course and accelerated towards it. "I won't let you down, friend," he silently vowed, his blood racing hot and swift, as he pushed his fighter to its limit. "Just hang on."

A prime specimen of his species, Kryzgh was a wild, clattering mass of razor-sharp, spiny fins, claws and fangs. Jorrin fell back, rolling, his flight suit torn open by the Kyll's wild onslaught. His fellow pilots surrounded Kryzgh as the wounded Kyll tore his way out of his damaged pilot pod in the launch bay. Jorrin gaped in fear and awe at Kryzgh's three sets of gnashing fangs, like triple heads, in a being that actually had no head, its central nervous system encased in a complex exo-skeletal frame. Jorrin started as his friend lashed out with bestial fury at the former comrades trying to restrain him. Kryzgh nearly blurred into a grey-silver shimmer, those razor-edged surfaces slicing faster than the eye could follow.

Kryzgh's fellow Kyll surrounded him, containing his fury until Rutann finally managed to get into position to stun him unconscious with neuro-electrical prods. Jorrin sighed deeply, wiping sweat from his brow. He was at once relieved and deeply concerned as his best friend fell senseless to the launch bay deck. Jorrin's mind swirled. It was all too much. He felt a comforting appendage on his shoulder and looked up into the huge, shaggy face of Zynn, one of the Zaarth pilots. A damn good one, he'd learned from multiple operations. And, a good friend. Zynn's six fluidic eyes shimmered bright purple, her three funnel-like speech orifices fluctuating as her translator implant converted her concern into human-recognizable speech. "Are you all right, Jorrin?"

"Yeah, Zynn, thanks," he muttered, stroking her thick, shaggy fur. The Kyll parted, making way for one of their analyzers to come to Kryzgh's side. The seconds ticked infuriatingly by as the Kyll medic ran extensive scans of Kryzgh's prone form. "Well?" Jorrin asked impatiently. "Will he be all right?"

He held his breath. The Kyll medic silently put away his instruments. Jorrin's blood turned to ice. "He is beyond help," the medic's A.I.-translated voice said. "Irreparable neural damage. The connection between host and symbiote are severed. Both are intact, but the connection is lost forever." Even Jorrin understood what that meant. The Kyll were a symbiotic lifeform. The symbiote in a Kyll was the center of its intellect, a soft inner core neurally linked with the exo-skeletal host that was the animal part. The two parts evolved in tandem over millions of years into a perfectly balanced being. Once that balance was gone, there was nothing left but agonizing madness, the two irreconcilable halves destroying each other. "There is nothing left but for him to pass on to the Horde."

Jorrin's heart turned to lead in his chest. His head bowed and tears formed in his eyes. Zynn's four-digit, black-shelled claw gently tightened on his shoulder. The surrounding throng of Kylls grated and ground and quivered, as they prepared. Jorrin's head sprang up. "No," he said through clenched teeth, stepping protectively between Kryzgh and the Kyll horde, that was even now preparing to devour him, to eat out the interior of his shell, as was their way; the individual returning to the Horde in the end, sharing his strength with his fellows. Nothing wasted. "Leave him alone," he warned, drawing his beamer. "You'll not take him. Not yet."

"Stand aside, human," one of the larger Kyll, apparently a horde leader, warned, bearing his fangs. "It is not for you to interfere. Kryzgh is one of us."

"He's my friend," Jorrin protested, his sweaty fingers tightening on his beamer. "He saved my life, and we pilots don't abandon our own!" As if in reply, the rest of the surviving pilots gathered around Jorrin. Men and women from his own squadron, Zaarth pilots gathering behind Zynn as she slithered up beside him, all with beamers drawn. "You want him; you go through us." He'd lost too many friends, damn it, to the Void. And, Kryzgh was a closer comrade in arms than any human he'd served with.

Jorrin looked around. None of the Kyll pilots stood with his group, though they hung at the fringes of the Kyll civilian mob, their beamers still holstered, their loyalties clearly divided. One of them, a veteran pilot named Skrygge, stepped slowly forward.

"Jorrin, my brother," the Kyll intoned slowly through his translator implant. "I understand your pain. But, you cannot understand Kryzgh's. Only anguish, madness and slow, humiliating death await him now. If you respect our comrade, then let him pass on with dignity. It's what he would want." The other Kyll ground and clattered in unison, their fangs glistening, as though in preparation for a feast that was for their kind both mourning and celebration.

Jorrin steeled himself, able to remember only the countless times Kryzgh had saved his life in battle. The many times they'd shared pleasure together in the neuro-stimulation chambers on leave. "I'm not ready to give up on him yet. Not while there's still even a bit of hope. He wouldn't give up on any of us!"

"What hope is there?" Skrygge asked. "You heard the analyzer."

"Maybe your medicine can't help him. But..." Jorrin clenched, scarcely able to believe what he was about to suggest. "Maybe..." His mouth went dry. "Maybe, if we take him to the Web."

A sickening, grinding screech rang through the Kyll horde. Gut-wrenching sounds the A.I. net translated as "blasphemy," "obscenity" and "unnatural" were discernable along with a Kyll word that loosely translated as "demon" or "hell". Cold sweat covered Jorrin as he tightened his grip on his beamer.

"Never," Skrygge intoned, his fangs clenching. Jorrin slowly lowered his beamer, in respect for a fellow pilot, to give Skrygge a fair chance on the draw. Jorrin licked his lips and waited.

Skrygge's claws knotted and tightened. Then, relaxed, moving away from his holstered beamer. Jorrin exhaled. "I will not draw the blood of a fellow pilot," Skrygge said through grinding fangs. "But, if you move against the Kyll, you stand without the Kyll squadron, Jorrin. As do all who stand with you."

The hairs on the back of Jorrin's neck stood on end as a sound spread rapidly through the Kyll horde. A sound he recognized as the rattling Kyll claws made just before they pounced on their prey. Skrygge slowly, haltingly moved aside, leaving Jorrin and the others defenseless before the blood-thirsty mob. Jorrin raised his beamer and set it on heavy stun force. The last thing he wanted was to kill any Kyll civvies. He'd probably be spaced for this as it was. And, as he was breaking Assembly law by interfering in the cultural practices of one of the three *Worldship* species, he knew he could expect no intervention from the Assembly Securitat forces. He looked left and right, beamers lined up all around him. His heart was in a vise as he realized that if Kryzgh were conscious and in his right senses, he'd probably surrender himself for execution rather than ask his comrades to shed their blood for him against his own kind. *Forgive me, old friend,* Jorrin thought as the horde charged and he fired.

Blue flashes shimmered in rippling pools through the shrieking crowd as all the pilots fired in unison. The civilian mob quickly deteriorated into a leaderless pack of wild animals, as intent on their purpose as the alien Swarm. Scores went down, unconscious, but the rest just kept coming.

Crackling white streams of neural shock pulses rippled through the crowd. Jorrin started and looked up as Rutann reared up to its full height, the Omega-class tactical robot blasting downward into the crowd. Its electrical probes extended, Rutann briefly resembled some nightmarish mechanical version of a gigantic praying mantis. The Kyll mob pulled back and regrouped behind the growing mound of unconscious bodies. Rutann gently gathered the still-unconscious Kryzgh in its metal claws and secured him on its platform, as Rutann assumed one of its several functional shapes. Becoming an aerial evac-sled, Rutann rose on a boiling shimmer of blue-white repulsion energy, its thruster jets extending.

"Assume defense positions," Rutann ordered, its programming as a tactical coordinator even now kicking in. *But, what else did its programming demand of it?* Jorrin wondered, his mind racing as he jumped onto one edge of the platform, firing into the crowd to shield Kryzgh from Kyll loners, who even now lunged at the lifting sled. Rutann was one of the newer A.I.'s, Jorrin remembered. Hard to understand sometimes, and more closely interfaced with the Web than earlier models. The primary program directive of all A.I.'s, to protect sentient life, seemed particularly strong in the Omega series. *Let's hope that's all it is*, Jorrin thought. He shuddered at the thought of handing his best friend over to the Web.

One of the other human pilots, Kazen, jumped onto the opposite edge of the sled, knocking aside a lunging Kyll attacker with his repulsion gauntlet. "Scatter," Jorrin called into his comm band, his voice echoing across the landing platform as he looked down at the scene of chaos playing out below. "Save yourselves. It's us they want. We got this covered. Go!" He saw his fellow pilots evacuating the landing platform, the humans fleeing on jet sleds and propulsion belts, the Zaarth taking flight, their wings unfurled.

Jorrin lurched and hung on as Rutann accelerated. They jetted across the yawning chasms, the centrifugal hydroponic farms, the free-floating spherical oceans, and the ancient, half-ruined cities that made up the *Worldship*. Or, rather made up only a tiny part of it, Jorrin realized. Only the outer sections, the extraneous layers built by the three races over the far more ancient aspect of the *Worldship*, which was still so much a mystery to all three of its adopted resident lifeforms. Jorrin shook off a wave of childish sorrow as he saw the blasted, decaying remains of Cartagna, the city where his parents had died. He dimly remembered the history vids he'd seen as a schoolboy, of the more ancient ruins that stretched beyond. Beresford's Hope, the revered first *Worldship* city. Some four thousand galactic years ago, the honored ancestors of humanity had first arrived there in their nuclear star jammers. They'd made a thousand-year journey in cryogenic cold-sleep, after fabled Earth's sun had flared and died. The radio signal of the blessed *Worldship* had been their one beacon of hope in the dark interstellar void, and the *Worldship* had been nurturing mother to humanity ever since.

Beyond stretched the ruins of Sorwanna, as the humans called it, Zrrghh-Brysshgh, as the Kyll called it. Its fallen towers still commemorated the first tragic war between the humans and the Kyll "invaders" as they were then known. Fleeing their own dying home world, the Kyll had arrived on the *Worldship* in their tachyon-drive hibernation ships, some six-hundred galactic years after the humans. And beyond that lay the ancient hive cities of the first Zaarth settlers, who had arrived in their fusion-drive multi-generational hive ships about a thousand years after the Kyll. For twenty-two centuries, the three races had fought over the *Worldship* in shifting alliances. In the past two centuries, the onslaught of the Swarm, the dark, enigmatic enemy from the Void, had forced all three races to cooperate in defending their common adopted home.

"Hang on, old friend," Jorrin quietly said, laying a hand gently on Kryzgh's still form. "We're getting you there, I promise."

"Jorrin, we've got incoming!" Kazen shouted, his long blonde hair flowing in the wind as he looked up. Jorrin saw Kyll attackers moving in fast on propulsion packs. Civvies, definitely; experienced pilots wouldn't be flying so clumsily, without any recognizable formation. *That's one point in our favor*, Jorrin thought. His heart sank as he saw more and more of them coming into view...at least a dozen, their thrusters shimmering blue against the ruins above.

"Attackers incoming," Rutann intoned. "Brace for evasive course corrections."

Jorrin crouched and held on tightly as Rutann turned sharply, swerving through the ruined, gutted towers of the ancient cities, as the Kyll swooped in, beamers blazing. An explosion ripped through a building side, half the ancient structure crumbling to dust. *Void, the devils are using kill settings*, Jorrin thought. Not that it really mattered; stun settings at this speed and height would be deadly. Jorrin and Kazen fired at will, stunning the first few attackers, who spun wildly out of control, some of them crashing into the surrounding ruins. Hearing Kazen scream, Jorrin turned just as a large Kyll dropped onto the sled, his claws clamping on hard. What was left of Kazen's body fell like a stone towards the ruins below. One swipe of the Kyll's claws ripped Jorrin's beamer from his hand. He swore at the top of his lungs, lashing out in rage even as the Kyll tried to pounce on Kryzgh.

Jorrin drove in hard, using his repulsion gauntlet. As he pounded the Kyll, the repulsion field shimmering silver gray on the rippling air, Jorrin flashed back to the last time he'd used the gauntlet, at a food riot in one of the central hydroponic pods. The starving mobs tearing at the stores, killing anyone who got in their way...he'd lost a brother in that skirmish.

As the Kyll fell from the sled, Jorrin leapt backward, just in time to avoid an over-hanging girder that would have taken his head off. Tumbling end-over-end in the neutral gravity of the *Worldship* interior, Jorrin pulled his cyber lash from his belt and activated it, the shimmering, electrically-charged metallic line playing out and coiling around one of the thruster jets. Jorrin had always hated those crowd-control weapons, having seen what they could do to living flesh. But, at the moment, dangling from the hurtling sled, he thanked the ancestors for including them in required ordnance. Hitting the rewind, he pulled himself up and swung over the edge onto the sled. He heaved a sigh of relief when he found Kryzgh was all right. It didn't stop the pang of guilt and anger that hit his gut a moment later, when he thought of Kazen and his family.

He roared in rage as a swarm of Kyll surrounded the sled and swooped in. "We'll go down together, friend," he said, clenching the lash. He recoiled as a rain of blue energy beams lanced down from above. He looked up and saw a swarm of Zaarth flying in their characteristically tight formation, beamers flashing. The Kyll quickly scattered and fled. Jorrin took a deep breath and came down on one knee beside Kryzgh. They were now in Zaarth territory. They were safe.

"I thought you might need assistance," Zynn said, her long, shaggy, serpentine form coming in alongside the sled, both sets of wings unfurled and stroking.

"I thought I told you to get yourself to safety." He smiled, holding his fist aloft in the traditional pilot's greeting.

"Since when do I take orders from you?" Zynn said, dipping her wings and gracefully angling downward.

As Rutann followed Zynn down, Jorrin saw that they had arrived at their destination. The Web stretched out for miles, its shimmering golden rays of energy extending to every section of the *Worldship*'s power grid. As the sled descended slowly, Jorrin could discern the many shimmering spheres of light that formed the nodes of the Web. And, inside the spheres were the acolytes, the Humans and Zaarth, who had directly interfaced with the energy source of the *Worldship*, in a way no one really understood. Through millennia of learning to tap the still-largely mysterious energy emanating from the *Worldship*'s power core, in order to fuel the hydroponic farms, factories and cities, the acolytes had evolved the Web.

For the acolytes, the Web had developed into a pseudo-religion. And, only the ancestors understood what it really was. A telepathic commonality, perhaps, like an immense living brain. Or, something more. Some believed that the intellects of the many individual beings comprising the Web collectively formed a level of thought that transcended the conventional dimensions of the universe. Some hoped it might eventually solve the ancient puzzle of how to control the *Worldship*'s navigation system, steering the *Worldship* where its occupants wanted it to go. Some even dreamed of circumventing the law of light speed, ultimately taking the *Worldship* in one lifetime to habitable planetary systems. Others feared the Web as a threat to the existence of free will and individuality. The military...Jorrin included...despised the Web for its subversive influence on the more radical scientists and the general population, sometimes even inspiring disaffection in the armament factories. But, whatever else the Web was, it was also the distributor of the *Worldship*'s energy, without which all three species would perish.

Rutann set down gently on a landing platform adjacent to one of the nearest nodes. Several of the acolytes left their spheres of light and gathered on the platform, floating down like motes of dust in a way that was also a mystery.

"I regret that we must re-unite under these circumstances, Jorrin," a familiar feminine voice said.

Jorrin's heart throbbed as he stepped from the sled, scanning the crowd. One of the human acolytes, a spare figure, indistinguishable from the others in the flowing white robes they all wore, stepped forward. Her small hands pulled back her cowl, and there she stood before him after what seemed an eternity. Jemma. Her triangular face was as strikingly beautiful as ever, its delicate cheek bones framing her penetrating, hypnotic eyes. Her clean-shaven head was marred only by the ovoid metallic object in the center of her forehead—the brain implant that linked all acolytes to the Web. As ever, her beauty seemed to hold his gaze captive. Yet, he could scarcely bare to look at her now, the sight of her in that costume, in that life...it nauseated him.

She approached him, reaching out to stroke his face. A part of him wanted to respond, but he reflexively pulled away. She sighed. "Your mind is still clouded by hatred."

"How did you know...?"

"I informed Acolyte Jemma Venturr of our impending arrival, and of our situation," Rutann explained, resuming its conventional configuration.

Jorrin ground his teeth, feeling oddly betrayed, as though that was possible where a machine was concerned. He at times found himself thinking of Rutann as more than just that. The robot, despite having demonstrated that it was directly linked to the Web, did nothing to ease his concerns.

"I came here because my friend needs help," he said through clenched teeth. "He was your friend once too, Jemma. Or, doesn't friendship mean anything to you, now?"

Jemma knelt by Kryzgh, her hand resting on his still body. She looked up at her fellow acolytes. They surrounded Kryzgh as though a single thought from Jemma was enough to summon them. They carried him, levitating his body with their inexplicable power, into the sphere of light.

"Will he be all right?" Jorrin asked.

"Who can say?" Jemma replied. "No Kyll has ever entered the Web before. I'll help him through it as best I can." She looked at Zynn, and smiled warmly. "Zynn," she said, running to her old friend and gently putting her arms around the Zaarth's broad, shaggy neck. "I have so longed to see you again."

"And I you, my friend," Zynn said softly, all six of her black exo-skeletal arms gently embracing Jemma. Jorrin shook his head. The Zaarth were cold and efficient killers in battle, but the capacity for hate didn't seem to exist in them. They valued beauty above all else, even in the form of an enemy. There were times when he envied them for that, as he sometimes envied the Kyll for their fierce sense of honor and their courage in battle. The Zaarth, with their hive-centered mentality, had readily accepted the Web. The Kyll, who valued their individuality above all, considered it pure evil. Could Kryzgh even survive this? Jorrin clenched his fists and cursed under his breath.

Jemma turned toward the sphere as several of her brother and sister acolytes returned. "He is ready," she said. "The implant has been inserted and Kryzgh's nervous system has accepted it. It is our hope that the Web will now serve as the connection between the animal host and the symbiote that is our friend's intellect." Jorrin stood and watched as Jemma walked towards the sphere. He gasped as Kryzgh appeared in the light, now apparently fully conscious. His fearsome claws extended as Jemma advanced towards him, his fanged maws open.

"No!" Jorrin shouted, reflexively bounding forward to pull Jemma to safety. Several of the acolytes, human and Zaarth moved to block his path. He reached for his lash, but a crackling burst of electrical energy from Rutann stayed his hand. "Let me through! He'll kill her!" He glanced over at Zynn. She was trembling, her appendages clenched, her wings rippling.

"Do not fear," Jemma said softly, approaching Kryzgh. Jorrin wasn't sure if his former lover was addressing him or Kryzgh. He held his breath as the woman he'd once loved...and still cared deeply about, he now realized...stepped without a twinge of hesitation into the center of Kryzgh's grasp. Jorrin couldn't believe his eyes as Kryzgh ever-so-gently laid his claws on Jemma's shoulders and arms, a loving caress. Jorrin realized those claws could shred her flesh, crush her bones in an instant. But, he sensed Kryzgh wished Jemma no harm.

"Jorrin," Kryzgh said, his translated voice a bit shaky, but growing steadily calmer. "You saved me, my friend. We are even now."

Jorrin fought back the tears. "Uh...by my count, you're still a few up on me, but I'm working on it." A smile spread across his face. "Anyway, Zynn really got us out of this one. Uh...are you...all right?"

"I am whole," Kryzgh answered, Jemma's small hands resting on his claws. "And at one with the Web. I now share the thoughts of the other acolytes. Jemma still loves you, Jorrin. You should not be so stubborn in your rejection of her, my friend."

Jorrin furrowed his brow. Was that really Kryzgh talking or...the Web? A chill ran through him. He looked around. The other acolytes had gathered around Jemma and Kryzgh. "Their thoughts form a pattern I have not read before," Rutann said.

"What?" Jorrin asked.

"Their thoughts gather in a conception of something they have never discerned before. They call it the Joining."

Tahim lurched as he emerged from the A.I./brain interface. He trembled, massaging his throbbing temples. "Run full system diagnostic," he ordered the attending A.I.'s. What he had just glimpsed in the numerical formulations of the Science Section's central intelligence's processing core could not have been real. It simply couldn't.

"Diagnostic completed," the cold A.I. voice droned through the speaker system. "Formulation 100% accurate."

The technician slumped into his chair, wiping the sweat from his upper lip. By the ancestors, it was true. Tahim's rigidly conformist upbringing had never permitted him to entertain such possibilities. In fear of losing all credibility with the Science Board, he had denounced his sister Jemma when she'd joined the acolytes. Deep down, the shame of that betrayal had weighed heavily on his heart. And, now...

He shook his head clear, forcing the rational part of his mind to calculate. Yes, it was real. The more advanced A.I.'s, the new experimental models interfaced with the Web, had translated the Web's group mind vision into mathematically provable scientific certainty.

Lifting himself out of the chair, he walked haltingly to the virtual reality interface and put on the cybernetic headset. He had to see firsthand what his mind could only half-accept in theory. He found himself in the depths of space beyond the *Worldship*. The crackling wave of the Swarm hurtled though the Void, seeking out the *Worldship* as though with conscious purpose and intent. As the swirling blue energies of the Swarm enveloped his mind, he saw a beauty in it he had never seen before. And, an intelligence he'd never known was there. A higher intelligence...comparable to the higher intelligence of the *Worldship*. Yes...the ancient theory was true, after all.

The *Worldship* was far more than an ancient, abandoned spacecraft. It was alive. Whatever alien civilization had created it millions of years ago had long since evolved into pure energy, pure thought coursing through the core circuitry of the *Worldship*, like brainwaves passing through synapses and neurons. The acolytes had managed to communicate with the alien super mind, if only on a very basic level. Now, the Web had gained a missing element that allowed it to see the whole truth at last. The Kyll symbiotic intellect, formed of a delicate balance of two completely opposite and seemingly irreconcilable perceptions, had given them the key. The Swarm and the *Worldship* needed to join. Like sperm and egg, like pollinating insect and flower. *They had to join.*

In his mind, Tahim saw the Swarm and the *Worldship* come together as one, the two alien intellects shedding the constraining cocoons of their physical casings and merging into a nova-like explosion of energy that formed a singularity. Like a black hole, but so much more.

Tahim pulled off the headset and slumped forward over the control console. *Jemma, my sister*, he thought. *Forgive me for having doubted you.*

He forced his hand to keep steady as he picked up the nearest comm link and addressed the other division chiefs. "Attend at once, on a secure channel," he said in a dry voice. "Everything has changed."

3 galactic years later...

Jemma Venturr screamed in pain as the explosion hurled her from the splintering base of the immense tower of the Star Lance, her sabotage target, into the yawning depths of the *Worldship* interior. Her body slowly descended in the neutral gravity, shattered debris and dead bodies surrounding her. Her mind swirled as she descended toward the core, so far below. Toward the Unimind. *The Joining must come*, the chorus of minds reverberated through her brain across the telepathic implant. She almost didn't notice the Securitat robots jetting towards her. *The Joining must come...*

Haig Starcross, Chief Counselor of the *Worldship* Assembly, reveled in his god-like power as he stood at the center of the virtual reality simulation of the Star Lance. This ultimate weapon tapped the grids of the Zaarth and Kyll sections, their power surging through its many channels, like the captive force of a supernova, finally concentrating into a beam of the purest, brilliant white energy, stabbing out across the Void and blasting the onrushing Swarm into cosmic dust. Haig chuckled with glee. The energy drain would all but destroy both the Zaarth and the Kyll. Humanity alone would rule the *Worldship*, as divine providence had always intended. Haig's heart swelled with excitement as he looked up at the dazzling explosion above him. History would remember him as humanity's savior.

"By your leave, Excellency," the gravelly voice of his aide, Cromm, broke his concentration, grating across his nerves like the droning buzz of some bothersome insect.

Haig cursed under his breath, mentally deactivating the virtual reality display. "What is it, Cromm?"

"An epistle from the Assembly counselors, Your Eminence," the thin little man said, handing Haig the crystal recording of the Council's latest bit of sniveling compromise. "They urge you to spare the life of the Web acolyte Jemma Venturr. They say we can ill afford a martyr now."

"Spare the life of a terrorist? A heretic?" He hurled the crystal against the nearest wall, shattering it into a million pieces. "No, Cromm. Now is the time for resolution. For firmness. Jemma Venturr will be spaced before the eyes of the populace, to show them that resistance to the Star Lance project equals death." He paced, looking out the viewport at the star fields beyond. "How are the repairs progressing?"

"On schedule, Excellency. But, that last demolition attack led by Acolyte Venturr set the Star Lance project back several weeks at least."

Haig clenched his fists and ground his teeth in frustration. He would not be denied his destiny by a rabble of fanatics. "Have you put a stop to those ship building projects, as I ordered?"

Cromm fidgeted and cleared his throat, his bony hand stroking his thin face. "The city state governments in all three sections are increasingly resistant, Eminence. They are under increasing pressure from their labor leaders and growing religious movements to continue the construction projects. It is becoming increasingly difficult for the Securitat to maintain order, particularly in the Kyll section, where the new religion is most intense. The Kyll are obsessed with the legend of Kryzgh, the decorated pilot who miraculously returned from the abyss, and of Jemma Venturr, the acolyte who saved him. More and more of the Kyll are becoming radicalized to this new belief as more of them enter the Web. Clashes between the new belief and the old are becoming increasingly bloody in the Kyll cities. And, the Zaarth resist us more every day."

Haig paced, his hands clasped behind his back. "You've been arming the traditionalist factions among the Kyll, I presume?"

"Yes, Excellency, but...it is also becoming increasingly difficult to hide our involvement from the Kyll. The more we are seen to be backing the traditionalist front...in direct violation of Assembly law...the more the traditionalist position is weakened among the Kyll workers and the military."

Haig stood with his back to his subordinate, staring out at the distant, seemingly mocking stars. *Am I being tested*, he wondered. "Increase the weapons shipments, and do all you can to fan the flames of conflict. The more violence erupts in the Kyll section, the more excuse we have to intervene with the Securitat forces. And, what prisoners we take from among the dissidents are that much more slave labor to complete the construction of the Star Lance."

"Chief Counselor, if I may...?" Cromm said in a faltering voice.

"What now?" Haig asked with disgust, turning to Cromm.

"This increasing use of slave labor seems to be breeding discontent in all three sections, especially with the Star Lance project draining the resources of the

Worldship. Our reserves are stretched to the limit as it is, and if we continue to cut back on supplies to the military..."

"Once the Star Lance is operational, we'll no longer need the military. Cast out your fear, Cromm," Haig said, clapping his hand heartily on the other man's shoulder. "Lack of resolve in situations like this has led to the downfall of many human governments on the *Worldship*, through the centuries. Always remember, fear is our strongest weapon. As long as the three races fear each other, our position is secure. Humanity is the largest and best established of the three. And, providing that the bulk of the sacrifice comes from the other two sections, our people will remain docile. And, once the two alien races are extinct," he said, pouring himself a glass of wine, "the *Worldship* is ours." He smiled and drank, savoring the flavor of the wine on his tongue.

"Excellency, that brings me to another rather disturbing point."

"Which is?"

"Construction of escape ships in all three sections is fueled largely by fear. Fear that there is no future for any of us on the *Worldship*. You see," The little bureaucrat drew closer, as though afraid for his words to be overheard. "Up until recently, the Securitat has been able to repress the concerns of the less doctrinaire scientists, but now, with this new religion stirring up so much chaos, we can't control the flow of scientific information through the comm net as effectively as we once did. More and more of the people, even the non-believers, are convinced that what the dissident scientists are saying is true. That in a few more centuries, pollution and depletion of resources will render the *Worldship* incapable of sustaining life."

Haig set down his wine glass and stepped over to his command console. "Then, what we need is more fear of today's consequences, to counter mounting fear of tomorrow's. You will double the production of clone troopers, Cromm. Deploy them in every city on the *Worldship*. Space any among the population who would spread dissent."

Cromm seemed stunned. "M-my lord..." he stammered, scarcely able to speak. "Is that wise?"

Cromm barely had time to react as Haig turned and cut him down with a beamer bolt. Stepping over the body, Haig finished his wine and summoned an attendant.

Representatives from all three sections were gathered at the main airlock by order of the Chief Counselor, to witness the execution of Jemma Venturr. She stood at the summit of the tower, directly under the great domed roof that in minutes would open to the vacuum of space.

"All my people are in position, Jorrin," Kryzgh whispered. He and Jorrin were hidden in the crowd and disguised under rough, dingy, hooded cloaks typical of factory and farm workers.

"Good," Jorrin replied, looking up at Jemma as she stood bravely at the summit, seemingly unmoved by fear. "Zynn says her people are set too. Remember, it all has to play out exactly on schedule. We'll only get one chance." As the seconds ticked by, Jorrin's mind swirled through the hectic memories of the past several months. The chaos had escalated in all three sections since the rebels had stormed the agro pods and processing stations to liberate the slaves, allowing Jorrin and a few of his comrades to break out of their slave pens. Jorrin had toiled at back-breaking labor in prison for nearly three years, ever since he'd shot his way through a Kyll horde to save Kryzgh. Only recently, he'd found his old comrade again in the madness. Jemma's plight had brought them together, through the growing resistance movement.

"So it is with all traitors!" the amplified voice of Chief Counsellor Starcross blared out over the roaring crowds.

The moment was close. Jorrin glanced at his watch, and looked left and right, taking note of the Securitat robots and military cyborgs stationed all around. Aerial drones buzzed around Jemma, carrying the picture for vid screens throughout the *Worldship. A grand show*, Jorrin thought with disgust, his hatred for Starcross rising like bile in his gut.

"The Joining must come!" Jemma cried out, her arms spread wide. The crowd exploded, guards firing here and there. Not always over the heads of the spectators.

"Kill the audio!" Jorrin heard one of the guard captains shout into his comm link.

Then, it happened. A dark line appeared in the domed roof. The airlock was opening. The static rippling in the air above him told Jorrin the force field was now activated, protecting the guards and spectators below from the suction of the air stream that would, momentarily, sweep Jemma out into the void.

"Now!" Jorrin shouted into his comm link. He and Kryzgh cast off their cloaks and opened fire with their beamers, taking out the robot guards on this side of the gallery floor. Positioned throughout the crowd, Kyll rebels opened fire with full kill settings. Robots and cyborg guards exploded as the crowd went wild and spectators stampeded for the exits.

Jorrin looked up as the explosions went off above, right on time. The Zaarth rebels had taken out the force field generators, just as planned. The crackling bolts and shimmer on the air told Jorrin the force field was down. Donning his jet pack, he fired his lift jets and rose high above the chaos below. He could hear the Kyll rebs roaring their religious proclamations even as they fired on the Securitat. "The Joining is at hand." "Our savior acolyte shall endure." He could see Kyll civilians joining the fray, tearing savagely into the Securitat guards. With Kryzgh leading the attack, there was no hope of the Securitat maintaining control.

Jorrin grit his teeth and accelerated. The split in the dome grew wider, Jemma standing at the center of it. Security drones moved into position, firing downward with kill beams. Jorrin weaved left and right, taking out as many of them as he could with his hand beamer. Zaarth rebs were coming up fast all around him, the air stream carrying them rapidly toward the air lock. They all fired, wiping out the last of the security drones.

"Jemma!" Jorrin shouted as she was lifted off the tower summit by the updraft sweeping her towards space.

Wings stroking wildly in the jet stream, Zynn circled in the updraft and caught Jemma in mid-air, forked tail coiling around Jemma and snatching her to safety.

Jorrin swept up from below and Zynn released Jemma into his arms. He turned and steered downward at a sharp angle. He could hear additional explosions. The rebs had blown open the maintenance hatches, opening the crawl shafts. In the rapidly dwindling air, Jorrin clamped an oxygen mask over Jemma's face. "Hang on, love," he said as he held her tightly against him. She smiled up at him. Love. The word had been so long absent from his tongue. He'd sorely missed it.

Weeks later...

At a rebel-held city near the edge of the human section, Jorrin, Kryzgh, Zynn and Rutann met with Tahim in a technical monitoring pod. "The Star Lance will be operational in a matter of hours," Tahim said, his brow furrowed and beaded with sweat. "And, the Swarm is on its way. This is our last chance."

"We couldn't ask for a better one," Jorrin said, fatigued but damn ready for a fight. "Since Jemma's escape, most of the human civvies have come over to us. We've taken out the last of Starcross's cloning labs, so he'll run out of cloned cyborgs soon enough. Most of the Securitat militia have either deserted or are fighting on our side."

"Starcross still has the more primitive A.I.'s," Rutann interjected. "They are numerous and heavily armed."

"Starcross has most of his robots attacking the space ports," Kryzgh put in. "That leaves only a light contingent protecting the Star Lance. We should be able to handle it."

"Where's Jemma?" Jorrin asked.

"She's rallying the troops in defending the space ports," Zynn answered. "She's also trying to keep the panicking mobs from clawing each other to death over space on the escape ships."

"You'll have to get your squadrons launched within the hour," Tahim said.

"We'll manage," Jorrin said.

"Together one last time, my brother and sister," Kryzgh said, extending a claw.

"To victory," Zynn said, placing an appendage on Kryzgh's claw.

Jorrin laid his hand on those of his two old friends, his only regret that he'd have to go into battle...possibly for the last time...without seeing Jemma again.

The last of the escape ships had launched and were moving away from the *Worldship*, carrying what was left of its civilian populations. The Swarm was already visible, a faint shimmer in the black void, as Zynn's rebel fighters and Rutann's tactical A.I.'s engaged the Securitat robot fighters in space directly over the Star Lance energy lens.

The black sky over the grey metallic curve of the *Worldship* horizon was a wild dance of energy beams and exploding spacecraft as Jorrin and Kryzgh launched from their space pods, leading the E.V.A. team. "Lay the thermite charges there, at the base of the phase conduit," Jorrin ordered, his rapid breathing fogging the plate of his space helmet as he fired his thruster jets, maneuvering around the base of the Star Lance.

"Star Lance now operational," Rutann's grating voice blared through Jorrin's head phones. "Energy charge at one hundred percent in three point five minutes. Swarm will enter range in six point seven minutes."

"Give it a rest, junk pile," Jorrin grumbled, licking sweat from his upper lip.

"Jorrin, behind you," Kryzgh shouted.

Jorrin fired his thruster jet and spun, just in time to see the horrific sight of a squad of cyborg troopers jetting straight towards him. In the light burst of an exploding fighter, he saw the cold, soulless expression of one of the cloned, cybernetically lobotomized zombies staring at him through its face plate, its eyes milky-white, its features still as death.

"No, Kryzgh!" Jorrin shouted, blasting out the brain circuitry of the lead cyborg even as it fired on him, its beam narrowly passing over his shoulder. "Finish laying the charges. I'll cover you." Jorrin launched a rocket grenade, taking out two of the cyborgs as they tried to attack his team. He killed a third with his beamer. The remaining two zombies flanked him. He got one, dead center. The other one nailed Jorrin with its beamer, taking out his life support unit.

His brain swam through waves of starlight and darkness. He was dimly aware of Kryzgh killing the cyborg trooper and towing Jorrin through space, just before the Star Lance exploded in a geyser of blazing light.

Jemma's face was the first thing Jorrin saw as he awoke on one of the escape ships, surrounded by his rebel comrades. "Jemma. Thank the Ancestors you're safe."

"Try not to move too quickly," Jemma said. "You've suffered oxygen depletion, but the medics have you back to normal now."

It was then he noticed the implant was gone from her forehead. He gently stroked her face, passing his hand over the healed-over scar where the implant had been. "Are you...all right?"

She shrugged, a look of sadness in her eyes, which were reddened with tears. "I feel...alone," she said. Zynn laid a comforting appendage on her shoulder and she stroked it.

"I'll help you through it as best I can," Jorrin said softly, taking Jemma's hand. "If you'll still have me." She kissed him lightly on the cheek.

Getting slowly to his feet, with Zynn's help, Jorrin found himself looking out a viewport at the *Worldship*, the Swarm drawing near. He looked around. "Where's Kryzgh?" Zynn was silent as the Void. Jemma lowered her eyes. Jorrin felt a coldness spreading through him, like death. "Where is he?"

"He's on the *Worldship*." Jemma answered, scarcely above a whisper.

For a moment, he thought he was having a nightmare. "What?"

"He left this for you," Jemma said, placing a crystal record into a reader and switching it on. A shimmering hologram of Kryzgh appeared in the center of the chamber.

"I'm sorry to be leaving you only a recorded message, my friend," Kryzgh said. "I deeply regret abandoning you and the rest of my brave friends. As you know well, I am no deserter, but as you also know, I have no choice. Without the Web to hold me together, only madness awaits me. I choose to die as I am. Whole, and remembering all of you. I choose also to break with tradition in denying my being to the Horde. I hope my people will not judge me a traitor for that. But, I choose to die here, at the birth of the future. Goodbye, my friends. Remember me." The hologram vanished.

Jorrin gasped, unable to speak, barely able to stand. Jemma and Zynn supported him as he stared out the viewport. The Swarm, a wave of black crystalline darkness and blue silver light, reached the *Worldship*. There was a blinding explosion of light and color as the escape ship trembled in the shockwave, even thousands of miles out in space. Like a nova star collapsing into a black hole, the Joining formed a shimmering vortex, like an aperture in the universe.

The A.I.'s guided the fleet through the newly formed star gate, the specially designed gravity wave shields of the ships protecting them as they entered a new dimension, outside the time/space continuum, where distance meant nothing. Into a cosmic labyrinth of wormholes leading to countless planetary systems throughout the galaxy. Like synapses for a cosmic intelligence of pure energy, perhaps. But, for the survivors of the three races...a gateway to infinite possibilities.

Tom Olbert lives in Cambridge, Massachusetts, home of Harvard University, M.I.T., wacky street performers, and kooky liberals. He loves it there. Tom comes from an interesting family. His father Stan Olbert is a retired physics professor and veteran of the Polish resistance. His sister Elizabeth Olbert is an accomplished visual artist, and his mother Norma Olbert is the author of the biography "The Boy From Lwow," the story of her husband's life during World War II.

Tom is a longtime author of science fiction and dark paranormal horror fiction. His short fiction has appeared in Lillicat Publishers' "Visions II: Moons of Saturn" and "Visions III: Inside The Kuiper Belt". His recent releases include:

<u>*Novel*</u>
Dissent: Book I of The Nexus *(Phase 5 Publishing)* ~
(http://www.phase5publishing.com/dissent)
<u>*Novella*</u>
Black Goddess *(Mocha Memoirs Press)* ~
(http://mochamemoirspress.com/black-goddess/)
<u>*Novelettes*</u>
Unholy Alliance *(Eternal Press)* ~
(http://www.eternalpress.biz/product/unholy-alliance-tom-olbert/)
Desert Flower *(Caliburn Press)* ~
(http://www.fishpond.com/Books/Desert-Flower-Tom-Olbert-Naomi-Clark-Edited-by/9781615726356)
<u>*Short Story*</u>
"The Arendall Horror", An Improbable Truth: The Paranormal
Adventures of Sherlock Holmes *(Mocha Memoirs Press)* ~
(http://mochamemoirspress.com/spookylock/)

About the Editor

Carrol Fix writes and edits for Lillicat Publishers. She is the editor of the *Visions Series*, science fiction short story anthologies describing human exploration of space, including *Visions: Leaving Earth, Visions II: Moons of Saturn, Visions III: Inside the Kuiper Belt*. She was an editor for *The Future is Short: Science Fiction in a Flash, Vol. 1*, and for a biography, *Sunshine & Shadow: Memories from a Long Life*.

Carrol is a short-story author and novelist whose science fiction work includes the award-winning novel, *Mishka: Book One of the Quadrate Mind*. She is currently writing the second book in the *Quadrate Mind Series*, while working on a young-adult fantasy novel, *Worlds Apart*. Her most recent short stories appear in *Visions: Leaving Earth, The Future Is Short: Science Fiction in a Flash, The Future Is Short 2: Science Fiction in a Flash, Twisted Tales IX: Wunderkind*, and *Perihelion Science Fiction Online Magazine*. A former computer consultant who has lived in six different states, Carrol currently resides near San Diego, California, USA.

CarrolFix@LillicatPublishers.com
http://www.lillicatpublishers.com
http://www.mishkabook.com

VISIONS III: *INSIDE THE KUIPER BELT*

VISIONS II: MOONS OF SATURN

VISIONS: *LEAVING EARTH*

READ

THE FUTURE IS SHORT:

SCIENCE FICTION IN A FLASH

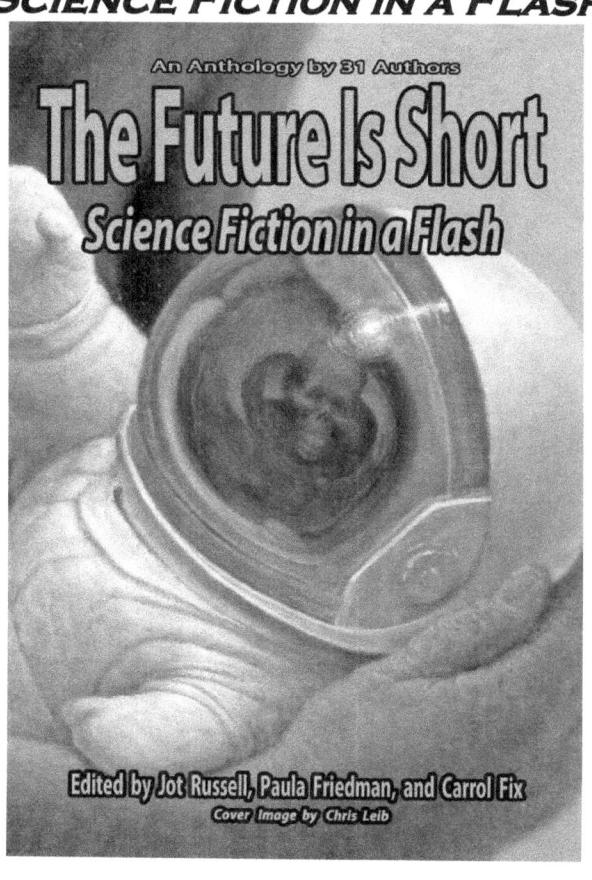

...and coming soon!

VISIONS V
MILKY WAY